WYATT

CHECK YOUR TRIGGERS

Your mental health and emotional well-being matters to me. You can find a list of possible triggers on the book's page on my website katerandallauthor.com or by scanning the QR code below.
Xoxo

For Matt. Always. Love you, babe.

CONTENTS

PROLOGUE
Maizie

"Shot, shot, shot," my roommates scream from beside me at the little Boston bar we wandered into. We're celebrating with a capital C. One, because it's my twenty-third birthday, and two, because we just took our last final of the semester. Emily and Taylor are two years younger than me. They both turned twenty-one a couple of months ago. Their birthdays are a week apart, and what a week that was...

I'm excited to celebrate with them, especially away from the confines of the life I'd been living in Shine. My own twenty-first birthday was spent with my parents at a Wednesday night church service in my hometown. Let's just say their birthday celebrations are significantly different from mine. The freedom I've found since moving away from Shine and my parents has been the absolute best thing about finally being able to go to college.

Boston has been good for me. At first, I doubted I'd make it here at all. My family isn't exactly rolling in money, and it took me a little time to save enough so that I wouldn't have to be working nonstop to pay bills and try to squeeze in classes where I could. That's a big reason I lived at home for so long after graduating from high school. It helped me save money and allowed me to only have to work part-time while living in Boston. And God willing, I'll never have to move back in with my parents.

Emily, Taylor, and I down the lemon drop shots, which the bartender graciously overpoured, before slamming our glasses back on the bar.

"This bar is way better than the last two," Emily says as she leans her back against the dark wood bar top. "Way cuter guys." Her eyes linger on a couple of guys who make their way past us, smiling as they meet up with a group of their friends.

"The last one wasn't so bad," Taylor interjects.

"Too many polo shirts and pressed khakis for my taste," I say, turning to Emily in agreement.

That's all I saw growing up in Shine. It was as though all the boys at church had the same strict dress code. Sure, I had dates after I turned sixteen, but they were the guys my parents set me up with. Usually they were the sons of the other members of our small church, and I'm pretty sure collared shirts and Dockers were the only things in their closets. I sure as hell never saw them in anything else. There were plenty who tried to get me to take off said Dockers, but anything other than a couple make-out sessions was a no-go. I remained steadfast in the church-required purity oath.

The entire idea that the members of the church were so focused on the girls proudly wearing purity rings as a sign of devotion is as absurd to me now as it was back then. At least it got me out of falling for the empty—and often annoying—promises that the boys I dated liked to throw around. They thought they were so clever and the girls didn't talk about who did what or who said what. We knew exactly which boys tried to get under our skirts, and we knew exactly who let them and what happened to them afterward. Nothing particularly nefarious with the leaders, but those boys would turn around and call the girls who fell for their lines *sluts* while simultaneously high-fiving each other. It was disgusting, and I never wanted any part of it.

"Well, look what we have here," Emily says, startling me out of the memories I often try to shove down.

I'm not a fan of remembering my high school days. Leaving Shine meant leaving behind the bullshit of my parents' strict rules and becoming a new Maizie—one who no longer felt the need to befriend only the girls they deemed appropriate, or spend time with the guys they thought would make good husbands someday. Once they'd sown their wild oats, of course—whatever that was supposed to mean.

Taylor and I shift our gazes to the group of men who walk in.

"That's more like it," Emily says, her eyes zeroing in on the four men. From what I can tell, they seem a little rough around the edges. They're all wearing jeans that look well-worn, and MC cuts, which I'm used to seeing.

The small town I grew up in is home to the Black Roses MC, and I went to school with a few of the kids who later joined. I never had much to do with them, seeing as my parents hated the club and everything it stood for—which, according to my dad, was ungodly lawlessness and perversion of our town. I never really agreed with him, though. The kids I went to school with were always nice to me, and their families showed up to every football game to cheer them on. My parents were there, too, to watch my band performances, but there was no missing the disgusted looks they used to throw the MC's way.

The cuts I see read *Bone Breakers* across the back, with a mean-looking skull dripping blood from its sharp teeth. *Arizona* is printed on the bottom.

Well, that certainly paints an image.

"Listen, I'm all for checking out guys who don't look like they're on their way to Sunday brunch, but those cuts are a little ridiculous," I say, turning back around and signaling to the bartender for three more shots.

"Oh yeah? And what do you know about cuts?" Emily asks.

"I grew up in a town that has an MC," I reply with a small shrug.

Through the two years of rooming with these girls, I've remained a bit vague about my past. Maybe I was afraid they would judge my meager beginnings, seeing as when we moved in, they both unpacked designer label after designer label. Or maybe it was because I was determined to leave the old me behind—the one who lived with her Bible-thumping parents and their suffocating rules.

"Girl, have you been holding out on us? The stories you must have!" Emily exclaims. Out of the three of us, she has a flair for the dramatics and thinks most people our age live their lives as a nonstop party. She couldn't be more wrong, at least where I'm concerned.

"It's not as salacious as you think it was," I say with a small shrug. "They were like everyone else I grew up around, working and raising their families."

"Did you ever date one of the bikers?" Taylor asks.

I laugh and shake my head. "No way. My parents would have completely lost it if the idea so much as crossed my mind."

"Well, your parents aren't here, and that man is fine as hell," Emily says, wiggling her eyebrows and nodding toward someone behind me. I turn and see the profile of a man ordering a few beers at the far end of the bar.

It's a profile that's...

Quite familiar.

I whip my head back in the direction of my friends. "I know him," I whisper-yell.

Nolan Dawson is standing in the same bar as me, wearing an MC cut. *The* Nolan Dawson, who is the brother of one of the only friends I had in high school. *The* Nolan Dawson, whom I had a huge crush on, but never dreamed of telling anyone about. He was popular and aloof. His sister, Mia, said he was a jerk, but I always figured it was the normal brother-sister rivalry thing. I didn't know him well—or at all, really. Even though I was friends with Mia in high school, we didn't hang out that much. I was always busy with church activities, and she seemed to have a lot on her plate, too.

Taylor looks behind me. "He's cute. You should go talk to him."

"You absolutely should," Emily agrees, nodding excitedly. "Have some fun. Hey, he could even dust off your pretty kitty."

My nose scrunches at the term she uses to describe that particular body part. My mother always called it a flower, which, in my opinion, is just as cringy. Personally, I've never called it anything because I don't talk about it. And no one has ever been close enough to "dust it off."

Emily laughs, and her attention is quickly captured by something behind me. "Looks like he made that decision for you," she says.

"I thought that was you," I hear a voice say behind me. When I turn, Nolan is standing next to me. "Little Maizie Wright," he drawls, a smirk tugging at the corner of his mouth. "You're not exactly the first person I thought I'd find at a bar in Boston."

"Disappointed?" I ask, returning his smirk.

My eyes wander over his face. The little dimple that used to make my heart beat a million times faster is prominently on display when his lips turn up into a full-fledged smile. Instead of blushing and turning away like I would have done all those years ago, I let him see the appreciative once-over I give him. I have no idea where the surge of confidence is coming from, but I don't hate it.

Nolan looks me over from the top of my head to the bottom of my black-heeled boots. "Not in the least," he says, shooting me a wink. "Can I buy you a drink?"

My inner teenage self is screaming *yes*, but I play it cool with a shrug and a slight tilt of my lips. "Okay."

God, I'm pretty sure he's gotten hotter since the last time I laid eyes on him—five years ago at my high school graduation. He's tall, with the same lean, firm build I remember—though I can't get a good look at his torso beneath the T-shirt and leather cut he's wearing. His sandy-blond hair is a little longer than the last time I saw him. But it adds to the carefree persona he's always had—as though he has better things to do with his time than worry about getting a haircut.

Nolan gets the bartender's attention and orders two beers. I'm not really a beer person, but when he hands me the longneck, I accept it with a thankful smile.

"What on earth are you doing in a place like this?" he asks before taking a long pull from his beer.

I sip mine and try not to wince at the skunky taste. "I go to school in Boston. It's my birthday, so my roommates and I are out celebrating. What about you?"

"Business," he replies, and his eyes drag over my body again as he shakes his head. "Damn, Maizie. It's really good to see you. And happy fucking birthday. Here I thought I was going to be bored out of my mind coming to a college bar." Nolan looks around and his gaze is filled with judgmental disinterest as he takes in the crowd.

"Not your scene?" I ask.

Nolan barks out a laugh. "Not at all, but a few of my buddies thought it would be fun to get under some college girls' skirts. I'm just here for the cold beer and to play wingman for the night."

I look over and see the group wearing the same cuts as him, talking to a couple of drunk girls who don't look a day over twenty-one, like most of the girls in here.

"You're not doing a great job with your wingman duties. They're over there, and you're here talking to me."

His gaze stays locked on mine, not bothering to spare his friends a glance. "You're much more interesting and a hell of a lot better looking than those assholes." He smiles again and takes a pull from the bottle in front of him. "So, how long have you been in Boston?"

"Couple years. Finally got out of Shine and started school here," I reply, sipping my own beer. This time it goes down a little easier, but it still wouldn't be my drink of choice. "So you're in Arizona now? That's where Mia is, right?"

"Yup. You still talk to my sister?"

"Not really." Through the years, Mia and I lost touch. I was working as much as I could and saving money to go away for school and she was busy with work and school herself. "She must like having family there with her, especially being so far from home."

Nolan scoffs. "She's as uptight as my parents. Always trying to control me even though I moved out there to help her out. She got pissed over some stupid shit, and we haven't talked since."

That doesn't sound like the Mia I knew, but it's been years, and it's not as though she and Nolan were particularly close growing up. They always seemed to be on different wavelengths, and it certainly isn't my place to judge their relationship after all this time.

"The last thing I want to do is talk about my sister."

"What do you want to do?" I ask, perfectly willing to drop the subject if it means having a good time with the guy I used to imagine being my first kiss.

"It's your birthday, sweetheart." Nolan nods toward something behind me. "I think your friends found someone else to celebrate with."

Turning around, I see Taylor and Emily chatting with a group of guys across the bar. Taylor has a coy smile on her face as she talks to a guy who looks about our age, and Emily is already draped across the lap of another guy. It's pretty much a typical night for those two once they have a few shots in them.

I shrug and turn back toward Nolan. "They like to have fun. Can't exactly blame them." Considering how hard we worked this semester, I'd never begrudge them a night of letting their hair down—or their pants. It's not as though I haven't thought of doing the same.

"What about you? You feel like having some fun tonight?" Nolan asks, and my cheeks feel like they're catching fire. I may not have much experience—okay, none—but it doesn't take a genius to figure out what he's saying, especially when he looks like a wolf ready to devour his prey.

"Depends on what you have in mind," I reply.

Nolan *tsks* and shakes his head, but the mischief never leaves his eyes. I remember him always wearing the same sort of devil-may-care look on his face in high school. It makes me feel just as enamored with him now as it did back then. But unlike back then, his smirk is turned toward me.

"Well, I think you should let me buy you a few more drinks. We can see where the night takes us."

Is this really happening? To me, of all people?

"Sounds good to me," I reply and turn to flag the bartender down.

When he comes over, I order two shots of tequila. Nolan doesn't exactly seem like a lemon drop kind of man. The bartender returns with the shots, and we hold up the small glasses.

"To unforeseen reunions," I say.

"And unforgettable nights," he says, and we clink glasses.

Holy shit, if I thought the beer was bad, the alcohol burning its way down my throat is ten times worse. I'm not much of a drinker, and when I do imbibe, it's usually some froufrou drink that the girls order.

Nolan laughs at the face I make when I bite into the lime. "That'll put hair on your chest," he says, and signals for two more.

"I don't usually drink tequila," I say, a little embarrassed by my reaction. This is not the cool, confident woman I want to appear to be.

Nolan shakes his head and holds up two fingers. Less than a minute later, the bartender comes back with more tequila. With the next round of shots in his hand, he hands me the glass. "After a couple more, you'll be a pro," he says, lifting his glass and pouring the liquid down his throat.

Blowing out a breath, I do the same. It burns a little less, but it's still far from being a pleasurable experience.

One of the guys wearing the same cut as Nolan comes over and slaps a meaty palm on his back. "We're heading out. Gonna party at the motel," he says, looking at the rest of the group who are heading toward the front door.

"I'll meet you there later," Nolan replies, and the other man looks at me with a knowing smirk.

"Yeah, okay, brother," he says before heading back to the group.

"If you have to go, I understand," I say, attempting to smile. I'm starting to feel a little wobbly on my feet from all the alcohol I've had tonight.

"Nah, I see those fuckers all the time. I'd rather stay and hang out with you."

"Hey, we need to steal Maizie for a second," Emily says behind me, looping her arm through mine.

Nolan chuckles and dips his head. "Don't steal her for too long." He winks and I fucking melt. Or it may be the tequila. I don't know and I don't particularly care at this point.

Emily and Taylor steer me toward the bathroom, and when we step inside, both girls squeal in excitement.

"Oh my God, Maizie. That man is fucking hot. I swear, if you don't go home with him, I'm signing you up for the monastery," Emily says, her eyes bright with excitement.

"I think you mean nunnery," I tell her.

"What the fuck ever." Emily waves her hand, and Taylor laughs.

"I know you probably didn't think ahead, so here," Emily says, reaching into her purse and pulling out a couple of condoms before handing me the foil packets.

"Do you really think I'm going to need those?" I ask, and Emily waves them in front of me before shoving them in the front pocket of my jeans.

"Maizie, I could practically feel the fuck-me vibes he's been sending you all night, and I was twenty feet away.

Yes, you are going to need them. You can't always rely on the guy to be prepared."

Taylor nods in agreement as she touches up her lip gloss in the mirror. "You better get back out there before another girl swoops in on him. That is one ride you don't want to miss out on."

"Jesus Christ," I laugh out. "You guys are weirdly invested in this."

"We just want you to have a good time. You work and go to school. That's it. Neither of us has ever seen you with a guy, and if anyone is due to let down her hair and have some fucking fun, it's you. Besides, it's your birthday. He looks like the kind of guy who could give you presents in the form of orgasms. *Several* orgasms," Emily says, wiggling her eyebrows.

I have no idea how she would be able to tell that just by looking at Nolan, but then again, it's not like I would know what the hell *that* looks like.

"Come on," Taylor says, opening the door. "I need another drink, and your man is waiting for you."

"Not my man," I say, walking out of the bathroom.

"Tonight he is," Emily says with a laugh. "And that's good enough."

The girls head back over to the group of guys they were hanging out with while I was talking to Nolan, and I walk back over to the bar. Nolan is leaning against the bar with one elbow propped against the wood as I weave my way through the crowd. His lips curl in a half smile as I approach.

"Hope they don't need you for the rest of the night." His hand slides around my hip and he squeezes. "I don't particularly enjoy sharing your attention."

"All yours," I say, and he bites his lip.

"Then let's get this night started."

My smile widens, and Nolan orders more shots. "Happy birthday, Maizie," he says, and we both down the alcohol.

Happy birthday to me.

In the morning, I wake in a motel I barely remember coming back to. Nolan isn't lying in bed beside me, but the shower is running in the bathroom. My stomach roils as I sit up and taste the remnants of the tequila from last night. Memories come rushing back. Saying goodbye to the girls after several shots, heading back to Nolan's motel, the party next door in his friend's room, then coming back to his room.

Oh fuck.

I look down and see that I'm completely naked.

Oh fuck.

The shower turns off, and Nolan strides out of the bathroom with a towel slung around his trim waist, heading straight to the bag sitting on the old wooden dresser.

"Hey," I croak out.

He spins and faces me. The smile from the night before is no longer teasing the corner of his mouth. In fact, he looks downright annoyed that I'm here.

"Hey," he replies, then turns back around and continues rummaging through his bag. He pulls out a dark-orange medication bottle, taps a couple of pills into his palm, tosses them into his mouth, then washes them down with a swig from a beer bottle.

I shift on the bed and look around for my clothes, feeling none of the excitement from last night. Nolan was charming and funny, and when we got back to his room, he was passionate—almost desperate—to have me, especially after I told him that I'd never had sex before. Gone is that man, though. This one can barely look at me.

He turns and offers the bottle of pills to me. "Need something for the hangover?"

"No, I think I'm going to get some breakfast. That usually takes care of it for me."

He shrugs. "Suit yourself."

"Um, are my clothes over there by chance?" The only thing I see from my place on the bed is my bra and shirt.

Nolan looks at the ground and grabs my jeans and panties from the floor, tossing them at me. I pull them under the sheet covering me and slip them up my legs.

"You don't have to hide from me now. Not like I didn't see it all last night," he says, dropping his towel and standing completely naked in front of me. I turn my head, and he chuckles, then turns back around and sniffs a pair of jeans before putting them on.

"God, you really were a virgin, huh?"

"Yeah," I breathe out.

There's a loud knock at the door, and a man yells, "Let's go!"

Nolan curses under his breath and pulls on a wrinkled shirt, then his cut, before zipping up his bag. He looks at me for a moment, then grabs a sheet of hotel paper and a pen, scribbling something on it.

"I gotta go, but if you're ever in Phoenix, give me a call. You were a good time last night. Wouldn't mind doing it again." He tosses the paper on the bed as I watch on in confusion and mild disgust. "Gotta go. Checkout's at eleven, so you should probably get going, too."

I nod and wrap the sheet around the upper half of my body that's still naked.

Nolan grabs his bag from the dresser and steps toward the door. "See ya around," he says, then opens the door and slams it behind him.

That's it. That's all I get. A half-assed goodbye and a hangover. I look at the paper with his phone number and shove it in my purse. I'm not really sure why. I seriously doubt I'll ever make it out to Phoenix, and after that little display this morning, I wouldn't call him even if I did.

Little did I know that about six weeks later, I'd have a reason to talk to him.

Chapter One
Maizie
Five Years Later

"Wait, you need to sing 'The Alphabet Song,'" I remind my son, Colby, as he's washing his hands. The little stinker always tries to lather up and then rinse right away after going to the bathroom, especially when we're at the park. I can't really blame him. There's a bright sun in the sky, and he's having a great time. But that doesn't mean I'm not going to make sure his hands are clean before I let him run back outside.

"I know, Mom," he says, like the very idea is equal parts annoying and exhausting.

"I know you know, son. But sometimes you like to tell me you forgot." My mouth tips up in a smile. You could fill a lake with all the things he "forgets" when he doesn't want to do them to begin with.

"Can we see if Pepper can come play?" he asks, begging me with his wide brown eyes.

Pepper is my friend Wyatt's puppy—the one Colby fell in love with. Hell, he even named the fur ball. I wish I'd thought to call Wyatt and ask if we could take him to the park with us. Those two tire each other out better than anything I could come up with. Pepper and Colby—not

Wyatt and Colby, though sometimes I think Wyatt is as much of a kid as Colby, and he's been known to stop by the park a time or two and run around with my son.

And I'd be lying if I said I wouldn't mind seeing Wyatt. Since moving back to Shine and getting a job at Thorn and Thistle—the bar owned by the club—he and I have had an easy friendship. Naturally, I found him attractive the moment I met him. I doubt any woman with a pulse could deny his boyish charm wrapped in a sexy-as-hell body, but he's a brother, and I have a strict no-biker rule.

That doesn't mean I don't occasionally let myself fantasize about wrapping my thighs around his tight shoulders and letting him do all the things I imagine a man like him would be very good at.

But that's where those thoughts have to stay—in my imagination.

"Not today, buddy. We're not going to be here much longer."

It's my day off from the bar, and I have a mountain of laundry on the couch that needs folding, plus a week's worth of dust and dirt that needs to be cleaned up around the house. Granted, we don't live in a pigsty, but if I've learned anything about keeping a house clean with a five-year-old boy, it's that if you don't stay on top of it, it turns into a disaster zone in no time.

Colby pouts, but I ruffle his sandy-blond hair and then tickle him behind his ear. His frown turns into a laughing smile.

"Next time we come to the park, I promise I'll ask Wyatt if we can bring Pepper," I tell him.

"When?"

"In a couple days."

"*What* day?" he asks, obviously annoyed with my lack of having a firm day.

"How about Tuesday after school?" I don't go in to work until five, so that gives us a couple hours at the park.

Colby tilts his head and squints his eyes as though he's considering the plan.

I chuckle. "I'm sorry, do you have a better offer that I don't know about?"

"I'm counting the days," he says. "Two days and I get to play with Pepper."

"Yes, son. Two days."

"Yes!" he exclaims, throwing his hands in the air as he runs out of the bathroom.

I laugh and follow him out. A man is talking with my friend Mia at the park bench where we'd been sitting, enjoying the afternoon sun and some iced coffees.

When he turns and faces me, my breath catches.

Nolan Dawson.

Fuck, fuck, fuck.

Colby runs over to the bench, grabs his water that's sitting next to Mia, and guzzles it down.

My first instinct is to grab Colby and get the hell out of here, but I'd look like a lunatic in front of my friend—and that would open up a can of worms I'm nowhere near prepared to take on. I hurry over, fear working its way through my entire body.

"Nolan, you remember Maizie, right?" Mia says.

Nolan doesn't answer right away—his gaze zeroed in on my son.

"Colby, go play a bit more before we have to go," I say, wanting my kid as far away from the man standing in front of him as possible.

"Yeah, uh, hey, Maizie. Long time."

"Hello," I reply coldly.

"I think you were about to tell me what you were doing here, Nolan," Mia says. Her tone is a bit gentler than mine, but not by much. No surprise there. From what she's told me, he really fucked her over when he was living in Phoenix.

"Business," he says, pinning me with his stare.

Heard that one before.

"Does our grandmother know you're here?" Mia asks.

Nolan finally shifts his eyes in her direction. "I was going to stop by and say hi. But I saw your car, so I thought I'd stop."

"How long are you in town for?" Mia asks.

Nolan shrugs. "Not sure. You want a departure date or something, little sis?" That air of overconfidence I found so attractive all those years ago makes me want to punch him in the throat now.

"Yes, actually, I do. After the shit you pulled in Phoenix, I don't expect Grandma is looking forward to a visit from you."

Don't mention the club, Mia.

I don't know what Knox—her boyfriend and the club's VP— has told her about the Bone Breakers, but they aren't exactly on *friendly* terms with the Black Roses. Not after a few of their guys went missing almost two years ago, before she came back to Shine. As far as I know, the Bone Breakers never found answers as to where their missing members disappeared to.

Hell, even I don't know the details. But I do know we were told to keep our eyes peeled for the patch Nolan is wearing on his cut and report back to the club prez—my boss—Ozzy if we saw anyone wearing it around town. I stay out of club business, but when that directive was given, I'll be the first to admit...it scared me. Especially considering what happened about nine months after the last time I saw Nolan Dawson.

"Jesus Christ, Mia. I was close and wanted to see my old stomping grounds and say hello to my family. I don't need a fucking lecture from you," he says. "That was years ago. Can't you just move on already?"

Mia shakes her head. "If you would have apologized or taken any accountability after the shit you pulled in Phoenix, then maybe I would have been able to let it go. But instead, you show up here in a fucking Bone Breakers cut, acting like you own the goddamn town. Newsflash—you don't."

Nolan laughs, but there's no humor in his tone. "What do you know about cuts, Mia?"

Don't do it.

"My boyfriend wears one. Only his says *Black Roses.* You remember Knox Turner, don't you?"

Goddamnit.

Nolan's mouth turns up in a sharp smile. "He's the VP, right?"

"Yup. And I know for a fact he wouldn't appreciate you lurking around town or visiting with our grandmother, though I doubt she'd even open the door for you."

Nolan's smile stays in place as he turns to me. "What about you, Maizie? Would you open the door for me?"

Before I can answer, Mia cuts in. "She absolutely would not, Nolan. Get the fuck out of here."

The man doesn't pay his sister any mind as he holds me with his knowing stare. He knows I opened the door for him years ago—or rather, my legs—and not a day goes by that I'm not reminded of that fact. I'll never regret having my son, but I'll regret who his father is until my last breath, and the fact that he laid eyes on Colby after all these years. I'm not a fucking idiot. Nolan took one look at Colby and I saw the wheels turning behind those shrewd eyes. They have the same light-brown hair and dimple on their cheek when they smile. It's not as though Nolan didn't know I was pregnant. He just never bothered to find out what I did about the pregnancy after I told him.

I've spent years without anyone knowing my secret. And he's a big enough asshole to spill it right here and now in front of one of my best friends, whose old man is not only the Black Roses VP but also one of my bosses.

And I'm so fucking terrified that all I can do is stand here and stare at him, praying he has a shred of human decency.

Nolan finally looks toward the street and steps back from us. "Pleasure as always, little sister. Make sure to tell your old man I said hello," he says, then turns and walks away.

Mia and I don't take our eyes off of him until he gets on his bike that's parked about a block away and rides off.

"I am so sorry. He's a pig," Mia says, turning to face me.

My brows draw together as I meet her apologetic gaze. "What do you mean?"

"The way he was flirting with you." She releases an exaggerated shudder. "Like you'd ever be interested in my loser brother."

I shoot her a weak smile. "It's okay. Guys like that are all talk anyways." I would know. "He was probably trying to piss you off more than anything."

"He certainly loves to do that," she says. "Do you want to come over for dinner tonight? I'm sure my grand-mother would love to see you and Colby. And I need to fill her in about her grandson being here. Knox is going to be fucking pissed." She blows out a breath and swipes a hand over her face. "My brother is in an MC that my boyfriend's club hates. Jesus fucking Christ."

I sit down, but keep my ears open for the sound of a motorcycle engine. "I know the clubs aren't exactly friends, but do you know why?" Even though I stay out of club business, it looks like their business has landed in my lap.

Mia shrugs and blows out a long breath. "Not really. I think it had something to do with Lucy and that cult she was raised in. Lucy said they used to buy meth from the leaders, and that's how she knew who they were. But she's honestly been pretty tight-lipped about them. I remember they were at a club party a couple years ago, and afterward, some other members came looking for the guys who went missing. But that was the last time I saw or heard anything about them."

Lucy is Jude's woman. She showed up in Shine with her best friend—Charlie—a few months before the bikers went missing. But we haven't seen any of the Bone Breakers around town since Jude and the rest of the club took out the cult that Lucy was raised in.

"Do you think the club had anything to do with the missing bikers?"

Mia looks me in the eye. "We know the guys aren't saints, and if they did have something to do with it, they had their reasons. If that club was dealing in meth, who knows what other shit they were doing."

I nod and look toward my son, who's hanging from the smaller jungle gym without a care in the world. Meanwhile, I feel like mine is crashing around me.

"So, dinner tonight?" Mia asks again.

"I can't." I offer her a small smile. "I have a ton to do at home." *Like not freak the fuck out that Nolan Dawson is in town and laid eyes on Colby.* "But let's shoot for next week."

"Sounds good." Mia releases a frustrated growl. "God, it's so fucking typical of my brother to show up here, out of the blue, expecting anyone to be happy to see him. I wish his sorry ass would have stayed in Arizona with the rest of the snakes."

You and me both.

Reading the pregnancy test in the little bathroom of my apartment has my stomach dropping to my feet. Or it could be the morning sickness I've had the last few days. Though they should really call it all-day sickness, considering my stomach likes to expel all of its contents at any time of day. At first, I thought it was the flu. But when I looked at my calendar and realized the date, a completely different realization smacked me in the face.

Who the hell gets pregnant their first time having sex? That doesn't even seem statistically possible.

Obviously it is, considering I'm staring at two very pink lines on a stick.

"Motherfucker," I whisper to myself before wrapping the pregnancy test in toilet paper and shoving it in the trash can.

Opening the bathroom door, I spot Emily and Taylor walking into the apartment.

"You feeling any better?" Emily asks as she sets her bag on the small leather couch in our tiny living room.

I look around at our apartment. The low coffee table we picked up at a yard sale where we spent countless hours poring over our books and Chinese takeout, the secondhand couch we bought from a couple of seniors who were graduating, the TV stand we made from old wooden crates, and the television we hardly watch because we're always so busy. This has been my home for the last year. My first taste of freedom from my parents' repressive home. And now it's all gone. Tears prick my eyes, but I try my damndest to hold them back. I'm not ready to say anything to them about what that test said. It could be a false positive. It could be... No, I know exactly what it is. I've never been one to talk myself out of the truth.

I'm pregnant.

"Yeah, not a hundred percent, but I'm getting there."

The next day, I walk into the student clinic on campus. I have no hope that the test is going to come back any different than yesterday's. Honestly, I don't even know why I decided to come here. Maybe to make sure the test I bought wasn't a dud. But in my heart of hearts, I know what it's going to reveal before the nurse walks back into the exam room.

"The test is positive. You're pregnant," she tells me.

The air whooshes from my lungs. Why am I surprised, or shocked, or whatever this feeling is?

She offers me a few pamphlets and a comforting smile before I walk out into the summer sun.

Emily, Taylor, and I live in Boston year round. We all work near campus, and about a month ago, I got a bartending gig that pays more in tips than their part-time coffee shop jobs. Not that they need the money as much as I do. Though my savings help me out during the school year, I rely on working as much as possible during the summer so I have time for classes and studying come September.

Or, I did.

There's no way in hell I can have a baby and live in a small apartment with Emily and Taylor. When would I work? When would I go to class? How the hell am I going to have a baby, live on my own, and do...anything?

By the time I make it back to the apartment, the girls have left for work. Fall semester is starting back up in a few short weeks, and there's no way I'm going to be able to make it work.

I walk into my room and collapse onto my bed, looking at myself in the mirror above my dresser.

"You're in one hell of a shitty situation, Maizie." Talking to myself is perfectly rational, right? Maybe I'm pregnant and losing my mind, too.

Blowing out a breath, I get up from my bed and open the top drawer of my dresser. I pull out the phone number that Nolan carelessly tossed at me before walking out of the motel room almost two months ago. I could go about my life and never tell him what our one night of drunken sex resulted in. I have serious doubts he'd care anyways. Or I can put on my big-girl panties and face my responsibilities.

I sit back on my bed and dial the number.

"Yeah?" he answers after the fourth ring.

"Hi, it's Maizie," I say.

Silence.

"Maizie Wright. From Boston. Or Shine, too, I guess."

"I remember. You in town, sexy?"

If I weren't nauseous before, that would do the trick.

"No. Listen, I need to tell you something. I'm pregnant." Might as well rip off the Band-Aid. God, that's the first time I've admitted it to anyone else.

"And?"

My brow furrows, and I look around my room as though searching for the answers to his weird reaction on my white walls.

"And I thought you should know?" Why wouldn't someone want to know that they fathered a child?

"Are you sure it's even mine? It was just the one time."

"Yeah, I'm sure. It was the only time for me."

"Oh, that's right. You were a virgin."

He fucking forgot?

"If you want money to get rid of it, I'm broke. Maybe in a couple weeks I can send you something, but I'm tapped right now."

"No, no. I thought..." What the hell was I thinking? "I just thought you should know."

"*And now I do. That all? I'm kind of in the middle of something.*" *A distinctly feminine laugh, followed by a long moan, comes through the phone.*

Jesus Christ. He has another girl there with him while we talk about this. And from the sound of it, he hasn't bothered to pause whatever he's "in the middle of."

"*Yup, that's it,*" *I answer with disgust rolling through my stomach.*

"*Okay. See ya around.*"

When I disconnect the call, I don't bother saying good-bye, and I'm sure he doesn't care or notice, for that matter. That conversation did nothing to ease my worries, not that there was ever a version of reality where it would have.

I toss my phone next to me and lie down on my side, my palm flattening against my lower stomach.

"*Well, I think we've established that your father is a complete jackass, and I'm not sure about my parents, but I'll figure it out. It's going to be me and you, kid.*"

Colby's loud laughter breaks me out of my momentary walk down memory lane. I look down and see that my entire shirt is covered with bubbles from his bath.

"You little stinker," I say, smiling at my son.

"Now we're both wearing bubbles," he says, grinning as a sudsy crown sits atop his head.

"I could have done without," I say dryly. He's completely nonplussed by my lack of enthusiasm over what I'm sure is the absolute best thing to be covered in—in his mind, at least. Hey, it could be worse. He could hate baths and run screaming from the tub. If I get covered because it makes him laugh, so be it.

"You almost done, monkey?" *Please be almost done.*

"One more minute," he says as he attempts a bubble beard.

When Colby is finally finished, I help him rinse the suds and dry off until he finds his motorcycle pajamas, which are his absolute favorite. Lucy got them for him last Christmas, and I've had to buy four more pairs since they're his favorite. Getting him to wear anything else is not an argument I like having right before bed.

"Three books?" he asks, hoping that I'm willing to forget about my two-book maximum. One of Colby's favorite times is lying in his little twin-size bed and having me read to him. If he had it his way, we'd stay up for hours past his bedtime so I could go through his entire collection twice.

"Two, son."

"Cece reads me three," he says with a little pout.

Cece is Lucy's sister and Colby's number one favorite babysitter.

I chuckle. "Way to rat her out, kid."

"I don't think she likes rats. She really hates mice. I 'member how loud she screamed when she saw one last summer." He opens his mouth, presumably to perform a reenactment of the fiasco, but I quickly cover his mouth with my palm.

"We all remember. No need for a demonstration."

I walk over to his bookshelves and pull two of his favorites, then settle into bed next to him. Halfway through the second book about a brave little caboose, Colby's breaths even out.

And my worrying begins.

Turning off his light, I shut his door firmly behind me. This afternoon freaked me the hell out. I know Nolan isn't the sharpest tool in the shed, but there was no mistaking the way he looked at my son. I haven't tried to reach out to him since the disastrous phone call we had almost six years ago. I'm not sure how much he remembers, but that little comment earlier makes it clear—he hasn't forgotten our night together.

Colby mostly takes after me, for now. He has my dark-brown eyes and the same straight, narrow nose. When he smiles, he looks just like I did at his age. There's no doubt that the bigger he gets, the more pieces of Nolan are going to come out, though, at least to anyone who knows he's the father. Not that anyone does. I refused to say anything about Colby's paternity when I showed up here two months pregnant and practically homeless. My parents kicked me out before I even had a chance to unload my meager belongings when they found out that I had sex out of wedlock and was knocked up. Don't even get me started on when I refused to tell them who "tainted" their daughter.

If it weren't for my grandmother, Rosemary, I would have been sleeping in the little pickup I bought before moving to Boston. When I showed up at her door in tears and scared out of my mind, she took one look at me and wrapped me in her arms. I lived with her until cancer took her from me and Colby. We only had two years with her before she passed, but I like to think we made them two of the best years of her life, watching her great-grandson grow and learn every day. I know they were two of my favorites.

I often thought I should give Colby the family he deserves. It's not like he doesn't have any. He has an aunt who already loves him and another great-grandmother who often tells me he's the smartest five-year-old she's ever met. Elaine Dawson, Mia and Nolan's grandmother, was friends with mine, and after she passed, Elaine was instrumental in helping me plan everything since my parents and I weren't on speaking terms. Shit, even my grandmother refused to speak to my mother for how she allowed her husband to treat me. My grandmother was never fond of my father. She thought he was some crazy religious zealot, and she wasn't far off. It's nothing compared to what Lucy went through with the cult she was raised in, but it was no walk in the park, either.

I've chosen to stay quiet about who Colby's father is. As far as I'm concerned, Colby is mine and mine alone.

Walking into my bedroom, I reach under my bed and pull out the small safe I have stashed there. When Lucy and Charlie came to town, Lucy made us learn to shoot. I met them both when they started bartending at Thorn and Thistle, and we became fast friends. Charlie found her happily ever after with Linc, the Black Roses enforcer, and has since quit bartending. The only time she works is if she's filling in for me or occasionally one of the other girls, since Charlie is in school getting her degree in family therapy. Maybe when all is said and done, she can unravel the mess my life is.

I don't regret my decision to become a mother, not for one second. Losing the freedom I'd finally found when I went away to college, yeah, that still stings a bit. But all I have to do is take one look at my kid, and I know it was worth it for me.

I'd do anything to protect my son.

I open the safe and check the chamber, then head into the living room of the house my grandmother left me. The three-bedroom, two-bathroom Craftsman-style home is plenty big enough for me and Colby. I haven't changed much since she passed. Personally, I love the floral wallpaper mixed with dark-blue walls in our living room. It's her style, and keeping it is sort of a memorial to the woman who loved and supported me no matter what.

I did update the furniture, though. And traded her brown plaid couch and matching recliner for a more neutral couch and two overstuffed chairs that are big enough to curl up in with a glass of wine and a good book. I kept the low oak coffee table she had for as long as I can remember. Thankfully, the house has a built-in entertainment center where our TV and all of her books still reside.

After turning off the lights, I sink into the couch that sits in front of the large bay window. It's not particularly late, but the street my house sits on is quiet after eight o'clock—not that I plan on sleeping.

Nolan saw Colby. There's no way he doesn't at least suspect that he's his son. And every time I think of the look he gave me before he turned to leave, a shiver runs down my spine. I don't know a lot about the Bone Breakers, but I know they're bad news, and my son's father is one of them.

If that asshole has any thoughts of coming for my son while he's in town, he'll have to get through me, and I'm a damn good shot.

CHAPTER TWO
WYATT

"Ozzy wants us in church," Cash says as Pepper and I are outside running around.

"Be there in a minute," I reply to our club treasurer.

If anyone had told me that I'd spend most of my days taking care of a puppy, I would have laughed in their face. He has nearly doubled in size since I picked him up while he was cowering next to the dumpster at Thorn and Thistle, but I couldn't leave the abandoned pup. I looked for his mama and potential littermates but came up empty. Probably a good thing, considering Ozzy would have killed me if I'd brought any more dogs home. But honestly, what did he expect me to do? I mean, he did tell me I could take it to the animal shelter, but that didn't sit right. This little guy had already been abandoned once, I sure as shit wasn't going to do it again.

"Pepper, come," I command. His golden ears perk up, and he trots over to me, sitting at my feet like I've trained him. "Down." He rolls over, and I kneel, petting his stomach. "Good boy," I tell him as he lies on his back and accepts all the love and attention.

"Funny, that's usually the face I make when Lucy rubs my belly, though we're usually naked and it's after—" Before Jude can finish his sentence, I pretend to cover Pepper's ears.

"Not in front of the children, you fucking pervert," I say.

Jude looks from me to the dog and shakes his head. "You've lost it, mate."

I shrug and stand, snapping at Pepper, who immediately rolls back over and sits next to my leg.

"You've trained him well," Jude compliments.

"A lot better than Lucy's trained your sorry ass."

"That's because I'm not the one who needs training. Lucy, on the other hand—"

"Lucy on the other hand, what?" the woman herself asks, stepping out into the expansive backyard with Charlie, Linc's old lady.

"Nothing, Lucifer. I was just telling Wyatt how much I like it when you rub my belly."

She quirks a brow and gives her man a flat look. "I'm sure."

"What are you guys doing here?" I ask, saving my brother from the dressing down his old lady is sure to give him.

"Target practice," Charlie answers.

That piques my interest. Most of the time when the girls come to practice at our outdoor range, Maizie is here with them. I look past Jude and the girls, hoping to catch a glimpse of the woman who's had me captivated since I first met her at Thorn and Thistle. Unfortunately for me, looking is all I'm allowed to do. Ozzy told me years ago—in no uncertain terms—that I wasn't allowed to take her to my bed.

My own fucking prez friend-zoned me before I even took a shot.

Lucy must see the expression on my face, and she smirks. "It's just the two of us today. Maizie said something about having to do a few things before her shift tonight."

I pretend that it doesn't faze me in the least that Maizie isn't with them. "Who's watching Colby tonight?"

"Me and Linc," Charlie answers. "Maizie said Colby wanted to come over and watch movies at our house since 'Auntie Charlie has the best snacks.' Why don't you come over and bring Pepper? They can run around the backyard and get nice and tired, so when Maizie comes to get him, he crashes out."

"Sounds good," I reply.

Knox peeks his head out of the back slider and gives us all a look that would terrify lesser men. "Church. Now."

Jude kisses Lucy hard on the mouth, and I follow him inside. Before heading into church, I stop in the kitchen to give Pepper his treat for being the best dog ever.

I slide into the seat on Ozzy's other side, directly across from Knox, who's sitting next to his brother Linc. On Linc's other side are Jude and Braxton—our sergeant-at-arms. Cash drops into the seat beside me, and our road captain, Barrett, settles in next to our treasurer.

I love this room. Always have. Gramps had the center of the giant oak table we've all gathered around carved with our club emblem—a skull with black roses for the eyes. This table reminds us that we're here for our brotherhood, that everything we do is to keep our family safe and taken care of. That we live our lives on our terms. As I look around the room at the pictures of the brothers that have come before us, it's as though they're all watching us, taking stock. I hope they know how much this brotherhood means to each and every one of us sitting at this table. There's a reason this is called church. This room is sacred, and I feel it every time I step foot in here.

Ozzy bangs the gavel on the table, and we all turn to him, giving our president the attention he deserves.

"I'm not going to beat around the bush. Looks like the Bone Breakers are back in town."

That earns a surprised look from everyone except Knox.

We haven't heard shit from those assholes in over a year. They came here looking to work with us for the Monaghans. Finn, the head of the Irish mob family we've worked with for years, wanted to expand out West. He wanted us to vet the other club since we didn't have a close relationship with them. Instead, they saw an opportunity for a payday and tried to take Jude's old lady back to the cult she was raised in. It didn't work out particularly well for them, seeing as Lucy isn't afraid to shoot someone in the face, and Jude, who found them trying to take her, is a fucking psychopath. Needless to say, the three guys they sent never made it back to Arizona.

"How many?" Cash asks. I look down and notice his giant hands clasped around the black leather armrest of the chair he's sitting in.

"One, that I know of. It's Mia's brother," Knox answers.

"What the fuck?" Braxton grits out. "Your old lady's brother is in the club whose members 'disappeared' last time they came to Shine? That's quite the fucking coincidence."

Knox turns that steely gaze that has petrified plenty of rowdy assholes on our sergeant-at-arms. "You *will* tread carefully, brother," he says in a dangerously low tone. "Mia had no idea he was part of the club. She hadn't spoken to Nolan in years."

Braxton nods, properly chastised for his implication.

"He cornered Mia at the park yesterday," Knox says. "Told her he was here on business. She didn't see anyone else with him. Could be he was passing through Shine on his way to wherever his club is. Could be he was having a look around. No one said anything to us about him or anyone else asking questions about their missing friends. I don't think they'd be that stupid—not after what we did to that compound."

"The fact that one of them stepped foot in our town doesn't bode well for their intelligence or sense of self-preservation," Jude says, flexing his jaw.

Hell, if it were me and anyone in that club showed up here after trying to take my woman, I'd be flying out of this room so fast and hunting down every last one of those motherfuckers. But I don't have a woman, and I don't teeter on the edge of sanity like the Englishman sitting across the table.

"So what do you think he was doing here?" Cash asks.

Knox shrugs. "We won't know until someone makes a move. I don't love the fact that anyone from that club even knows the name of our town, let alone used to live here, but we can't go to war with a club just because one of their members is here visiting his family."

"We should have taken out the lot of them when they went after Lucy," Jude says.

Uh-oh.

"We were a little fucking busy at the time, Jude. Or did you forget your old lady had a cult after her?" Ozzy says, his gaze pinning Jude where he sits. To question Ozzy means... Well, I actually don't know what it means, considering no one's ever done it.

Jude nods. "Sorry, Oz. I hate the thought of any of those arseholes being within a hundred miles of Lucy. Or any of our old ladies, for that matter."

Jude's apology seems to temper Ozzy's anger for the time being.

"So what happened yesterday exactly?" Cash asks.

"Mia was at the park with Maizie and Colby," Knox starts, and I immediately sit up straight. That piece of shit was near Maizie and her kid? That I don't like at all. Not one fucking bit, actually. "He said he was here on business, but didn't specify what type of business. Then Mia gave him the what for, and he took off."

"Are you sure she didn't see anyone else?" I ask.

"She didn't," he answers.

We don't know much about the Bone Breakers, but it would be highly unusual for any club to send only one guy to check out a rival club. If it's only Mia's brother here, he's probably just in town for a visit.

"Did he show up at Mia's grandmother's place?" I ask, hoping that we can put this to bed.

"Nope," Knox says. "But Mia told him she doubted her grandmother would even want to see him, which her grandmother confirmed when Mia told her that he was in town. Mia and Elaine have written Nolan off, especially after the shit he pulled when he and Mia lived together in Phoenix. The only family that still gives a shit about him is his parents, and they moved to Boston years ago."

"Maybe he was on his way there?" I offer.

Knox shrugs. "Anything's possible. But the fact remains—he's a Bone Breaker. There's no way in hell he doesn't know that three of their men went missing here. The fact we haven't seen any of them in almost two years? That's pure luck."

And thank God for that. We've been a bit busy the last couple years. Not that we can't handle it, but it's nice to think they've bought the whole *they disappeared after leaving Shine* story we sold them. Though I'm beginning to think it isn't that easy.

"I'm going to increase security at Midnight Rose and Thorn and Thistle," Ozzy says. "To be on the safe side. If the Bone Breakers have proven anything, it's that they aren't afraid to go after the women."

That idea calms me by the slightest margin, considering Maizie works four nights a week at the bar.

"Do you think they're a viable threat?" Cash asks.

Ozzy considers the question for a few moments. "I can't be sure. Like I said, this could be a one-off. It's Nolan, and he has ties to the town that don't involve us. But if he's here for his club, then we're going to make damn sure everyone is safe until we have a clearer understanding of the situation. The last thing I want is to go to war with them, but like hell I'm going to let us get caught with our pants down."

I look around the table at my brothers. Jude and, surprisingly, Cash, are the most on edge, but there's definitely tension rolling off each brother. War is dangerous and deadly. We've had a pretty good run of being able to avoid it throughout the years—with the exception of helping the Monaghans eliminate the threats they've faced—but it's been a long-ass time since we were the main player.

I suppose all good things come to an end at some point.

I pull up to Linc and Charlie's house, and through the front window, a little face is peering out when I park my truck. It's a beautiful night and perfect for a ride, but then I'd be responsible for disappointing a certain five-year-old by not showing up with his best bud.

Colby comes barreling down the front porch of Linc's one-story cottage as I open the passenger door of my truck. Without waiting for a command, Pepper jumps down and runs straight to Colby, jumping and running circles around the kid.

"Pepper, down," I command, and the dog sits next to Colby. I can see the energy vibrating off him, but he listens nonetheless.

"Come on, Wy, he wasn't being bad," Colby pleads.

"I know, bud, but if he gets any bigger, he'll knock you over. Then your mom will be mad at me, and I'll be in trouble."

The last thing I want is to get on Maizie's bad side. She has many sides I'd like to be on, but those aren't appropriate thoughts to have in front of her son.

Charlie comes outside and smiles. "Oh, come on, Wyatt. Don't torture the poor kid."

I look at Colby, who is begging me with his big brown eyes.

"Okay, Pepper," I say, and the pup and kid immediately start running around the front yard.

"Where's your old man?" I ask Charlie.

She nods toward the garage. "Staring at his new girl-friend."

I narrow my eyes in question and head in that direction to find Linc and Jude huddled around a bike that sits in parts over Linc's work table.

Linc looks up and grins. "Look what I picked up."

"A bunch of spare parts?" I ask, seeing the mess in front of him.

"Hell no. When all is said and done, this thing is going to be show worthy," Linc says, looking over the parts as though he can already see it all put together.

"Whatever you say, mate. You definitely have your work cut out for you," Jude says.

"A little hard work never scared me."

It's been a long time since Linc had a project like this laid out in front of him. He and Knox used to love finding old bikes for cheap and rebuilding them. I don't think he's done anything of the sort since he got out of prison a couple years ago. Though I enjoy working on my bike and will often lend a helping hand to my brothers when they need it, the way Linc looks at everything in front of him is on another level. It's as though he's a kid in a toy store, staring at a giant puzzle that he can't wait to solve.

"Who's at Thorn and Thistle tonight?" I ask. I love that Linc has a new project, but that doesn't mean we don't have bigger issues to worry about.

"Braxton," Jude says, and I nod.

Since Brax is six-five and at least two hundred fifty pounds of pure muscle, it puts me at ease knowing he's the one hanging out with Maizie tonight. Naturally, I'd rather it be me, but that's Ozzy's call. Besides, it gives me a chance to let Pepper run around with Colby. They can have some fun and tire each other out.

It's not much, but it's one thing I can do for Maizie.

"What about Lucy and Cece?" I ask.

Jude shakes his head. "I have no fecking clue where Little Bit is. She's been in the habit of taking off without telling her sister where she's headed. And she doesn't like to answer questions about where she's been when she gets home."

"Still not going great on that front?" I ask.

"Nope. But I'm staying out of it. If Lucifer wants me to step in, she'll tell me, but I think she's at as much of a loss as I am."

Jude isn't what I would call warm and fuzzy. Shit, neither is Lucy, for that matter, but when it comes to Cece, both of them have been treading lightly. I just hope like hell it doesn't blow up in their faces.

Lucy steps into the garage. "Dinner's ready," she informs us.

"What did you make me, Lucifer?"

She rolls her eyes. "Chinese takeout."

"Ah, my favorite," Jude says, walking to his woman. "What about dessert?"

She winks at the man and turns to walk back to the house, adding a little sway in her step for him. When he lets out a growl, she takes off in a sprint and he lunges after her, laughing until I hear a door slam.

"Those two have some serious issues," I say, and Linc nods.

"Try living next door to them," he replies, and I chuckle.

No fucking thanks.

Three hours later—after the takeout has been demolished, the cupcakes devoured, and Colby and Pepper have passed out on the floor in front of the TV—there's a quiet knock at the door.

Charlie unravels herself from Linc. "That must be Maizie," she says quietly, so she doesn't wake Colby.

Pepper lifts his head, and as soon as Maizie walks through the front door, he settles back down with Colby.

"Looks like it was quite the party," she says, smiling at her sleeping son.

"Pepper has been bugging me to hang out with Colby, so we stopped by."

Maizie releases a light laugh. "Pepper, huh?"

I love that I can make her laugh even after a long night of working. The sound brings a smile to my face.

"He's very talkative once you get to know him," I tell her.

She shakes her head and walks over to her son, kneeling next to him. "Hey, buddy," she says in a quiet voice. "Time to wake up."

Colby opens his sleepy eyes a bit and smiles. "Hi, Mommy. Can Pepper spend the night?"

"Not tonight, son," she says, lifting him from the floor.

I stand from my chair and hold out my arms. "Let me. It was my dog who tired him out," I say.

"It's okay. I got him," she replies.

Colby is already asleep again in her arms, not that he really woke up in the first place.

"Maizie, you've been working all night. Let me, yeah?" I hold out my arms again.

She looks exhausted. I haven't seen her in over a week, and she has dark circles under her eyes. Still beautiful, but very tired.

"Thank you," she breathes out. "Careful, he's heavier than he looks," she says, handing him over.

Colby doesn't so much as stir, but Pepper gets up and follows us out to her car.

"Here you go," Charlie says, handing Colby's backpack over to Maizie.

Maizie leans in and gives her a hug. "Thank you so much," she says. "You sure you're still on for watching him tomorrow night, too?"

Charlie grins. "Of course. I love having the little guy around. Gives me someone to hang out with now that Linc has a new project."

When I lean in and set Colby in his car seat, he opens his eyes and smiles at me. "Can we play again tomorrow?"

"Sounds like a good plan to me, bud," I reply and buckle him in.

"Mm-kay."

I watch as his eyes flutter closed again. Damn, I wish I could fall asleep that easily. Even when I was his age, sleep never came as easily as it does for this kid. My only guess is, when you grow up like Colby—with a mom who loves him and a group of people as close as any blood-related family—it's easy to feel safe enough to let sleep take over. Not exactly the way I grew up.

I shut the back door, walk around to the driver's side, and open the door for Maizie.

"Well, thank you, kind sir," she says, offering me a tired smile as she sits down.

"You okay?" I ask, noting the way her shoulders are slightly slumped forward, as if the weight of the world sits there.

"Didn't sleep well," she says, scrunching her adorable nose.

"Are you worried about something?"

Maizie lets out a humorless laugh. "I'm a single mom. I'm always worried about something."

I wish like hell I could take some of it away for her, give her some sort of reassurance that whatever's on her mind will work itself out, but what do I know about being a single parent? Shit, I *wish* my mom had been single when I was growing up. It would've been better than staying in a shitty marriage with my dad. At least Colby has a mom who loves him and puts him above everything else. It sure beats having two parents who yelled at each other night and day.

I smile and resist the urge to run my finger under the circles under her eyes and lean in to give her a soft kiss, promising everything will be okay.

"Night," she says as I step away from her car.

She shuts the door and takes off down the street back to her house, which is a few minutes away.

When I turn around, Charlie is giving me *the look*. The one that says she knows something I don't want her to know.

"What?" I ask.

She stares for a beat then shakes her head. "Nothing," she says with a smile. "Nothing at all."

CHAPTER THREE
Maizie

It's been three days since I saw Nolan at the park. Three of the longest days and nights of my life. I've been sleeping on the couch with my gun close—if you can even call what I've been doing sleeping. It's mostly been me dozing off for an hour at most, then being jolted awake by any noise I hear outside. Then I check through all the windows and settle back on the couch, only to do the whole thing all over again with the next noise. I will say, I didn't realize we had so many fucking raccoons around my house.

Nolan hasn't tried to contact me, thank God, but the look he gave me when he walked away said that it was a distinct possibility that he has some assumptions and I should probably expect to hear from him. Or maybe I'm imagining it. His sudden appearance caught me off guard. I've known they were on the outs ever since Mia came back to town. Any time he had been brought up, she sounded determined to keep it that way. But what if he slides back into Elaine's good graces? What if he decides that he misses Shine so much, he wants to put down roots here? What if I have to tell one of my best friends and the rest of the club that I've been keeping a secret from everyone for years?

It's not as though I intended to keep it a secret that Colby's father is a member of a rival club. I didn't even know the Black Roses had any issues with the Bone Breakers when I came back to Shine until everything happened with Lucy. But when I found out, I was more determined than ever to never tell anyone about Colby's parentage. Never in a million years did I think Nolan would come around Shine, or see Colby and me at the park.

I don't know how many more nights I'm going to be able to give my friends the flimsy reason for having them watch Colby rather than having Cece come over to the house to watch him like she usually does. Colby loves Cece, and I trust her implicitly with him, but I've been terrified that Nolan will show up at my house when I'm at work and try to see Colby, which would scare the shit out of Cece and my son. Not that he knows where we live, but it's also not like Shine is a big town, either. He could easily track us down if he wanted to.

Jesus. There's really no reason to think he'd want to in the first place. He never called to check on me. He probably assumed I'd "take care of it" as he so callously put it, when I called him six years ago, scared out of my mind. I doubt Nolan has any desire to suddenly be strapped with the responsibility of a five-year-old kid, especially if he's been living the life his sister told us about. It's not as though I've called him asking for money, and I never would. I take care of my son. No one else. My grandmother left me a small inheritance and her house, much to the ire of my parents. But it's a blessing that allows me to not have to work two or three jobs in order to keep a roof over our heads.

Throughout the years, my mom has come around a bit, but my dad is still staunchly in the *I'm a Jezebel of the highest order* camp. Mom contacts me and sees Colby a few times a year. He thinks my parents live far away. It was a conclusion he came to on his own, and I've never had the heart to tell him any different. How do you explain to a five-year-old that their grandmother has to sneak away to spend time with him? At least, that's what I'm assuming she does, since we don't discuss my father.

It was my grandmother who sat with me during the hours of labor and my grandmother who babysat for me when I started working at Thorn and Thistle when Colby was a few months old. She insisted that I didn't need to work, but kids are expensive, and I didn't want her shouldering my financial responsibilities.

When my grandmother got sick, it was Ozzy who came up with some ridiculous "fund" they have for all their employees that allowed them to still get a paycheck if they were taking care of a sick family member. At first, I tried to argue with him about it, but it was like talking to a brick wall, so I accepted the club's generosity with a grateful—yet not at all fooled—smile.

The club has done more for me and my family than I could ever repay. Well, that's not entirely true. I've been repaying their kindness by lying to them, haven't I?

I always told myself the end justifies the means. That by not telling anyone who the father of my child is, no one would pass judgment on our situation—not that they didn't judge me anyway—and I would have full control over how I raised my son. That I wouldn't be forced to share weekends with someone who was nowhere near capable of being a parent. Maybe it sounds selfish, but I was doing it to protect my child. After knowing what I know now about Nolan, I'm convinced I made the right call.

The bar has been quiet tonight, which isn't necessarily uncommon for a weeknight. And I can't say I'm upset about it. I'm paid well above minimum wage, which certainly helps when the tips aren't rolling in on nights like these. Tonight though, I simply don't have the energy to deal with people. I can barely keep my eyes open as I grab a couple beers for the two lone patrons sitting on the other end of the bar when the front door opens.

Wyatt, Barrett, and Braxton come sauntering in. Seeing Braxton isn't a surprise. He's been hanging out here a lot more since Mia told Knox, who told the rest of the club, that Nolan is in town. It has nothing to do with my fear, but he is a member of the Bone Breakers, and the clubs aren't exactly what you would call friendly.

"Hey, Maizie," Wyatt says, leaning against the bar. "Can I get three beers?"

I nod, and Wyatt shoots me a smile. I've always loved that smile and wondered what it would feel like pressed against my mouth. I hope he doesn't see the blush that I feel creeping up my neck. Usually I'm better at hiding my reaction to Wyatt, but I'm exhausted and my defenses are seriously lacking, along with my sleep.

Friends. You're just friends and can't be anything more.

Wyatt is handsome with a perpetual tan, dark hair, and brown eyes so deep you can get lost in them. *Jesus, girl. You must be tired if you're waxing poetic about the man's eyes.* He's tall too. Maybe not as tall as Braxton, but I've always loved standing next to a guy and feeling petite, which is hard to come by when you stand five-nine. He has long legs and thick arms. Arms I've imagined being wrapped in while he kisses me with that smirk on his face he seems to always wear. But he's also a biker, and technically one of my bosses.

Though I mostly answer to Ozzy, Wyatt is in the club and still has a say in what happens with my job, should we start something that ends up crashing and burning. Not to mention, Colby loves him and his damn dog. I would never be responsible for breaking my kid's heart when Wyatt realizes dating a single mother is nothing like the girls I'm sure he's used to. I'm not free to take off at a moment's notice and ride down the coast. I can't hang out at parties all night and sleep in the next day as though I don't have any responsibilities. He might be nice to look at—very nice, actually—but that's all it will ever be. Me looking and him living a free and easy life.

Handing the beers over to Wyatt, I give him my best attempt at a smile. "Here you go."

Wyatt takes the beers and tilts his head, studying me. The boyish smirk is gone, replaced with something that looks like concern.

"You okay, Maiz?"

"I told you. I haven't been sleeping well, remember?" I reply with a little more bite to my tone than he deserves.

"It just looks like it's something more than being tired."

"So you're saying I look haggard?" I ask, raising my brows.

"No...I'm saying if there's something you need to talk about, I'm here."

Gah, he's fucking gorgeous and nice as hell, even when I'm being a wretched bitch.

"I have raccoons," I blurt out.

Wyatt lifts an eyebrow, confusion written on his face. "In your...house?"

I bark out a laugh, and that relieves some of the tension on Wyatt's face. "They're outside, and they keep waking me up. That's why I haven't been sleeping." Partly true, mostly not.

He nods. "I'll send someone over to get rid of them."

"You don't have to do that."

Wyatt rests his elbows on the bar and leans toward me. "I know I don't have to, but they're causing my favorite bartender to lose sleep and snap at me." And the smile is back. It would be so easy to lean forward and put my mouth inches from his to see what happens. Just throw caution to the wind and let the chips fall where they may.

Friends, Maizie. Just friends.

Lack of sleep and the temptation of Wyatt are too damn much right now.

Shaking myself out of my wayward thoughts, I re-focus on the conversation we're having instead of the curve of Wyatt's smile. I should argue and tell him I'm going to take care of it, or I could accept his offer and say thank you. Either way, if I know anything about how these guys operate, it's as good as done.

"They won't kill them or something, will they?"

That pulls a laugh from Wyatt. "No, I'll make sure he just removes them from your property. We don't need Colby coming across the murder of a raccoon family and being traumatized for the rest of his life."

And he cares about my kid. Damn him.

"Thanks, Wyatt. I appreciate it."

"Anything for you, Maiz."

Wyatt straightens and turns, walking over to the table Braxton and Barrett are sitting at, completely oblivious to the riot of butterflies taking off in my stomach. The idea of *anything* sends thoughts swirling around in my head. Thoughts I have no business thinking.

Two hours later, and I think I've passed the point of exhaustion and have gone into that weird phase where you feel like everything is some sort of fever dream.

Thankfully, it's closing time and since it was a slow night, the only thing I have to do is take the trash out and lock up.

"Let me do that," Wyatt says, standing from his seat.

"Absolutely not," I tell him. "It's my job, and no way in hell am I going to have you telling my boss I'm slacking."

Wyatt chuckles and sits back down. "Didn't realize you were so territorial over the dumpsters."

"Now you do," I tell him. "If you want to do something helpful, though, you guys can flip the rest of the chairs."

He salutes me, and I roll my eyes, then walk through the hallway where the bathrooms are to the back door. I toss the giant bag into the dumpster and turn around to find Nolan standing between me and the door leading back inside.

"What the hell are you doing here?" I hiss, trying to keep my voice low, at least for now. I don't want anyone knowing that Nolan is lurking around to talk to me. There would be questions that I really don't want to answer.

"I came to talk to you about the kid," he says, looking behind him at the door.

It looks like Nolan is alone, but there are three members of the Black Roses just on the other side of the door he's standing in front of.

"Is he mine?"

Every muscle in my body locks, and anger courses through my blood. "No. He's *mine*."

Nolan holds his hands in the air as though he's surrendering. "I'm not trying to take anything from you."

"My child is not 'anything.' He's my son."

Nolan blows out a breath; this conversation probably not going as he expected. "Listen, I'm going back to Arizona tonight. I didn't come here to start trouble."

"Why are you here, then?"

"I had some business that I needed to take care of. I take it you haven't told anyone who his father is."

"Like I said, he's *my* child. End of discussion."

Nolan nods a few times and stretches his neck. "Yeah, alright. The last thing I need is a kid weighing me down, anyways."

I don't move. My eyes stay laser-focused on him, hoping he sees the fury burning in them. I would do anything for my son, and I swear to God, if it means killing this man where he stands to keep him away from Colby, I'll fucking do it.

"See ya around, Maizie," he says, then heads down the small alley and turns the corner.

That's when I finally exhale and nearly collapse next to this fucking dumpster. That conversation was less than a minute, but I'm pretty sure it shaved about ten years off my life.

The back door opens, and Wyatt peeks his head out. "Hey, you okay?"

Holy shit, had it been ten seconds earlier, he'd have walked out when Nolan was here, and I'd have had a shit ton of explaining to do.

"Yeah, just getting some fresh air."

Wyatt's eyes dart to the dumpster then back to me. "Out here?"

I nod and smile, shrugging. "Fair point. Come on. I need to grab Colby from Lucy's and head home."

"I'll call Jude and have him bring Colby to your house. That way you don't have to drive over there."

"It's no big deal. It's not that far out of the way."

"Really, I'm sure he'd be hap—"

"I said I got him. He's my son. I will go pick him up, then I will take him home and put him to bed." My tone is sharp, a lot sharper than the one I used earlier tonight. But for fuck's sake, I don't need a white knight biker trying to invade my life right now. I don't need anyone playing savior.

"Okay, Maiz," he says, that placating tone making me feel two inches tall all over again. He opens the door wider without meeting my eyes.

Fuck, now I feel like an asshole. But here's the thing. If I start to depend on Wyatt, then I'll be setting myself up for disappointment. And not just me, my kid, too. Wyatt is handsome, charming and sweet. If I make a list of everything I want in a man, I'd basically be listing everything I like about Wyatt. He's also completely and utterly unattached. He doesn't even have his own place. Not that he needs to own some fancy house or something. But he still lives at the clubhouse and can pick up and leave whenever the mood strikes.

I...can't, not with any of it. I just can't.

The next night, I'm at work, and Colby is at Charlie's house. Again. Until I know for sure that Nolan has left town, I'm not comfortable asking Cece to come stay at my place. It's a little busier, but I'm just as tired as I've been all week.

At least I have one of my favorite people here to keep me company.

"You know, I'm a little offended that Colby hasn't asked to come to my house to hang out while you've been at work," Mia says from the other side of the bar.

It's not that he hasn't asked, but Mia lives on the same property as her grandmother. and with Nolan in town, I'm nervous he'd show up there.

I laugh in an attempt to deflect from the unease I feel. "Don't blame him. Charlie and Lucy ply my kid with junk food."

"Hey, I'm the baker in this group. And he loves my chocolate chip cookies," she grouses.

"True, but it also helps that Charlie and Lucy live right next door to each other, so I'm pretty sure he's getting double the sweets."

She nods. "I can see the logic in that. So, did I tell you my brother is officially on his way back to Arizona?"

"You didn't. How do you know?" That's the confirmation I was looking for, and she doesn't realize how much

I've needed to hear it. How could she when I still haven't told her why I want him gone so bad?

"I guess my mom called him, and he told her he was in some little town in Kansas. Naturally, my mom called my grandmother and bitched her out about not being able to keep him in Shine, where he belongs. Jesus, my parents really have no clue."

Thank God. Kansas is states away from me and Colby.

"He didn't even try to come see my grandmother. I don't think he was in Shine for more than a day or two. I never saw him again, did you?"

My head rears back. "Why would I see him?"

"Uh, you work in one of the only bars in town and he likes to drink."

"I work in a bar owned by another club. This is the last place he'd come to wet his whistle."

It's not like he was stopping by for a beer when I saw him last night, so I'm not *technically* lying.

The front door opens, and one of my other favorite people walks in with her man. Then comes Mia's, and trailing behind is the guy who hijacked way too many of my thoughts last night.

"Hey, sis," Lucy says as she sits down next to Mia. "Wyatt said you're having a raccoon problem at your place."

I nod as Wyatt sits a couple chairs down from Lucy.

"I have a guy stopping by in the morning to take care of it, if that's okay with you?" Wyatt says, giving me a cautious smile.

Guilt instantly shoots through me. I was a complete bitch to him yesterday when he offered to help me out with Colby. That conversation played over and over in my mind last night as I was sitting on the couch at my house, where I've spent the last couple nights. Though I'm still firmly of the belief that Wyatt is the last person I should let myself rely on for a myriad of reasons, I also know that I didn't need to be so rude about it.

"Thank you so much. I really appreciate it," I say, offering him a smile and his favorite beer.

He nods in thanks, and I move on to make drinks for Knox, Lucy, and Jude.

"So, I was thinking," Lucy says after taking a sip of her whiskey.

Mia snickers. "Oh, this should be good."

Lucy purses her lips and gives Mia a hard side-eye. "As I was saying, I'm going to sign you up on one of those dating apps."

Mia laughs, nearly spitting her drink out, and from the corner of my eye, I see Wyatt stiffen in his chair. I'm not the only one who notices, either. Jude eyes Wyatt and then gets what I can only describe as a devious twinkle in his blue eyes.

"Lucifer, I think that's a great idea," he says.

"Right? I'm brilliant." Jude leans over and kisses Lucy on the mouth. "And I may have already set up a profile for you," she says, grabbing her phone from her purse.

"You did not," Mia says, shaking her head as Knox chuckles beside her.

"Of course she did," Knox says. "This is Lucy we're talking about."

"Did you run this by Charlie? Usually she talks you down from your ridiculous ideas," Mia comments, looking over at Lucy's phone.

"That's exactly *why* I didn't. She's a buzzkill."

"By buzzkill, do you mean she's the one who keeps you in line? We all know it wouldn't be your old man," I say.

"Exactly. She's been shackled to Linc for too long to remember what it's like to get out there and date."

"Wait a second, Lucifer. What's that supposed to mean? We've been together for nearly as long."

"Just that my friend is single, and I want her to find someone who cares about her and wants to give her the world like she deserves. And maybe a roll in the sheets, too."

"Jesus Christ, Lucy. There's more to life than sex," I say, wholly uncomfortable with where this conversation is going.

I've been out on a couple dates since I had Colby. I've even had sex. There was a perfectly nice guy who used to come in here when he was traveling through town for work a couple times a month. We struck up a conversation, and he took me out. We would've even maybe made a go of it, but he got a new job that required travel and a home base six hours away. Then again, now that I think about it, I wasn't particularly devastated by his change in employment. That was...Jesus, how long ago was that?

"I'm not talking about regular sex. I'm talking about knock-your-socks-off sex. And that, my friend, is some life-altering shit," Lucy says.

Jude preens next to his woman. We all know how they started—and the way they like to settle arguments. Lucy is hardly the *don't kiss and tell* type.

"Oh, look. You have some interest already, and I just set this up a few hours ago," she says, holding her phone in my face. There's a picture of a perfectly handsome man staring back at me.

"Let me see that," I say, grabbing her phone from her hand. I exit out of the picture she was showing me and find the profile she made. The picture is one of me laughing at Knox's birthday party a few months ago. It's actually not too bad. In my profile, she's written that I'm twenty-eight and work in the hospitality industry. I live in the greater Boston area, and I love kids and enjoy nature when I'm not working.

"See, I didn't put where exactly you live since, you know, there're weirdos on the internet who pretend to be people they aren't."

"Like you pretending to be Maizie?" Mia asks.

"It's for the greater good," Lucy retorts. "And I said you like kids, which you do, but I didn't say that you have one since, you know...weirdos and all that."

"What about this part of me liking nature?" I ask with an arched brow.

"We go to the park a lot with Colby. That's nature," Lucy replies.

"No, that's me getting my kid outside to run the wiggles off. Two totally separate things."

Lucy shrugs. "Close enough."

I release a deep exhale and hand her back her phone. My friend is certifiable. Well-meaning but absolutely batshit.

"Look," Lucy starts as she crosses her arms and rests them on the bar, leaning slightly toward me. "You aren't going to meet the man of your dreams working in this bar," Lucy says.

"Hey, I like to think this is where we fell in love," Jude says, staring at his woman with a dejected look on his face.

She swivels her head in his direction. "No, this is where you wore me down to finally agree to let you take me on your bike. The love part didn't come until way later." She turns back to me. "All I'm saying is, you're young and beautiful and more than a bartender at Thorn and Thistle. You're more than Colby's mom. You're also a woman who needs to be reminded there's more to life."

I scoff. "I don't need a man for that."

Lucy throws her head back in laughter. "Sister, no one *needs* a man. But they sure can be fun to have around," she finishes with a wide smile.

I shake my head and laugh, holding my hand open in front of her. "Fine. I'm too tired to fight with you when you're obviously—and might I add, strangely—fixated on this."

Lucy's smile is beaming as she does a little happy dance in her seat and hands her phone back over to me.

Leaning across the bar, I hold the phone so we can both see the screen and scroll through the pictures of the men who have liked my profile. Some of them are pretty cute. And some look like they live in their mom's basement.

"All you have to do is swipe on their picture, then you'll be matched and can start messaging each other," Lucy says.

"How the hell do you know that?" Jude asks.

"I did my research. Do you really think I would let one of my friends go into this blind?" she asks as though she's offended that he would assume such a thing.

"*Let* is a bit of a stretch. You basically forced this on her," he volleys.

"To-ma-to, to-mah-to," she replies, waving him off. "Oh, how about this guy?" she asks me.

I look at the picture. Not bad. He has light hair, not the dark that I prefer, but his profile says he's six-one, so at least he's a bit taller than me. And it looks like he lives about forty-five minutes from here, so not so close that I'll run the chance of bumping into him at the grocery store if it doesn't work out.

"Do it," Lucy goads, making a swiping motion with her finger.

I look at her, then the phone, then back to her. "Will this get you off my back?"

"I make no promises."

That's honestly the best I'm going to get from her.

"Fine," I say, and I swipe.

The next morning, Wyatt shows up at my door with two cups of coffee and holds one out to me when I open the door.

"I come bearing coffee and exterminators," he says with a half smile.

I look behind him as two men get out of their truck with traps. "You're a saint," I tell him as I reach out and grab the coffee from his hand. "Never thought I would be so happy to see a pest control truck in front of my house."

Colby comes running to the front door still in his pajamas, his brown hair sticking out at every odd angle imaginable. "Where's Pepper?" he asks, looking past Wyatt.

"He had to stay home today. We're getting rid of your raccoon problem, and I wouldn't want one of the guys to mistake him for a raccoon and put him in one of the cages," Wyatt answers.

"I would have protected him," Colby says, obviously a bit put out that Wyatt would show up without his dog.

"I know, bud. But I have a few things that I have to take care of today, and Pepper can't come along."

"He could have stayed with us, and you could have come back later to pick him up," Colby argues.

"Colby," I say in a firm voice. The last thing Wyatt needs is my son giving him grief when he's here to do us a favor.

"You're right," Wyatt says. "That's what I should have done. Next time, okay?"

Colby nods, appeased with the promise of a next time.

"Come on in," I say, moving away from the door. I look down at the nightshirt I'm still wearing without a bra. I cross my arms over my chest while nonchalantly taking a sip from the coffee Wyatt brought me. I may not be the fullest up top, but the thin shirt does nothing to hide what I do have. "Um, I'm going to go change real quick."

Wyatt nods toward the kitchen. "I'll be in here."

I walk back to my room and change out of my pajamas and into a T-shirt and denim shorts. When I walk back into the kitchen, Wyatt is watching Colby carefully as my son pours milk into his cereal bowl.

"He said it was okay for him to do it himself as long as an adult supervises," Wyatt says, looking between me and Colby like he isn't sure he's doing the right thing by letting Colby get himself a bowl of cereal.

I wave off his concerns. "It's fine. We're in the *I can do it myself* stage, but still in the *not-so-great hand-eye coordination* stage," I tell him.

"I didn't spill any, Mommy," Colby announces.

"Good job. Now take it to the table carefully."

We all have a seat at my kitchen table, Colby on one side of me and Wyatt on the other.

"Thank you so much for doing this for me," I tell Wyatt.

"What did I tell you? Anything for my favorite bartender." He smiles and takes a sip of his coffee.

There's no mistaking the heat that spreads from my neck up to my cheeks. And he doesn't miss it either if the smirk on his full lips is anything to go by. *What I wouldn't give to not wear my emotions all over my body.*

"So, um...how was the rest of your night?" I ask in an attempt to get myself under control and into more neutral territory so I stop blushing like a schoolgirl.

"It was fine. I needed to get back to the clubhouse and take Pepper out," he replies.

A couple minutes after Lucy made me swipe on the dating app, Wyatt threw some bills on the bar and headed out. He wasn't what I would call angry or anything like that, but his mood had definitely shifted, a little like it is now that I brought up last night.

"How has your garbage disposal been? Any more problems?" he asks. The change in topic isn't lost on me, and it makes me wonder why he seems to care. We're friends. He's never made a move. Not that I would allow myself to get swept up in him. I need him as a friend more than I need him in my bed. Or so I keep telling myself.

"No more problems. Thank you again for fixing it for me," I reply.

A few weeks ago, I'd mentioned to Lucy that the damn garbage disposal was giving me issues, and about an hour later, Wyatt showed up at my front door with a tool belt and a smile. He's been doing little things like that for me for the last few years. I'd usually thank him with dinner or a beer, and over that time, we've gotten to know each other. Ever since he rescued Pepper, we see him at least once a week, either at the park or at one of our friends' houses, and Colby gets to play with Pepper.

He's always been here when I needed, without me having to ask, and he's the brother I've become closest to and know I can always rely on. Because we're friends.

Just friends.

There's a knock at the door, and I get up to answer it.

"All set, ma'am," one of the exterminators says.

"That was fast. Hold on, let me grab you some cash," I say, turning away from the door. "What do I owe you?" I call as I walk into the kitchen to grab my purse.

"Nothing, ma'am. It's been taken care of," he replies. "Let us know if there are any other problems."

I turn to Wyatt and crook an eyebrow. He's carefully studying his paper cup with the Cool Beans logo—my favorite coffee shop in Shine.

"Wyatt?"

He looks at me and smiles. "Yes?"

My brow quirks in question. "Did you pay to have my raccoons removed?"

"Well, technically they aren't *yours*. At least not anymore," he replies.

"Mommy, when someone does something nice for you, you're supposed to say thank you," Colby says before he lifts his bowl to his mouth to drink the fruity-flavored milk.

I let out a breath and chuckle. "Thank you, Wyatt."

The man shrugs. "Like I said, anything for you, Maiz."

CHAPTER FOUR
MAIZIE

Okay, I'll admit it. This dating app thing is actually kind of fun. It could all be bullshit, but it's a lot better than what I have going on, which is absolutely nothing. Dating in a small town is hard, especially when you've grown up with most of the guys around here. Or when you've been harboring a crush on one of your friends that you know you can never act on—but I'm not going to think about that.

In Shine, my pickings are slim. There are the guys I went to school with, who I've known practically my entire life, or there are the guys who come into Thorn and Thistle. Those two groups tend to have a significant overlap. This town isn't really a place where single people move to. Most of the men who live in Shine have been here their entire lives, or have moved away and then have come back to raise kids like me. And they're either happily married, bitter from divorce, or they just never grew up. None of that bodes well for a single mom who may or may not want to find a partner.

Honestly, I've never given much thought to putting myself out there until Lucy brought it up—a.k.a., harassed me mercilessly. I figured I'd meet someone eventually. I was a young mom—still am—and it always seemed like one of those things I'd have time for later. But Lucy has made the point over and over: I'll never meet someone if I don't put myself out there. So last week, I finally gave in to one of her harebrained ideas. And it actually hasn't blown up in my face.

With the threat of Nolan destroying my world gone, I can finally relax again. I didn't sleep for days. Becoming a mom hasn't been great for my sleep, but those few nights on the couch were miserable. When Wyatt came over with the exterminator to get rid of the raccoons, he made a comment about me finally being able to get some shut-eye. Little did he or anyone else know that it wasn't the raccoons I needed gone, it was the threat of Nolan showing up and blowing my life to pieces. Now that he's gone, I can get back to business as usual. Well, mostly usual. This whole dating thing is out of the ordinary, but I'd be lying if I said it wasn't the first time in years I've felt a little more like the girl I was becoming before I got pregnant and had to move back to Shine.

It's not that I don't love my life and what I've built here. I love my son, my friends, and my job. But for the first time in years, I'm letting myself do something a little out of the ordinary, something for *me*—not the mom, friend, or kick-ass employee. Just me.

"*Moooom*, when is Cece going to get here?" Colby asks, popping into the bathroom as I put the finishing touches on my makeup.

"Soon, monkey. I don't need to head to work for another thirty minutes."

Colby has missed spending time with Cece. When I was worried about Nolan being here, I'd made arrangements for him to spend last week rotating between Lucy and Charlie's houses. Being a single mom, I make sure to have everything set up in advance, so I couldn't very well say never mind and have Cece come over. Things were back to normal, but I didn't want to raise suspicions about why I was bringing Colby to them in the first place. It's entirely possible that I'm overthinking this entire thing, but I suppose that's what happens when you're avoiding telling your friends the truth about why you're scared to leave your kid home with a babysitter.

"I'm going to finish painting her a picture," Colby says, then takes off running out of my bathroom.

I smile in the mirror. He's such a sweet kid. Then it hits me...

"Colby," I call. "You mean draw, not paint, right?" No answer. "Colby?"

My question is met with silence. It's that scary kind of silence that screams *your kid is getting up to something he knows he shouldn't be doing and doesn't want to say anything.* I'm fine with him expressing his creative spirit; hell, I encourage it. He loves using paints, but I'm always there to supervise and make sure we don't suddenly have a new mural of handprints on the wall.

Walking into the kitchen, I find my son sitting at the table, papers scattered across the cloth I keep handy so accidents don't ruin the wood. Well, at least he thought to do that much.

"What did I tell you about painting while I can't be here to watch?" I ask.

He looks up at me, and I notice the line of blue across his cheek. "I forgot."

"You forgot what I said, or you forgot you weren't supposed to get all this out by yourself?"

He sticks his bottom lip out and looks to the side. "Both?"

"Yeah, I'm not buying it, kid." I shake my head and sit across from him. "You know the rules with the paint. Next time you break them, there won't be any more painting, understood?"

"Sorry, Mommy. You were busy, and I really wanted to paint a picture for Cece. She loves my paintings."

"I understand, but you still have to ask."

He slouches in his seat at the table. "Can I keep painting, or do I have to put it away?"

"Do you promise to ask next time?"

He nods with wide eyes, imploring me not to take his paints away.

"Okay." I look at what he's working on. "That looks great, buddy. Tell me about your picture." That's a little trick I learned after about the tenth time that I would try to decipher his drawings—ask him to explain so I don't inevitably get it wrong. Though Colby is artistic for a five-year-old little boy, he's more of an abstract artist than a realist. That could also be because he's five.

"That's me," he says, pointing to a smaller figure on the page. "And that's Cece." He points to a figure with yellow hair.

"Who's that?" I ask, pointing to the blob of yellow.

"Pepper," he says as though it should be obvious. I suppose I can see it if I squint one eye and close the other.

"What are you guys doing?" The only thing he's painted with the figures is a huge green ground.

"We're playing at the park, but I still need to paint the swings." Colby grabs a brush and dips it in black paint.

"Okay, bud. Why don't you finish your painting, and I'll make you a snack."

"Carrots, please," he requests.

"You know, you're going to turn orange one of these days," I tell him as I stand from the table. Most moms would be happy their five-year-old is interested in vegetables at all, but the only thing this kid eats is anything orange.

"Really?" he asks excitedly, kicking his feet back and forth under the table. "That would be so cool."

I should *not* have told him that. It's going to be more of an incentive now.

"How about an apple, too?"

"With peanut butter?" he asks without looking from the black paint he's now using to line a swing set.

"Duh." I smile, walk over to the refrigerator, and pull out an apple and a bag of carrots, then set them on the counter that separates the kitchen from the small dining area where Colby is set up.

The entire time I was pregnant with Colby, I ate apples and peanut butter. It was one of my only cravings, and my grandmother was convinced he would come out of the womb with a spoonful of peanut butter. The memory of her making that joke sends a sharp pang of grief through my heart. God, I miss her.

My grandma never knew who Colby's dad was because I refused to tell anyone. But I know that if she were here, and I had told her how scared I was last week when Nolan showed up at the house, she would've done everything in her power to reassure me we were safe. She would have gathered me in her arms and told me that she knew I had my reasons for not saying anything—just like she did a hundred times before. And it breaks my heart that Colby doesn't remember her. That she won't see him grow into this adorably sweet and occasionally mischievous little soul who she loved from the instant I told her I was pregnant.

"Mom, why are you staring at me?"

A laugh escapes, and I grab a knife from the butcher block next to me and begin cutting his apple. "I happen to like looking at you."

He gives me one of his goofy grins and goes back to painting his masterpiece.

I bring his snack over to the table, and he grabs a carrot and bites into it, munching as he concentrates on his painting. After putting everything away, I take a seat at the table across from my son to supervise while he paints. He's engrossed in his project, only stopping to take a bite of either the apple or carrot on his plate and examine his work of art.

My phone dings with a notification from the dating app. There are a couple messages from the guy who I matched with. Steven Sheridan, age thirty-five, never been married, and no kids. He's good-looking with dark hair, and his bio says he's six-one. Not bad. He seems nice enough. I told him I am, in fact, a single mother, and he was completely nonplussed by the idea. Lucy didn't put that in my profile, but I don't feel right lying to any-one about being a mom or omitting that fact while we get to know each other online. It seems disingenuous, and though I've spent the last several years keeping a secret from those closest to me, I'm painfully truthful in every other area of my life.

Almost as though I'm overcompensating for the last five years of a huge omission.

Steven: *How do you feel about Thai food?*

Me: *Love it. There was a little Thai restaurant in Boston that had the best Pad Thai I've ever tasted in my life.*

Steven: *Are there any good Thai restaurants where you live?*

Me: *Lol. No. It's been years since I've had Thai.*

Steven: *There's a great spot about twenty minutes from me. Maybe we can have our first official date there.*

Me: *Well, I'm pretty sure to go out on a date you'd have to ask first.*

Steven: *I'm working my way up to it.*

"Okay, Mommy. All done." Colby holds up his painting, and I put my phone down to give him my full attention.

I'm pretty sure he used all of the blue paint he had for the sky, and he added another figure.

"Who's that, buddy?"

"It's Cash. Sometimes he comes to the park with me and Cece."

Interesting. I wonder how Lucy feels about the MC treasurer hanging out with her sister.

"Let's put this on the front porch so it dries faster, yeah?" I grab the painting by the corner and walk out to the porch, laying it on the small table that sits between two rocking chairs. I've always loved this porch. It's where my grandmother and I would sit in the evenings when the weather was nice and enjoy the golden hour together. When I was little, I remember her out here knitting while she rocked and listened to me babble on about whatever was on my mind.

Sitting in one of the chairs, I close my eyes and take in a deep breath, remembering how simple I thought life was. I think about the day she and I sat in these chairs when I was seven months pregnant and we were talking about whether or not to decorate Colby's room with bears or trains. It was so simple then, yet it wasn't. I was having a baby by myself, which in and of itself was completely daunting. But I had my grandmother at my side, and she made sure I knew just how much I was loved and how excited she was to have a great-grandson.

Then she left us, and I was alone and heartbroken, and the club stepped up. Ozzy made sure I was paid while on leave, and Tanya—Linc and Knox's mom—would come over and help out with Colby while Elaine Dawson and I planned my grandma's funeral. Tanya helped me find babysitters when I went back to work, and the brothers made sure to keep my tip jar full. During a time when I thought for sure I was going to drown, they held me up.

"What are you doing out here?" Colby asks as he comes and sits in the other chair. He starts rocking, but his feet don't touch the ground, so he's swaying his body back and forth to make the chair move.

"Just thinking about Grandma," I reply and watch this little person I created in the same chair I used to sit in when I was his age.

"What song did she used to sing to me?" he asks.

Colby doesn't remember her, but I do my best to tell him about her, and he loves it when I sing the songs that she used to.

"Come here," I say, patting my lap. He hops off the chair, and I set him on my legs, wrapping his little body in my arms. I start singing the same song my grandmother used to rock him to sleep with, and he rests his head on my shoulder. I'm not going to have many more years like this with my son, so I revel in these moments with him while I still can.

"How much longer till Cece gets here?" he asks.

"She should be here any minute, actually," I reply. "Let me go check the time." I pat his leg and he stands from my lap. "Can you go wash the paint off your hands and face, please?"

I walk to the kitchen, where I left my phone, as Colby trudges to the bathroom. I swear, what do kids have against soap and water?

The time on my phone reads 3:40 p.m., which is about ten minutes after Cece was supposed to be here. I dial her number, and it goes to voicemail. Maybe she's on her way.

I begin cleaning up the paints that Colby had out. Usually this would be his job, but if Cece's late, then I'm going to have to run out of the house as soon as she gets here, and I don't want to leave her with a mess. I take care of the few dishes that are in the sink and still haven't heard anything from her. I try to call her again, and again, there's no answer, so I call Lucy.

"Hey," I say when she answers her phone. "Are you at home?"

"No, Linc and Jude surprised me and Charlie with a trip to the beach. You okay?"

"Yeah, but I tried to call Cece, and she isn't answering her phone. She was supposed to be here ten minutes ago."

"Hmm. I'll give her a call," Lucy says with a slightly worried tone to her voice.

I'm a bit concerned with her not being here as well. Cece has been going through a hard time lately, but she's always been on top of it when it comes to watching Colby for me. Lucy has said the only time she's really her old self is when she spends time with my kid.

"Okay. I think I'm going to call Mia, though. I'm supposed to be at the bar in a few minutes, so I kind of need someone here right away."

"That's probably a safe bet. I know Cece was up late again last night, so she might be sleeping." Lucy doesn't sound so much worried as she sounds irritated that her sister would be blowing me off.

"Okay, have fun." I hang up the phone and dial Mia's number.

"Hi, friend," she answers.

"Hey. So remember when you said you were a little offended that Colby never asked for you and Knox to watch him?" I ask in a cheery voice. "Good news. He'd love his favorite auntie to spend the evening with him while I'm at work."

Mia laughs. "I wish I could, but Knox is taking me to the beach. I guess Charlie and Lucy went down earlier today with Linc and Jude, and when I mentioned that I was jealous, Knox called and made a reservation so we could meet them there."

"Shit," I breathe out.

"What's going on?" she asks.

"Honestly, Cece flaked on me, and I don't have anyone to watch Colby for the night."

"So he didn't want to spend time with his *favorite* aunt?" she asks, humor lacing her tone.

"I'm sure he'd love to, but no, it was my idea. Thought if I buttered you up, you wouldn't be able to resist saying yes."

"First of all, you never have to butter me up to hang out with my favorite five-year-old. Second, I'll be there."

"No way," I tell her, leaving no room for an argument. "You guys have plans, and there's no way I'm going to be the one responsible for you being stuck here watching Colby instead of enjoying the ocean."

"Knock it off. We'll go down tomorrow. Besides, I made a new batch of chocolate chip cookies yesterday that will go to waste if I don't bring them over."

"That's a flimsy reason for postponing your trip and doesn't make me feel better about anything in the least," I say, blowing out a long breath.

"Too bad. I'll be there in ten minutes," she says and hangs up the phone.

Laughing to myself, I make my way down the hallway filled with family pictures of me, my grandmother, and Colby, and find my son in his room changing out of his paint-splattered T-shirt.

"Hey, buddy. Mia is going to come hang out with you while I work tonight instead of Cece."

Colby sticks out his bottom lip. "But what about the picture I painted for her?"

"You can give it to her when we see her next. Mia said she made some cookies that have your name on them, so she wanted to come over tonight."

Obviously, I'm not going to tell him that his favorite babysitter is MIA.

He tilts his head back and forth, considering the change of plans. "What kind of cookies?"

A huff of laughter escapes me as I lean against the doorway of his room. "Chocolate chip."

A wide grin stretches across his face. "My favorite!"

I shake my head and feel my phone vibrate in my pocket. When I pull it out, Wyatt's name flashes on the screen.

"Hey," I say, answering the call.

"Hey, Maiz. I heard you were short a babysitter tonight. Thought me and Pepper could come hang out with Colby."

"Mia already said she was coming, and she promised cookies so…"

"Yeah, but Pepper misses his best friend, and I happen to be at Knox's place where said cookies were baked, so I can bring them with me. This way, Knox and Mia don't have to cancel their plans, Colby still gets his cookies, and Pepper gets to play with his favorite human."

It would make more sense to have Wyatt come. I hate the idea of Mia having to cancel her plans. Lord knows we all need a little getaway every now and again.

"I'm sure Colby would love it." It's not as though beggars can be choosers at this point.

Hearing his name, Colby turns to me with curiosity in his gaze.

"How about if Wyatt and Pepper come over instead?" I ask my son.

"Yes!" he exclaims, throwing his little fist in the air.

Wyatt's deep laugh comes through the phone. "I take it he's okay with the plan?"

I watch Colby hop up and down before he runs out of the room. "I'm going to paint Wyatt a picture of me and Pepper!" he yells.

"No more paints. You can use crayons," I call to him before answering Wyatt. "You could say that."

"Okay. See you in a few minutes."

Wyatt hangs up, and before I slide my phone back into my pocket, it dings with a text notification from Mia.

Mia: *If you're not okay with Wyatt watching Colby, I'll still come over.*

Me: *It's completely fine. Have fun on your trip.*

It's not that I don't implicitly trust Wyatt with my son. I do. Wyatt has been incredible with Colby, and he's always here to lend a helping hand. I haven't seen much of him since the other week with the raccoons, which is a little strange. Usually he's at the bar a couple nights a week, but I know he's been busy with club business. Not that I know exactly what that entails, nor would I ever ask. But it hits me that I've missed seeing him around. And those are not feelings I should be having. Especially when missing him proves my feelings are turning into more than friendship, and I'm not ready to look too closely at that. I *can't* look closer.

I remind myself once again that Wyatt is a brother in the Black Roses, and I'm the single mom who bartends at the bar his club owns. Acting on my fantasies would be a recipe for disaster. It's sure to blow up in my face, and that would hurt my kid, and possibly even put me out of a job. Not to mention, it would be so easy to let my little crush on Wyatt turn into something deeper, only to be...well, crushed. Nope. He needs to stay firmly in the friend zone. The stupidly hot and funny and charming friend zone.

"Get it together, Maizie," I whisper to myself as I walk into the living room where Colby has his crayons strewn across the coffee table as he furiously colors the paper in front of him.

"What are you drawing, buddy?"

"Wyatt on his motorcycle with me and Pepper on the back."

God, he really loves that dog. It almost makes me want to get him one of his own. Key word being *almost.*

I look at the picture and stick-figure Wyatt holding onto the handlebars, wearing a helmet. Colby is behind him with a huge smile on his face. A yellow dog sits behind him with its tongue hanging out of its mouth, wearing a helmet.

"Where's your helmet?" I ask.

"I gave it to Pepper. I want him to be safe," he says as he continues to color in the sky.

"Okay, but if you ever ride a motorcycle, you know you have to wear a helmet, right?"

"Of course, Mommy. When Wyatt let me sit on his bike, he made me put one on even though we weren't moving. He said I always need to practice safety, even if I'm just pretending."

Well, if that doesn't just punch me in the heart, I don't know what would.

I look at my phone and see the time. "Okay, buddy. I'm going to finish getting ready."

I walk into my room, put on my black boots, throw my hair into a high ponytail, and then there's a knock at the door.

"It's Wyatt and Pepper," Colby yells excitedly.

Moments later, I hear Colby laughing hysterically and Wyatt asking him where I am and if he's allowed to open the door for people.

"He knows it's safe for you," I reply for my son. I walk through the hallway from my bedroom to the front door, where Wyatt is standing. He's wearing a pair of faded jeans that mold to his long legs and a black T-shirt that hugs his chest.

It's positively sinful that this man looks this good in something as simple as a pair of jeans and a damn T-shirt. His colorful tattoos dance over his corded muscles as he reaches out and ruffles Colby's sandy-blond hair. The affectionate smile he gives my son melts my heart. When he turns that smile toward me, a flutter of excitement swirls in my chest.

This is bad. Very, very bad.

"You look nice," he says, letting his gaze trail over my entire body. That one look turns the little bit of excitement into a flurry of butterflies.

"I always look like this," I say, obviously terrible at taking any sort of compliment.

"And it's always good." Wyatt gives me one of those half smiles that makes it seem as though there's more meaning behind his words than what he's saying. Like men do when they flirt with a woman.

Wait, is he flirting with me?

Do I want him to flirt with me?

No.

Jesus, I just went over all the reasons why starting anything with him is a bad idea. Then three seconds into him being in my house, saying something sweet, and I'm questioning my own resolve.

"There's money on the counter for you guys to order food," I say, walking into the kitchen and away from Wyatt and the temptation I have no business feeling.

When I slide my phone out of my pocket to throw it in my purse, I see a message from the dating app.

Steven: *So if I were to ask you to dinner next week would you say yes?*

I smile at the message. This is more my speed. Someone who isn't involved with the club, who works a nice, normal job, and isn't one of my bosses.

Me: *I would definitely check my schedule. You know, if you were to ask.*

Steven: *Okay, how about dinner next Saturday? I'll send you the address of the restaurant, and we can meet there.*

Me: *You've got yourself a date.*

This is good. This is safe. This isn't giving me the butterflies that the man standing in my living room does, but that's okay. I haven't met Steven in person yet, but I'm willing to give him a shot. It's not as though I have anything standing in my way, like, say, a six-four biker. One who is currently standing in my entryway with his dog, here to watch my son for me. Nope, nothing in my way at all.

Steven: *Great, I'll send you all the information. I'm really looking forward to meeting you.*

Me: *Me too.*

I turn around, smiling down at my phone, and when I look up, Wyatt is standing less than a foot from me with a slight frown on his face. He's looking at the phone in my hand. When he notices me looking at him, his expression quickly clears, and he offers me a charming grin. But there's something in his eyes that wasn't before.

"You talking to a guy from that dating app Lucy set up for you?" He makes it sound casual, but that look is leaving me wondering if it is.

"Yeah, I actually agreed to dinner with one of the guys."

Wyatt nods. "Good, good. That's..."

"Good?" I finish for him.

"Yeah. It's all good, Maizie. You should get out there and meet some people." The way he says it tells me he isn't at all thrilled about the idea. And I don't love hearing it, but what can I possibly expect? I have no idea what to do with that, so I shrug and grab my purse and keys.

"Okay, I really need to get going. Thank you for coming. You have no idea how much I appreciate it."

"Of course, Maiz. I'm always here to help you out."

He really is. And that fact thrills me and kills me at the same time.

CHAPTER FIVE
WYATT

When Mia came into the workshop at Knox's place and told him that they needed to postpone their trip for a day because Maizie needed a sitter, I jumped at the opportunity to make myself available. It didn't hurt that I had Pepper with me, and Colby loves that dog as much as I do.

Since the night at the bar when Lucy signed Maizie up for that dating app, I've been doing a lot of thinking. And aside from showing up at her house the next day with the exterminators, I haven't seen her. I've been working security at Midnight Rose, the strip club that the club owns. And I had to make my monthly trip to check in on my parents, which never leaves me in a good mood. I didn't want to bring my shitty attitude around Maizie. She's my friend, but I know damn well there's some sort of spark between us. And I know she feels it, too.

Maybe I was selfish in thinking I had time. Maybe I figured there was no way she was going to meet the man of her dreams working at a little bar in Shine. I've never made a move, but there are a million reasons why. Answers to questions I still haven't quite figured out. After all, it isn't just Maizie I worry about hurting, it's her son, too. I grew up with parents who fought all the time until finally getting divorced. When I was younger, times were better, but things changed and I was caught in the aftermath. A part of me is scared that I'll repeat my parents' mistakes, and the idea of putting Colby through that breaks my fucking heart.

Truth be told, I've been interested since I met her almost five years ago. She was hot, and I was single. I didn't know much about her the first time I saw her working at Thorn and Thistle, but Ozzy was quick to tell me that she was off-limits when I asked about her. He made it clear that she'd just had a kid, and the last thing she needed was anyone fucking with her head. I respected my prez and the brotherhood enough to listen. I was free and single and had every intention of keeping my life that way.

But now...now things have changed for me.

When her grandmother passed away, the club did what it always did and rallied around one of our own. Even though she was an employee of the club, she was still ours.

She started coming around the clubhouse with her kid for family dinners Tanya liked to arrange. The employees from the shop and the bar would get together and eat massive amounts of food and hang at the clubhouse with their families. Obviously, Maizie never stayed for the festivities that would take place later in the evening, and I found myself less and less inclined to as well. When Linc got out of prison, and his old lady came into the picture along with Lucy, they started working at the bar as well. The two girls and Maizie hit it off and became fast friends. Since my brothers were spending more time there, I tagged along.

That's when I admitted to myself that my feelings for Maizie started to change. Somewhere along the way, I saw her as more than just our hot bartender who had a kid, and instead started seeing her as a friend. As a gorgeous and strong woman who took care of herself and her kid.

Whenever she needed something, I'd make sure she had it without her having to ask. Oil change on her car? Check. Leaky faucet? Turns out I'm a great plumber. Her lawn mower took a shit and she needed her grass cut? Never let it be said I don't love to do a little landscaping for my favorite bartender. It wasn't that I was doing any of this in the hopes of getting her in bed, but she needed a helping hand, and I have two.

The small things I did for her would turn into a beer when I was finished or dinner if she didn't have to head into work. If I was coming by the park to let Colby play with Pepper, I made sure to stop and get her favorite coffee from Cool Beans. Not because I wanted her to feel indebted to me, but because we're friends—and that's what friends do.

But I want more. Have for a while. Since my feelings have changed into something more than friendship, I've tried to figure my shit out. Tried to come to terms with my shitty upbringing and wondered several times over the last couple years if I could even be the man she deserves. If I have it in me. Ozzy couldn't possibly take issue with me dating her if my head is on straight, right?

But she's never really seemed to look at me as anything more than a friend.

Until I showed up at her place tonight.

There was no mistaking the heated look in her stare when she came down the hallway and I was standing in front of her door after Colby let me in. When I laid eyes on her in her tight black jeans and loose T-shirt that hung off one shoulder, the urge to run my tongue over the bare skin of that shoulder was strong. Maizie is beautiful, there's no denying it, and it's getting harder and harder for me to not walk up to her and press my lips against hers to see how she'd react. Would she open her pink lips and let me taste her, or would she push me away? I always thought there was time for me to make a move, more time for me to figure my shit out, but my window is closing thanks to Lucy and that damn dating app.

She was messaging with a guy she matched with when she was leaving. He put a smile on her face, and I wanted to punch *him* in the face. Granted, I have no idea who the hell he is, but I hate him already. Maybe I could have Jude's brother break into her account and find out his information. It wouldn't be too hard, I'm sure. Then I could pay him a little visit and...Okay, that might be too far. Although now that the idea has formed in my mind, I'm not sure it's entirely off the table.

Instead, I did the dumbest thing I possibly could and told her she should meet people. Why I said that, I have no idea. I don't want her meeting anyone else. I want her to finally see what's between us. But she seemed happy and a little more relaxed than I've seen her lately and I'm...an idiot.

"Come give me a kiss, buddy," Maizie calls into the other room as we're standing face to face in her kitchen, awkwardly waiting for Colby to come say goodbye. Why is it so strained between us all of a sudden? It's never like this with me and Maizie. But she wasn't messaging other guys any time we hung out before, and I wasn't telling her it's a good thing she's making plans with other guys.

Colby comes bouncing in with Pepper hot on his heels and throws his arms around Maizie's waist. "I love you, Mommy," he says, and she bends to kiss the top of his head.

"I love you too, monkey. Be good for Wyatt, yeah?"

He looks up at her with a wide grin. "Can he take me to the park?"

"Not this time, bud. He needs a car seat for his truck, and I don't have time to put mine in there."

He gives her a little pout.

"Don't worry, Colby, we're going to have so much fun here that you won't miss the park at all," I tell the disappointed little boy.

"What are we going to do?" he asks.

"Uhh…" Shit, I've never watched Colby on my own. I feel like I should ask for a list of age-appropriate activities we're allowed to do.

"How about you and Pepper run around the backyard? We still have a rope and a few balls for him back there. Then I'll bet Wyatt will build you a fort in the living room, and you guys can watch movies. After that, you can pick out two books for Wyatt to read before you go to bed."

Sounds easy enough.

"Okay. Come on, Pepper," he says and hightails it through the kitchen to the door that leads to their expansive backyard.

"Shit, I really have to go," Maizie says, looking at the clock on the wall. "You sure you're good with this?"

I give her the most reassuring smile I can muster and hope she didn't pick up on the moment of doubt I had. "Of course. I was a five-year-old boy once. I'm sure we'll be fine."

"Okay, I'll see you around eleven," she says, and once again we're left in an awkward limbo.

"Have a good shift," I say and step aside so she can move past me. I follow Maizie to the door and watch her get in her car and send her a small wave before shutting the front door.

I make my way to the backyard and have a seat on Maizie's deck. Colby is running around, playing with the dog, as I enjoy a warm evening in the house of the woman I've been pining over without her.

Colby runs over with Pepper trotting behind him. "Can I have a soda?"

"Does your mom let you have soda before dinner?"

"Can I have dinner?"

"Of course, buddy. You should have told me you were hungry." That unlocks another fear. Has this kid been starving the whole five minutes I've been here and didn't tell me? Would he tell me? Does Maizie have him on some sort of feeding schedule she didn't tell me about?

"I'm not that hungry, but I really want a soda," he says.

"Do you know what time you usually eat dinner?"

He shrugs. "I dunno. Whenever I tell my mommy I'm hungry, she usually just gives me something to eat."

Okay, so he knows how to ask for food. That's a relief.

Jesus Christ, Wyatt, he's five, not a baby who can't talk. Get a grip.

I may be overthinking this whole food thing, but this feels like a test. Not one Maizie set up, I volunteered after all. But still. I think being able to take care of her kid when she's not around is pretty damn important.

"How about I order us some pizza, and I'll let you have half a soda before it gets here and the other half with dinner?" That seems reasonable.

"Okay. Come on, Pepper, let's order pizza."

Colby leads the way into the house, pulls the menu from a drawer, and hands it to me.

"What do you like on it?" I ask.

"Chocolate," he answers with a sly grin. "And marsh-mallows."

I shoot him a dubious look and he giggles. "How about sausage and mushrooms?"

He scrunches his nose and shakes his head. "No mushrooms, but me and Pepper love sausage."

"Pepper doesn't eat pizza."

Colby tilts his head to the side. "He did when we were at Lucy's. He stole it right from my plate." Colby giggles and pets Pepper on the head as the dog leans against him with his tongue hanging from his mouth.

"Well, he's not supposed to." I grab my phone from my pocket and dial the pizzeria, placing an order for a large sausage pizza and some cheesy breadsticks. Turning toward the fridge, I grab a can of soda and find a glass in the cupboard next to it. "Alright, deal's a deal," I say, pouring half the can into the small plastic cup and handing it to Colby. He turns to walk into the living room with it, watching the top carefully so it doesn't spill.

"Are you allowed to have that in the living room?" I call and he turns around and walks back into the kitchen.

I smile as he has a seat at the kitchen table and drinks from his cup. When he's about halfway through, he stops and lets out the biggest burp, then laughs. A chuckle escapes me, which makes Colby's smile wider.

"Mommy says that's gross, and I should say excuse me. I don't think girls think that's funny. Sarah in my class says it's gross, too." He shrugs but seems rather nonplussed about this Sarah girl calling him gross.

"Pfft. What does Sarah know? Take another sip. Let's see if you can make it louder."

Colby laughs and downs the rest of his soda. When he opens his mouth, a loud burp escapes, and then he giggles so hard he nearly topples over.

"You do it, Wyatt!"

I shrug and stand from my seat to walk over and get my own soda. I chug half of it and then hold up a finger, signaling for Colby to wait. When I open my mouth, I release a long and very loud burp of my own. Colby laughs hysterically, slapping the kitchen table with his little palm. I shake my head and realize entertaining a five-year-old isn't that hard after all. Hell, it's practically the same as hanging out at the clubhouse, but instead of beer, we're downing sodas and laughing at stupid shit.

"Do it again," he yells with excitement.

Man, this kid's easy. I chug the rest of my soda and burp as loud and for as long as I possibly can. Colby is laughing ridiculously hard, and this time he does fall off his seat, but he rolls on his back and continues to giggle. Pepper, not wanting to be left out of the fun, starts licking Colby's face, which only serves to make Colby laugh harder. Once his laughter has settled, he sits up on the floor and Pepper lies down next to him, turning on his back for belly rubs.

"Come on, kid. Didn't your mom say something about building a fort?"

"I love forts. And farts!" He laughs hysterically at his own joke, and I can't seem to keep the smile off my face.

"I'll build a fort if you promise not to fart in it."

That gets him laughing even harder. "No farts in the fort. No farts in the fort," he sings as he jumps up and runs to the closet. I grab the soda cans and his cup from the table and rinse it out before sticking it in the dishwasher. I know how easily messes can pile up, and if you stay on top of it, it won't overwhelm you the next day. At least that's the case at the clubhouse. I assume living with a kid is the same to some extent, and I don't want Maizie coming home to a mess.

I head into the living room and move the low coffee table to the side. Colby walks in with blankets and pillows stacked on his little arms higher than his head.

"Woah, kid," I say as I grab everything from him. "The last thing I need is a trip to the ER because you tripped over something and busted your head. I don't think your mom would be too pleased to get that phone call."

"I've never been to the hospital. Have you?" he asks with wide eyes.

How do you tell a kid the last time you were in a hospital was when you were visiting your brother, who was shot because his woman's crazy ex was after her? Answer is simple: you don't.

"Nope," I say, lying through my teeth. The little white lie isn't going to hurt him, but the truth would scare the shit out of him. "So how does this usually go?"

Colby taps his finger to his chin. "My mommy takes the chairs in the kitchen and spreads them out here"—he points to a corner of the living room—"here"—he points to the other corner—"and over there."

"Sounds easy enough."

I turn and walk into the kitchen, and Colby darts past me, grabbing a chair and lifting it, but he only gets it about three inches off the ground before he turns around with it.

"I can do it," he says, struggling to walk with the high-backed chair in his arms.

"Uh, how about you let me? Remember, we're trying to avoid accidents while your mom's gone."

Colby sets it down and wipes his forehead with the back of his arm. "Okay," he says, a little out of breath. "That's heavy."

"Don't worry. Give it another year and you'll be carrying all kinds of stuff around."

"Really?"

I honestly have no clue. "Yup. Keep eating your veggies and you'll grow up strong." That sounds like the right thing to say.

"I love carrots. And apples. And peanut butter. And chips. And cookies," he explains as I carry the chairs two at a time into the living room.

"How about pizza?" I toss the pillows Colby brought on the floor between the chairs.

"That's my biggest favorite."

I drape the blanket over the chairs, and voilà, we have ourselves a living room fort. "Phew, because we have one coming."

As I finish my sentence, the doorbell rings. Colby runs to the door.

"Let me open it, buddy."

The young delivery driver is on the other side, and I hand him the money from my pocket—because no way in hell is Maizie paying for anything—then take the pizza into the kitchen.

"One slice or two?" I ask the little guy standing next to me, who is practically salivating over the delicious scent of cheese and sausage.

"Three," he answers.

I look at the pizza and back to him. "How about we start with two and you can have a third if you're still hungry?"

Colby nods. "Deal."

I fix him a plate and give him another half of a soda—I'm the adult here, so I make the decision to bend the rules just a tad—and send him into the living room where he crawls into his fort. Walking into the living room with my plate, I ask what he wants to watch. He picks some kids cartoon I've never heard of, and I cue it up on the television. Colby's eyes are glued to the TV as he sits on the pillows with Pepper lying next to him, the dog's eyes following the slice of pizza Colby brings to his mouth then sets back on his plate as he chews.

As I settle into the couch with my own plate, I feel my phone vibrate in my pocket. Lucy's name flashes on the screen.

"I'll be right back, bud," I say, pulling the phone from my pocket before heading into the kitchen.

"Hey, what's up?" I ask.

"Hey. I talked to Cece. She was asleep and didn't hear her alarm or the million phone calls from me and Maizie. If you want her to, she can come and relieve you of your babysitting duties."

"Nah, I'm good. We just got pizza, and now we're watching some cartoon with talking cars."

"Jesus, I think I've watched that movie at least a dozen times with him," Lucy says with a laugh. "So you volunteered to watch Maizie's kid, huh?" Her tone isn't so much a question as it is a statement laced with meaning.

"I did. He's a cool kid, and Mia and Knox wanted to get out of town to meet up with you guys."

"Uh-huh. I'm sure it was you just being helpful to your VP and his old lady."

And there it is. I shouldn't be surprised. There have been a couple moments when we've been at the bar and my gaze has lingered a little too long on Maizie, and Lucy's noticed. She didn't say anything then, but apparently she was biding her time. And apparently, that time is now.

"What can I say? I'm a nice guy," I tell her without taking the bait.

"Of course you are. You're also as transparent as a windshield," Lucy says with amusement in her voice.

"I don't know what you're talking about."

"Yeah, okay." She doesn't buy it for a second. "Have fun with Colby. And if you're so inclined to do something for Maizie when she gets home, she has a bottle of red in the cupboard above the fridge. She likes to have a little glass after a shift sometimes to help her wind down."

A small smile tips my lips. "Good to know."

"I thought it might be."

Lucy hangs up, and I make my way back into the living room. I peek my head in the fort and see that Colby has already wolfed down one slice of pizza and is working on his second.

"Wow, bud. You were hungry."

He nods. "Can I have another one now?"

"Of course."

I hand him one from my plate and sit back down.

This babysitting thing is a walk in the park.

A couple hours and several homemade cookies later, Colby can barely keep his eyes open. It's around nine o'clock, and I figure he'll let me know when he's tired enough for bed. When I look inside the fort, he gives me a tired smile.

"Ready to hit the hay?" I ask.

"Yeah."

He gets up from his cocoon of blankets and pillows and trudges into his room.

"Let me know when you're ready," I say, giving him some privacy to change into his pajamas.

"Okay, Wyatt."

I walk in, and the kid is under the covers with three books sitting on the bed.

"Can you read me a story?"

I nod and sit next to him, picking up a book with a bear on the front. It looks as though it's been well read, the cardboard pages frayed at the edges.

"Is this your favorite?"

He nods slowly, the sugar crash from the cookies hitting him hard.

I read him his book, surprised that when I get to the end, he's still awake.

"Another?" I ask.

He nods again, and again, when I get to the end, he's still awake.

"One more?" he asks with pleading eyes.

"Okay. Just one though, and then you need to close your peepers and get some sleep."

This time, when I get to the last page, I look at Colby and he's out cold.

Carefully, I stand so I don't wake him up and signal for Pepper to follow me out of the room, shutting the door behind me.

When I get into the living room, I begin cleaning up the mess we made. It's not really that bad, and I'm done in less than ten minutes. Maizie won't be home for a while still, so I turn on the TV and start watching some baseball highlights to pass the time.

About half an hour later, the headlights from her car illuminate the living room through her front window. I open the curtain and watch her get out of the car and make her way up the front porch. Heading into the kitchen, I open the cupboard above the fridge and pull down the bottle of wine Lucy told me she keeps there. I grab a glass from the cupboard and pour her a healthy amount, then walk back into the living room as she slides the key into the lock of her front door.

I take a seat as she opens the door, and when she sees me on the couch with the TV playing quietly in the background, she smiles.

"How was he?" she asks as she sets her things down on one of the overstuffed living room chairs.

"He was great. He and Pepper played, then we ate pizza and watched the same movie almost three times."

Maizie releases a breathy laugh. "*Cars?*"

"Yup. I was digging those talking cars. Especially the judge. Kind of reminds me of Ozzy."

Maizie bursts out laughing and sits on the other end of the sofa. I hand her the glass, and she looks at it then back to me. Her expression is soft as she takes the glass from my hand and sips.

"Ah," she breathes out and leans against the cushions. "I could get used to this."

I want you to get used to this.

"My services are at your disposal." The corner of my mouth tips up in what I would like to think is a charming smile.

Maizie shakes her head and chuckles. "You never know. I might need you here again."

Shrugging, I watch as she takes another sip. "Anytime. I mean it, Maiz. Colby's an awesome kid."

"Yeah, he is pretty great."

"You're doing a hell of a job raising him."

She swallows and blows out a breath. "Thank you. Honestly, that means a lot. It's not easy doing this alone. I worry that I'm screwing him up all the time, and I'll have nobody to blame but myself."

"Trust me. He's far from being screwed up, Maizie. Sometimes having one parent is better than having two who are bitter and angry that they're forced to be together to raise a kid neither really wanted in the first place."

Her head tilts to the side as she studies me. "You sound like you're talking from experience."

I shrug. "My folks weren't exactly going to win any parenting awards. When my dad lost his job, my mom about damn near lost her mind. He started drinking and cheating, and she started gambling. They stayed together a lot longer than they should have for 'the sake of our family.'"

"You seemed to turn out okay, though."

"That depends on who you ask, I guess." I let out a humorless laugh. "They got divorced when I graduated high school. He lives right down the street from her in a little duplex with another guy in the other unit. And somehow they still find the time to make each other miserable at every turn. They don't really have a reason to interact at all since I'm not around, but I guess toxic cycles are hard to break. And they love trying to drag me into their shit."

"When was the last time you spoke to them?"

"Yesterday, actually. I went to visit my mom and she was complaining about my dad and his new flavor of the month and how the entire neighborhood is talking about it. Then I went to see him, and he was talking about my mom spending her entire paycheck at the casino and trying to get him to pay more in alimony because the cost of living went up." I shake my head and roll my eyes. "According to him, one of the neighbors saw her at the casino."

Maizie leans her head against the back cushion of the couch and brings her knees up, resting them next to me. "What do you do when they're like that?"

"I nod along and try to stay neutral. No use getting on either of them about their shit at this point. Not that they'd listen. Then I slipped an envelope of cash into my mom's mail slot and came home. And I'll probably do it all over again next month when I make my way out there."

She wrinkles her nose. "Jesus, I'm sorry, Wyatt. That's really shitty."

I shrug. "It is what it is. I could write them both off, but then who knows where they'd end up. My mom would probably be homeless, my dad would feel bad and offer to let her move in, and the whole thing would start all over again." I resist the urge to pull her feet into my lap and run my hand over her tired calves.

I think back to all the times my dad would be between girlfriends, and he'd end up staying with my mom. They said they were going to try to work things out, but sure enough, she'd be throwing his shit on the lawn a couple weeks later.

"Well, I think that despite everything, you've turned out to be a pretty decent guy," she says, smiling as she reaches over and rests her hand on my knee. The heat from her palm travels up my thigh, and I shift in my seat—because if I don't, she's going to see just how much that simple touch is affecting me.

Her hand falls away, and a second later, her face curls into a grimace. She grabs her T-shirt and pulls it over her nose.

That's when I smell it.

"Jesus, Pepper," I say as I pull my own T-shirt over the lower half of my face.

Pepper looks up from his place next to the couch, completely unbothered by the stench he's gassed us with.

"God, what do you feed him?" she coughs out.

"He hasn't had dinner yet." Then I think back to the amount of food I *thought* Colby shoveled in his mouth.

I let out a chuckle and wipe at my watering eyes. "Pizza."

Chapter Six
Maizie

"That one. That's the perfect first date outfit," Mia says while I have her on a video call.

"You don't think it's too, I don't know... casual?" I ask.

There are three outfits laid out on the bed, and I can't decide between two of my favorites. Mia vetoed one of the dresses right away. Said it was "too much" for a date at a Thai restaurant and that it should be reserved for a third or fourth date in the city or something. I laughed and told her we might not make it that far. She was quick to inform me that if we didn't go out again, it would be my decision, because any man would have to be a complete moron not to want to.

"No. The off-the-shoulder top is perfect. And those jeans look amazing on you. Plus, it's a good idea to wear flats just in case you need to make a break for it."

I laugh. "Jesus, Mia." She might have a point, though.

"You never know. He could be a total dud. What if you need to escape through the bathroom window?"

"Oh my God. Has that actually happened to you?"

"The dud part, yes. *The Great Bathroom Escape*, no. But I've been on a couple dates where climbing through a window would have been preferable over going back to the table."

I sit on the bed and let out a breath. "I'm not sure I'm cut out for this. Maybe I should cancel and delete that app. This seems like a lot of work for something I could potentially be trying to run away from."

"Oh, come on. I'm kidding. No one actually does that. Besides, how are you going to meet someone if you don't try? A couple duds is par for the course."

"You're really selling this," I deadpan.

"It'll be fine. I'm sure Steven is going to be a perfect gentleman, and you're going to have the best time ever."

"What am I doing, though? I have a kid who needs me around. I shouldn't be taking off to hang out with some random guy I met on the internet."

"Maizie, Colby is fine. Auntie Mia is going to come over, and we're going to bake cupcakes and watch movies. Then I'm going to read him *four* bedtime stories, and I'll be his favorite again."

I burst out laughing. "So my date is really only an opportunity for you to be number one on Colby's list of favorite people?"

She gives me one of those looks that says I'm an idiot for thinking anything else. "Naturally."

I shake my head and run my hand over my face, letting out a tortured groan.

"Listen, sister," Mia starts, interrupting my internal freak-out. "You are an amazing mom, but you're also a woman. You have every right to want to go out and meet someone. Find a partner. Shit, if you want to go out, get laid, and never talk to the guy again, you have every right to do that, too. Whatever you decide isn't going to take away from being a great mom. But you have to take care of yourself, too, and there's no reason for you to feel the least bit guilty about that."

My eyes meet Mia's through the phone, and she gives me her librarian stare—the one that says I need to listen to her and not argue because she's the expert.

"Okay, okay," I concede. "Enough about this date. You and Knox are coming to Colby's game, yeah?"

My son started Little League this year. Even though I was never particularly into sports growing up, there's something ridiculously adorable about watching a bunch of five-year-olds hitting a ball off the tee and trying to figure out where to run.

"We'll definitely be there. Actually, I think everyone is coming."

She has no idea what that means to me. Colby doesn't have any family other than me—well, none that anyone knows about—so when my friends show up to support him, it makes me feel a little less alone in this whole single-parent thing.

"Okay. I need to get him ready. See you in an hour," I tell Mia, and we hang up.

As I'm putting the outfits away that I won't be wearing tonight, my phone rings again.

Elaine Dawson's name flashes on the screen.

"Hello?"

"Maizie, sweetheart. How are you?" she asks in a cheerful voice.

"Fine. How are you, Mrs. Dawson?"

"What have I told you about calling me Elaine?"

"Sorry," I say with a little chuckle. "Habit."

"Well, break it, dear. You're making me feel old."

We both laugh. Elaine reminds me so much of my own grandmother. She was never one to stand on ceremony, just like Elaine isn't.

"I heard young Colby has a baseball game today," she says.

"He does. I was just about to finish getting him ready so we can head over there."

"You know, it's been so long since I've seen a game in person," she says wistfully.

"Well, this isn't exactly the big leagues. The kids still hit off a tee."

"Everyone starts somewhere, and it's a beautiful day for a game."

"Do you want to go? I know Colby would love to see you." Even though Elaine doesn't know she's Colby's biological great-grandmother, she treats him like one anyway. In the few times we've spent with her, she's given him the kind of attention my own grandmother used to shower on him when he was a baby.

"I'd love to. Thank you for inviting me. How about you pick me up in thirty minutes? I'll go early with you so we can scope out the future all-star players together."

"Uh...sure. Sounds great."

"Wonderful," she says in that cheery tone again. "See you then."

She hangs up, and I stare at my phone. That woman is a master, and I kind of love her for it.

When I pull up to Elaine's house, Colby undoes his car seat straps and hops out of the car to greet her on her front porch. She was already waiting outside, enjoying the fresh air and warmer temperatures in one of her rocking chairs. Colby holds her hand as she walks down the steps. I don't think she needs the extra support, but I'm teaching him to be a gentleman, so this is great practice. And of course, Elaine absolutely eats it up.

They make their way to the car, and Colby opens the passenger door for her before getting in his own car seat.

"Hello, dear. It's such a gorgeous day for baseball," she greets, her voice chipper.

I smile and nod. "That it is. I'm glad you can come with us."

"Of course, dear. Thank you again for inviting me."

I have to stifle that laugh that threatens to escape. She knows damn well she angled that entire conversation earlier so she could get an invite.

"You strapped in, bud?" I turn and inspect Colby's car seat harness before putting the car in drive.

"Yup," he says with an enthusiastic smile on his face.

"Alright, here we go," I say as I pull around the circular driveway.

On the way to the game, Elaine starts talking to Colby about the finer points of the game. She tells him the stats of her favorite players and talks about her favorite moments from the games she's gone to. He soaks up the attention like he does every time we spend time with Elaine.

"Maybe you and your mom could come to a game with me this summer. I still have season tickets," she says.

"I want to go to a real baseball game, Mommy," he exclaims.

"We'll definitely do that this summer, buddy," I answer as I pull into the parking lot of the Little League field.

The sight in front of me warms me to my very soul. Motorcycles line the parking lot, as well as a couple of familiar trucks. The Black Roses have shown up en masse for my kid.

We pile out of the car, and Colby grabs his baseball bag, lugging it over his shoulder.

"Want me to carry that?" I ask.

"Nope. I got it," he says with a wide smile as he walks over to say hello to everyone.

Arthur Lewis, or Gramps as most of us call him, strides over to us and holds out his arm for Elaine. "It's a beautiful day for baseball, and I get to spend it with a beautiful lady at my side."

"Oh, Arthur, you are an incorrigible flirt," Elaine says as she slides her hand in the crook of his arm.

"You make it easy, Elaine."

I smile as I trail behind.

"Told you everyone was coming," Mia says when I meet her at the gate, along with Lucy and Charlie.

"I can't tell you how much I appreciate you all coming out to support Colby." My friends are the absolute best.

"We're family. Of course we're here," Lucy says, giving me a hug.

I walk over to Colby, who is getting high fives and words of encouragement from all the brothers.

"Kick their asses, kid. And remember, if the other player is crowding the base, just run right into him. That'll teach him," Jude instructs my son, and Lucy shoots him a withering look. "What?" he asks when he turns his gaze to her.

Lucy chuckles and shakes her head. "Nothing." She looks at Colby. "Don't listen to him," she says, pointing at the Englishman.

"I don't think they even keep score at this age," Charlie says.

"Maybe not, but there's nothing wrong with showing the other team who's boss," Jude replies.

"Right now we're working on teamwork and good sportsmanship, right, son?" I ask Colby before shooting Jude a look.

"Yup. And we do our best and cheer for everyone," he answers.

"What kind of bull—" Jude starts.

"It's what's important to teach five-year-olds, asshat," Knox says, wrapping an arm around Mia and pulling her closer to his chest.

"Okay, guys. I'm going to take Colby to his team before you impart any more words of wisdom to my son," I say, laughing as Colby and I walk over to his coach.

Colby runs over to greet the other kids, and the coach smiles as I approach. "We don't usually get this kind of turnout for T-ball," he says.

I turn and look at all the bikers and their old ladies—at my friends who have become our family.

"Yeah, we're lucky to have a big family."

Then a shot of fear runs through me. The same fear that I've felt since I saw Nolan just a few weeks ago.

Would we be so lucky if they knew the truth?

Watching the way Colby lit up when he hit the ball and everyone cheered for him as he ran the bases filled me with so much happiness I could've burst.

It was almost enough to drown out the lingering fear: if they knew who his father really was—or that I'd been keeping it a secret all these years, especially after everything that happened with the Bone Breakers last year—would they still be here?

Colby is on cloud nine after the game, and everyone tells him what a good job he did. It reminds me of when we were in high school and I'd see the entire club show up for Ozzy, Knox and Linc's football games. I would be there playing in the marching band, and I'd see nearly everyone who was here today cheering for the guys back then. When I was pregnant with Colby, I never imagined he would have that in his life, but I was wrong, and I've never been so happy about being wrong in my life.

We drop Elaine off at her house with a promise to pick her up next weekend. She tells Colby what a great game he played, and if he works hard, she has no doubt he'll make it to the majors.

Then she turns to me and says something that has me nearly in tears. "Your grandmother would be so proud of you."

I swallow hard and nod, not trusting my voice in that moment.

Elaine smiles and looks back at Colby. "He's a great kid, Maizie. No one will ever be able to take that away from you."

When she gets out of the car, I wonder what she means by that. I've made damn sure that no one can take him away, and as long as her grandson stays out of the picture, no one ever will.

After getting home, I make Colby a snack and then start cleaning the house to keep my mind occupied and off the impending date I have tonight with Steven. Jesus, *impending*? That's a horrible way to think about it. I'm just nervous. And second-guessing saying yes.

It's not as though I have many offers from guys around here, and it's not as though I've been interested in anyone I know. Well, except for one guy, but he's out of the realm of possibilities for me, and I need to stop thinking about the what-ifs that will never be.

No, this is good. It's exciting. At least I *should* feel excited. No, I *am* excited. I blow out a breath as I'm scrubbing a spot on my stove that was probably clean several minutes ago. This whole dating thing isn't off to the best start if I'm standing here having to convince myself that I'm looking forward to tonight.

"Mommy, can you put my movie on?"

Colby's voice breaks me out of the surge of self-doubt that's been plaguing me since we got home from the game.

"Yup."

We head into the living room, and I put his favorite movie on. Then I make my way to my room to take a shower. It's not an *everything* shower since there will be nothing happening tonight that would require that, but I'd like to show up not smelling like furniture polish.

As I'm finishing up my makeup, Mia texts me.

Mia: *We'll be there in 30. Heads-up, Wyatt and Pepper are coming too, if that's ok.*

I'll never say no to my kid spending time with his favorite furry friend. I saw Wyatt at the game, but Pepper wasn't with him. Before we left, Colby asked Wyatt if Pepper could come over tonight. Of course, he said yes, and I told Wyatt that Mia was watching Colby tonight since I have a date. I saw what looked like disappointment turn down the corners of his mouth for a brief second, but it was gone and replaced with a smile before I could make heads or tails of it.

Me: *Yeah, Colby invited him.*

Mia: *Okay, see you soon.*

I toss my phone on the bed and look at my outfit. I wore something similar when Wyatt came over to watch Colby for me last week. I remember that flash of heat I saw in his eyes. How much I liked seeing it there.

Not thoughts you should be having right before a first date with another guy, Mia.

When I change into my outfit, I'm instantly glad this is the one Mia picked. I'm comfortable and don't feel like I'm dressing up and putting on a show. It seems to take some of the pressure off, and I'm definitely all for that.

Heading into the living room, I see Colby sprawled on the couch, staring blankly at the bright colors on the screen.

"Why don't you take a little nap, bud. Then you'll have energy to play when everyone gets here."

He turns on his side and pulls the blanket over him, cocooning himself. He's always done that, even as a baby. I used to call him my little burrito because he'd wrap himself tightly in any blanket lying around and fall asleep within two minutes.

I head into the kitchen, make myself a cup of tea, and grab my phone. Might as well do a little doomscrolling before Mia gets here. I don't post on social media much, but I always make sure to stick one of those smiley face emojis over Colby. There are too many weirdos out there.

My old roommate, Emily, posted a picture of her in a bikini on some tropical vacation. Emily, Taylor, and I haven't stayed close throughout the years. Not that I blame them. Our lives took completely different turns, and we're all busy. I love seeing their accomplishments, even if it's just on social media. They will always hold a special place in my heart. Seeing their posts reminds me of a time when I took control of my future and escaped the confines of my parents' rules. Even though I'm back in Shine, it's because I made that choice—no one forced me.

The caption on her picture reads: *I'm never leaving.* Good for her. I wish I had the time and money to take a vacation like that. Hell, I wish I had the confidence to wear a bikini like that and post it.

After having Colby, there have been changes to my body. Not that anyone saw my pre-baby body—except on the night he was conceived. The stretch marks and dimples that appeared after pregnancy haven't troubled me too much, but I'd be lying if I said they didn't make me a little more self-conscious, especially now that I'm dipping my toe in the dating pond.

I wish I could say I was the kind of person who doesn't care if someone sees an imperfect body and feels less attracted to me. But the truth is, it would sting.

The few times I've been naked around anyone other than Colby's father, the lights were off and we were under the covers. I didn't do it intentionally, but I can't say the darkness didn't help me feel just a little more secure.

Jesus, I'm really getting ahead of myself. No one is seeing anyone naked anytime soon.

I look up from my phone, and from where I'm sitting at the kitchen table, I have the perfect view of Colby's head lolling to the other side of the couch. He's passed out cold. I do the most mom thing ever—walk over, kneel beside him, and just watch him sleep with a small smile tugging at my lips.

I used to do this every night when he was a baby. I'd sit next to his crib for what felt like hours, memorizing the rise and fall of his chest.

Sometimes, if my grandmother happened to pass by the open door, she'd step in and rest a hand on my shoulder. No words—just a quiet moment between generations. She knew. She understood that once you laid eyes on the little human you made, your life would never be the same. I know it broke her heart when she cut contact with my mother. That was her baby, but she couldn't stand to see what my mother and father did to their scared, pregnant daughter. Colby and I became her center until the day she died.

The sound of a motorcycle stopping in front of my house pulls me from my thoughts. Mia and Knox get off his bike while Wyatt's truck pulls up behind them. He walks around to the passenger door and opens it, allowing Pepper to jump out and make his way through my yard, stopping and sniffing every couple of feet. Wyatt strolls over to where Mia is unpacking the saddlebags on Knox's bike. She starts handing him a few things that look like ingredients to make the cupcakes she was bragging about using to get her the number one spot on Colby's list. When Pepper gets a little too close to my neighbor's front yard, Wyatt whistles, and the dog comes trotting over to him.

I open the door, and Pepper notices me right away. I can tell he wants to run inside and find who he's really here to see, but Wyatt hasn't given him the command yet.

When Wyatt looks at me waiting in my doorway, his smile turns up the corner of his mouth.

"Hey, Maizie," he greets as he makes his way over. "Where's Colby?"

"Sleeping on the couch," I say, nodding toward the inside of my house. "Come on in and wake him up."

"Inside," Wyatt commands, and the dog takes off running past me and into the living room. Seconds later, giggles erupt from Colby.

"Pepper!" he exclaims.

Wyatt climbs the stairs, and before he brushes past me, his gaze travels the length of my body. The heat in his eyes is unmistakable, and so is the moment his gaze shutters. "You look nice."

The nearness of him stutters the breath in my lungs. "Thank you," I reply lamely.

He gives me a tight smile then ventures into the house to set the bags he's carrying in the kitchen.

"Hey, sister," Mia says, walking into the house with a couple more bags, followed by Knox.

"What's all this?" I ask, peeking inside. I see more than just cupcake ingredients.

"Just some stuff I had lying around. When I see something at the store and think Colby might like it, I pick it up. I figure I can use it for his birthday or Christmas or something," Mia says nonchalantly. I don't buy it for a second.

I pull a box out of one of the bags. "You spend much time in the Lego aisle?" Then I pull out a puzzle box with a motorcycle on the front. "Or the puzzle aisle?"

"Sometimes I like to see what they have. Figured it would give us something to do tonight," she responds.

"You're not trying to buy his affection?" I ask.

"Oh, she one-hundred-percent is," Knox answers for his woman, leaning down to kiss the top of her head.

Mia smacks him in the chest, and I smile. "He'll love it." I look at the time on my phone. "Shit, I gotta go." Walking into the living room, I find Colby on the floor petting Pepper, who is furiously wagging his tail. "Come give me a hug." I open my arms and Colby hops up and wraps his around my waist.

"Bye, Mommy."

I kiss the crown of his head. "Be good. And try not to feed Pepper any human food tonight," I add in, remembering the other night when that dog nearly gassed me out of my own house.

Colby giggles. "Come on, Pepper, let's go play."

My son and the dog take off through the kitchen, briefly giving Knox, Wyatt, and Mia a quick hello before I hear the back door slam shut.

Mia walks into the living room as I'm putting my phone in my purse. "Nervous?" she asks.

"A little."

She gives me a warm smile and a hug. "It'll be great," she says. "You'll see."

The date is, in fact, not great. It's not necessarily bad, but I think I need to make a new note to myself that the last thing I should do before a date is see Wyatt. Getting butterflies in your belly for the man you can't have when you're about to meet a man who is a possibility isn't the greatest way to jump into the dating scene.

The food is delicious, and Steven is kind and funny. But there's no...spark or sizzle. Shouldn't there be something along those lines the first time you meet someone? He's attractive, there's no doubt. And he didn't lie about his height, which I've heard happens on these apps. His dark hair sets off his light-brown eyes. But the color isn't the deep whiskey color with flecks of gold that I find incredibly sexy on a certain biker...*Oh my God. Stop it.*

"Okay, here's an important question," Steven says, setting down his fork and staring me in the eye. "Cats or dogs."

"Dogs," I reply immediately, thinking about the way Colby laughs around Pepper.

"Ohh, I'm a cat guy."

"Cat guy?" I've never heard someone put it like that.

"Cat...man?"

We laugh, and I shake my head before taking a sip of my iced tea. "Honestly, I don't have the time for anything living in my house other than my son. A friend of mine has a dog that Colby loves, so he brings him over a lot."

"Maybe Colby would like cats, too. I can bring mine over and see," Steven says, then grimaces. "Sorry, that was a little forward. This is a first date. I guess I just feel like I kind of know you already. It's been a real treat getting to know you through messages. Gives me something to look forward to." His smile is sweet...but other than that, I don't feel much of anything. His smile doesn't hold the cool confidence of—*Nope. Not going there.*

I shake my head and redirect my thoughts before returning Steven's smile. "I completely understand. But there're a lot of steps between now and meeting my son."

Steven nods. "Absolutely. I would never presume that you would be comfortable enough with me right away."

"Thank you. Honestly, this is the first date I've had in years. And I never made it to the stage of introducing Colby to someone." I groan and immediately cover my face with my hands. "I probably shouldn't have admitted that, huh?"

Steven chuckles and pulls my hand away from my face. "Hey, it's alright, Maizie. I'm sure being a single mom keeps you plenty busy. I'm just glad you carved out a little time for me today."

My smile widens. He really is a nice guy. There're no creepy vibes coming from him, and so far he's been the perfect gentleman. "Thank you. I'm having a good time."

I would probably be having a better time if my thoughts didn't keep straying back to Wyatt and the way he looked at me when he came over today. Or the flutter in my chest when he had a glass of wine ready for me after a long shift at the bar.

Stop it, Maizie. You're here with Steven. A nice accountant who is interested in you and isn't a biker or your boss.

We finish dinner, and Steven walks me to my car. He doesn't try to kiss me, but he does lean in for a hug. It's a nice hug...but still no flicker of attraction.

"Drive home safely," he says, opening my door.

"You too." I give him a smile, and he shuts my door.

I'm not sure if he'll ask me out on a second date, but he seemed to have fun. I'd give it another shot. It could just be an off night for me. It could be me being so nervous. It could be a million things that're keeping me from feeling the excitement that should be there.

Problem is, I have a very strong feeling it's one thing in particular—or to be more precise, one person.

CHAPTER SEVEN
WYATT

Why did I agree to come hang out here while Maizie is on a date? Hell, why do I do half the things I do when it comes to this woman? When I slipped past her to walk into the house, I had to tamp down the urge to brush her curled hair behind her ear, to pull her into me and tell her that she should cancel. But I didn't. I sent her on her way instead and stayed to hang out with her son and our friends.

Thankfully, Mia was here tonight, because after making the cupcakes, Colby was a mess from head to toe. I thought it was hilarious when I gave him the bowl of chocolate batter to lick, and he stuck his entire head in. Mia and Knox got a kick out of it too, but when he pulled away, there was batter stuck in his hair and smeared all over his face, even in his ears.

I knew the kid was going to need a bath. I've never bathed a kid. Do you have to sit in there the whole time with them so they don't accidentally drown? What if you get soap in their eyes? I'm sure it would hurt like a bitch, but would it do permanent damage? What if you made the water too hot and gave them third-degree burns? It all seemed very complicated, but Mia knew what she was doing, and by the end of the night, Colby was tucked in bed, clean and tuckered out.

There's a knock on the door, and when I pull it open, Charlie and Lucy are standing on the other side with a bottle of wine.

"What are you doing here?" Lucy asks.

"Figured I'd come over with Pepper and hang out with Colby. What are you guys doing here?" I ask.

"Linc roped Jude into helping him with the new bike, which means they're sitting in our garage, drinking beer and fantasizing about Linc's new project," Charlie answers. "Decided we'd come over to get the scoop about Maizie's date."

"She's not back yet," I tell the girls as they walk past me to the kitchen.

"I know. She texted a few minutes ago that she was on her way home," Lucy states.

I follow the girls into the kitchen and look at the clock hanging on the wall. It's not even eight o'clock yet. Can't have been that great of a date if it lasted less than two hours. *Doesn't matter, Wyatt. It wasn't your date.*

"Hey, guys," Mia greets, coming in from the patio where we were hanging out, enjoying the warm evening. "Oh good," she says, pointing to the wine on the counter. "You brought a bottle."

Charlie grabs wineglasses as Lucy rummages through one of Maizie's drawers, then triumphantly holds up the wine opener.

"Is Colby asleep?" Lucy asks.

"He just passed out. He said he wanted to stay up until his mom got home, but once he was done with his bath, he couldn't keep his little eyes open," Mia answers with a soft grin.

"It doesn't hurt that he ate his weight in cupcakes," I say.

"That never hurts anyone. Where are these cupcakes you speak of, by the way?" Charlie asks.

Mia's smile widens as she lifts the lid of the container sitting on the counter. "Double chocolate, as per Colby's request."

"Kid after my own heart," Lucy says, reaching in and taking a bite of the frosting-covered dessert. "Oh my God, I need you to take these away or I'm going to eat all of them."

Mia laughs and grabs a couple, putting them on a plate. "Can you take these to Knox?" she asks, handing me the plate.

My brow tips up in suspicion. "Why do I get the distinct impression you're trying to get rid of me?"

"Because she is. Here, take these too," Lucy says, grabbing a couple beers from the fridge and handing them to me.

"Mmm. Beer and chocolate cupcakes. Sounds perfect," I say. It actually sounds disgusting.

"Shoo," Charlie says, waving her hands to the patio door.

I shake my head and take my beers and plate of cupcakes to the back patio.

"The girls kicked me out, but they sent me with this, so I guess we can consider it a win," I say to Knox.

I sit at the table, and Knox nods his thanks when I hand him a beer.

Knox is eyeing me like he has something he wants to ask. It's not like my VP to remain quiet about anything, not that he's necessarily a man who throws around words like confetti. But if he has a point to make or a question to ask, he's not one to shy away from speaking his mind.

He tilts his head to the side and another beat passes before he finally asks, "What are you doing here?"

My brows dip in confusion. "Uh, right now I'm having a beer with my brother."

He shakes his head. "No, what are you *really* doing here? And don't give me some bullshit answer. You've been hanging out here quite a bit lately."

A light chuckle escapes me. "You keeping track of my whereabouts? I don't know if I should be flattered or a little nervous."

"You're a fucking smart-ass," he replies.

It's my turn to shrug because it's not as though I'm going to argue. I'm also really good at deflecting conversations I don't want to have. Learned that one a long time ago.

"Is there something going on with you and Maizie?"

Okay, either I'm losing my touch or Knox is like a dog with a fucking bone tonight.

"She's a friend. And she's out with another man, so I can safely say no," I reply.

"That all?"

"Yup."

"But you want it to be more." Most people would frame that as a question, but most people aren't Knox. I haven't talked about this with anyone. I know Lucy suspects my feelings toward Maizie are a bit more than strictly friendship or employer-employee, so I assume the other girls have some inkling as well.

I let out a breath and take a sip from my beer. Knox is eyeing me, patiently waiting for me to give him an explanation.

"Yeah, I do," I finally admit to someone other than myself. "But there's a lot of shit in our way."

"Such as?"

"Such as Ozzy, for one," I say. "He was pretty adamant when Maizie started working at Thorn and Thistle that she was off-limits."

"It was a vulnerable time for the girl. He didn't want anyone to think she was up for grabs or to make her uncomfortable. He knew who she was when he hired her. Knows her parents and what fucking assholes they are. The whole town knew the story of her coming back from Boston pregnant and unmarried. In her parents' world, that was some sort of betrayal to them."

"Better than her settling for some asshole who knocked her up then treated her like shit." I would know a little something about that.

"You sound like you have experience there."

I tilt my head back and forth. "It's no secret that I didn't come from a loving home. That my dad shouldn't have married my mom when she got knocked up. He was a cheater and thinks he missed out on being young and free. She thinks she wasted her life with him. Both of them are right, too. Though they probably should have figured it out a hell of a lot sooner and saved us all the trouble."

Knox narrows his eyes, studying me. "What about you? Do you think tying yourself to a woman means you aren't free?"

I take another sip of my beer. I'm not sure if I like this chatty side of Knox. "When I joined the Black Roses, I did it because I believe in what the club stands for. The brotherhood. Living life on our terms, and fuck everyone else. Yeah, the idea that tying myself to someone and all of a sudden there're rules and questions and—"

"Accountability?" Knox interjects.

"Maybe." I scrub my hand over my face. "Fuck, man, I don't know. I know I like her. I know I want to make her life easier. I know I fucking hate that she's on a date right now with some other guy."

He takes a long pull from his beer bottle. "That sounds like interest to me."

"But it needs to be more than that." I pause and look toward the sky then back to my VP. "She's got a kid who is fucking awesome and doesn't deserve to have his life upended because I might decide it's too much or she decides she can't handle someone in this world."

Knox hums, considering his next question. "Do you think it would end up being too much? Being accountable to another person and having the responsibility of having a woman with a kid?"

"Honestly? I'm not sure." I blow out a sharp breath. "All I ever heard when my parents were fighting was how much my dad hated feeling strapped down. He viewed having a family as a burden. And I'm not saying I would feel the same way, but what if I do? Can't exactly change genetics."

"Wyatt, your dad being an asshole has nothing to do with genetics. Look at Linc. His dad was a piece of shit, but he'd sooner cut off his own hand than raise a finger to Charlie."

I shake my head. "That's different."

"How?"

"He had you and Tanya to protect him. To show him that's not how you treat your wife and kids. Tanya left and took you guys out of that shit. My mom stayed, and I dealt with the fallout every time they had a fight. Every time my dad cheated. Every time my mom got back at him by blowing money at the casino or charging a bunch of shit we couldn't afford to his credit card. I didn't exactly have a role model for being a good parent or partner."

"When you talk about the brotherhood and living life on our terms, maybe that means doing the opposite of what you grew up with. I would trust you with my life, with the life of any of our brothers and our women. That counts for something. Maybe living life on your terms means you decide what genetics dictate, and the rest is up to you." He shrugs. "Sure, you might look like your dad, but that doesn't mean you need to make your dad's mistakes. You had shit role models? Do the opposite of what you grew up with and see where that takes you."

"I can't exactly *see where that takes me* when there's a kid involved."

Knox lets out a light chuckle. "You're so fucking dumb sometimes."

"Thanks, asshole."

"You're already ten times the man your father was, and you don't even realize it. It doesn't sound like your old man gave two shits about making you and your mom feel like a burden." He waves his hand in front of me. "But here you are, tangled in knots because you're afraid of causing Colby and Maizie any hurt. You think your dad would care this much?"

I scoff. "That man never cared about anything more than himself and what skirts he could chase."

"Listen, I'm not saying it's a bad thing you aren't looking at this from all angles and playing out the what-ifs. Maizie is a friend, an employee, and a single mom. I would be pissed if you just wanted to get in her pants a few times and be on your merry fucking way. But I don't think that's what you want."

It's not. Not by a long shot.

I look through the window and see Maizie has just returned. She's inside, smiling at the girls and looking happy. Doesn't look like she experienced the worst date of her life. Lucy hands her a glass of wine, and she laughs at something.

She's fucking breathtaking when she laughs.

My gaze travels back to Knox, who is eyeing me with that scrupulous expression that tells me he sees something, but I'm not sure what.

"Yeah." Quiet laughter rumbles out of him. "I think you know exactly what you want. Too bad you're too chickenshit to do anything about it."

My head rears back. "Is this some sort of tough-love thing you're trying out? Gotta say, I'm not a fan."

"Just calling it like I see it. Although I'm not opposed to being proven wrong."

I give him a flat look and stand. "Want another?" I ask, pointing to the bottle in front of him.

He nods. "Sure."

I walk into the kitchen and the girls are in the living room. Grabbing two bottles, I'm about to head back outside, but their conversation stops me.

"Aw, honey. It was the first date. The first one you've had in years. I'm sure there were a lot of nerves," Mia says.

"Yeah, I don't know. I wouldn't say no to a second, see if maybe I was just in my head too much." Maizie groans. "There wasn't that instant spark, though. Maybe I expected too much right out of the gate."

"I don't know. There's something to be said for an instant attraction," Lucy chimes in.

"Did you feel that way when you first met Jude?" Maizie asks, and I hear Charlie laugh.

"Hell no, she didn't. She couldn't stand Jude when they first met," Charlie answers.

"If you recall, sister, he didn't make the best first impression—and there was that whole gunfight that erupted not too long after. But yeah, I thought Jude was a complete ass."

"Wow, never a dull moment," Maizie says in a flat tone. "Steven was nice, though. He's an accountant. I doubt he has much use for firearms."

"You sound less than thrilled when you say his name, sweetie," Lucy says.

I feel like an absolute creep standing in Maizie's kitchen and eavesdropping on her private conversation. Does that mean I walk back out to the patio with the beers I'm supposed to bring Knox? No, it does not.

"Ugh, I don't know. Maybe I'm not ready. It's not like I don't have a happy life. I'm not desperate for a man or anything like that," Maizie says.

"It's not about being desperate, it's about finding someone to spend your life with. Or at the very least, someone to spend the night with," Lucy says, finishing with a laugh. "But if he doesn't do it for you, there're plenty of others who would. I can think of one in particular."

Excuse me?

"Don't start with that again," Maizie says on a sigh.

"It's not like he isn't interested. Hell, it's not like you aren't either," Lucy argues.

What moron wouldn't be interested in Maizie? Who wouldn't jump at the chance to make this woman and her kid a part of their life?

"It's not that easy. He's a brother and one of my bosses," Maizie says. "And he's not exactly relationship material. Besides, if anything happens and it falls apart, Colby would be devastated."

Which one of my brothers am I going to have to kill?

"Yeah, but this is Wyatt we're talking about. He doesn't strike me as the type who would disappear from your life, or Colby's," Mia says. "And it's not like we don't all see the way he looks at you."

"Looking and acting are two different things. He finds me attractive. So what? It's not as though I don't come with a kid. Maybe he's scared to be with a single mom. Maybe he thinks I'm tainted somehow."

"Woah there, sister. Those are your parents' words coming out of your mouth. You aren't tainted, and there's no way in hell Wyatt thinks that. If he did, I'd—" Lucy says before she abruptly stops.

Pepper must have walked out of Colby's room to see who's home—and probably to see if he can beg for some food. Instead of going into the living room, he turns toward the kitchen and finds me hiding behind the wall that separates the kitchen from the hallway, which opens up into the room where the girls are sitting. It would have been fine if he would have just walked into the kitchen. But no, the dog is wagging his tail and looking up at me from the hallway, in plain view of the girls.

"Knox?" Mia calls

"Nope," I say, stepping into the hallway. "It's me. I was just grabbing a couple more beers for us. Pepper must have heard the door."

Each of the girls has varying degrees of embarrassment on her face. Maizie's is the reddest of the four.

"Hey, how was your date?" I ask, attempting to be as casual as possible, like I hadn't been standing here for the majority of their conversation.

"Uh, good. It was good. How was Colby?" Maizie asks.

"Awesome as ever. Hope you don't mind that I let Pepper sleep in his room. I can't guarantee he didn't jump on his bed."

Maizie chuckles. "It's totally fine. I can throw his sheets in the wash."

We stare at each other for a couple beats. She's probably wondering if I heard what she said, and I'm wondering if she suspects that I was listening in.

"Okay, I'm going to bring these to Knox," I say, holding the beers up.

I turn and head back to the patio.

So she's interested, but scared. Sounds familiar. But maybe she has the right idea. It's not as though anyone would consider me a sure bet. What if I'm too much like my dad and end up ditching her and Colby when shit gets too real?

Chapter Eight
Maizie

When Wyatt turns and heads to the backyard, we all stay completely silent until we hear the door shut. Lucy even gets up from the couch and walks across the hall to the kitchen, peeking her head around the corner to make sure he isn't in there.

She turns back to us and gives us a thumbs-up. "All clear," she says, then has a seat in her spot.

"Do you think he heard us?" I ask.

Lucy shrugs as though she couldn't care less either way. Shit, she'd probably prefer he did hear us so we could stop "dancing around this attraction," as she likes to put it.

Mia and Charlie sip their wine, neither answering my question.

I grab the pillow from behind my back, press it to my face, and scream. When I lower it, my three friends are watching my mini freak-out with soft, understanding expressions. Well, except Lucy. She's sitting next to me with a smile on her face.

"What's the worst that could happen if he did hear you? Then he would know how you feel," Lucy says.

"I'm not even sure how I feel. On the one hand, I want nothing more than to throw caution to the wind and crawl up his body like a tree frog, and on the other, I'm terrified of the implications and the fallout."

"A tree frog?" Mia asks.

"I took Colby to the library last week, and he found a book about frogs that I've been reading to him every night. It's the first thing that came to mind."

"Okay, I'll drop it then," Lucy says. "Tell us about your date."

"It was fine. We ate some Thai food, had a good conversation, got to know each other a little more. There was definitely attraction on his end. But for me...I'm not sure. Fireworks weren't going off. I think I kept things light and open enough for him to feel comfortable enough to ask me out again."

"What do you think stood in your way? Lack of chemistry or..." Lucy prods.

I've never been one to lie to my friends. Well, that's not entirely true, but when it comes to this stuff, I need someone to talk to.

"And I kept thinking about Wyatt. About how he looked at me, how he's great with Colby, how seen he makes me feel. How sometimes when he looks at me, it's almost as though he's holding himself back from wrapping me in his arms and kissing the holy hell out of me." I let out a breathy chuckle. "That last part might be wishful thinking. But then I tell myself it's complicated as hell and probably all in my imagination."

"The only thing in your imagination is the idea that he hasn't been salivating over you for years," Lucy says, not so helpfully.

"He's a friend. He's attractive. He's nice to me and my kid. That doesn't mean he wants to get in my bed, Lucy."

"Christ on a cracker. Why are you trying to talk yourself out of this so hard? He's hot—never tell Jude I said that—and interested. You're beautiful and have so much to offer. He knows you're a mom, adores your kid, and has a fucking dog. He's made for you. What is the fucking issue?"

"All of it," I exclaim before I lower my voice. He might have heard what I said earlier, but he might not have. *Yeah, I'm going with that.* "My kid loves him, which is great in theory, until he decides it's too much. He's technically one of my bosses, so if it does blow up, I could be out of a job, or it would be excruciatingly painful for me to keep working there. He's a brother—like your men—so if things end between us, it could affect the relationship I have with all of you, too."

"Maizie, if you think we'd ditch you if things didn't work out between you and Wyatt, you haven't been paying attention," Charlie says. "We love you, and we're not going anywhere."

"But it would be different," I argue. "I wouldn't be going to family dinners anymore, and things would be awkward between me and the guys. What if it doesn't work out and he starts seeing someone else and they don't like that I work at the bar or hang out with you guys? What if she gets upset that his brother's women are friends with his ex? What if it gets weird for you guys, trying to be nice to his new girlfriend and maintain a friendship with me? What if your men make you choose to keep the peace or something?"

"Wow, this new girl kind of sounds like a bitch," Lucy says. "I don't want to be friends with her." She sends me a smirk and rolls her eyes. "Who do you think you're talking to? Have the three of us ever given you the impression that our men dictate our lives or our friendships? They would never dream of it. What else is scaring you?" she prods further.

So many things. So many things that I can't explain.

"What if I fall in love with him and he sees all the parts of me and decides he doesn't want me?" I ask in a low voice. Being independent, taking care of myself and my son on my own is safe. No one can turn their back on me like my parents when I don't meet their expectations.

"Then fuck him," Lucy says with a shrug. "If he's an idiot who would let you slip through his fingers, then he deserves to lose you and end up with whatever heinous asshole you conjured up for him." She reaches her hand over and rests it on mine. "But what if none of that happens and he ends up loving you the way you deserve to be loved and giving you and Colby the world?"

"That scares me, too," I admit out loud for the first time.

"I can't tell you what to do," Lucy says. Charlie coughs dramatically and Lucy shoots her a withering glare. "I know how hard it is to let someone in after being on your own for so long. How hard it is to trust someone to see all your messy pieces and not run in the opposite direction. But I also know that if you don't at least open yourself up to the possibility, you'll always wonder what could have happened. What you could have had."

She makes a good point. But I'm still not there. Not saying I won't be someday, but that day is not today.

When everyone leaves and I make sure the house is locked up, I crawl into bed, exhausted from the day. Wyatt didn't say much when he made his exit, just sent me a smile and a wave as he filed out the front door with everyone else. Lucy made sure to give me one last loaded look before she and Charlie hopped in his truck so he could give them a ride home.

Now that the house is quiet, my mind is loud as ever. Usually, this is the time I can lie in bed and reflect on the day, relax, and think about tomorrow. I'm doing a whole lot of thinking, but it's not as relaxing as usual. My mind keeps going back to my date and who I was thinking about on said date. I keep remembering what Lucy was telling me and the way Wyatt left without so much as a backward glance. He must've heard us talking.

My mind wanders to the way he looked at me when I was leaving for my date. When he showed up at my house with his dog and a smile. He knew I was going out with another man. If he were as interested as Lucy seems to think, wouldn't he have stopped me? These guys aren't exactly known for *not* being possessive of their women. Not that I'm Wyatt's woman. Not by a long shot. But he seemed so unaffected watching me leave. Then again, he could have been putting on a mask. The same one I wear when he's around and I don't want anyone to know how badly I wish I could kiss him with the ease that Lucy does with Jude. Or have him wrap his arm around me in that possessive way that Knox does with Mia.

I imagine the way his T-shirt hugs the corded muscles of his arms, and the way his jeans sculpt his long legs. I imagine what's underneath, and how it would feel to have him without a stitch of clothing on, trailing his smiling lips down my body. What it would feel like for him to make me come with his mouth then his cock.

I'm feeling hot and uncomfortable under the sheet I have over me. *Achy.* That's what this feeling is. Every part of me is craving something I want from him.

I reach over to my nightstand and pull out the vibrator I keep stashed in there for nights like these. Nights where I want to imagine, for a few moments, what it would feel like to be filled by the man who spends so much time trying to make me smile—make my life that much easier, that much better.

I run my finger through my slit, finding that I'm already wet. The shaft of the vibrator slides inside of me without any resistance. I imagine Wyatt sitting on the end of my bed, watching as I pleasure myself with the toy. I think about the burning look in his eyes from earlier. How his mouth would be parted as he took deep breaths while he watched me move the toy in and out of my dripping pussy. I may never have seen the faces he makes when he's in the throes of sex, but I have a vivid imagination.

When I turn it on, my back immediately arches off the bed. I was halfway there even before I pulled out the toy. My eyes squeeze shut as I run my hand from my stomach, under my nightshirt, and over one of my breasts. My fingers twist my nipple to add a touch of delicious pressure—all the while imagining it is Wyatt's hands exploring what I like, what makes me gasp, and what makes me cry out in pleasure.

It doesn't take more than a few moments, and my toes are curling, the sensation of my orgasm quickly taking over my entire body. I pulse around the toy and come long and hard with Wyatt's name on my lips.

The next three days are spent with Colby, enjoying some much needed quality time with my son since I don't have to work. We spend one of the days at the lake with Linc, Charlie, Knox, and Mia. Knox bought Colby a fishing pole for his birthday last year, and with the summer weather in Massachusetts, it's the perfect time to catch some fish.

I love watching the way the brothers take Colby under their wings. They grew up with a single mom, then they had Trick and Gramps to look out for them when they landed in Shine as kids. That was something that worried me when Colby was a baby. Would he have any positive male role models? It's not like his father would—or could—ever be one. And even if his paternal grandfather lived here, from the stories Mia's told us, it doesn't sound like he would be particularly hands-on. And don't even get me started on my own father. To this day, he's never reached out to meet my son.

Colby asked before we left if Wyatt and Pepper were going to be there. I didn't call to ask him if he'd like to join us. After the little rendezvous I had with my toy—and one of the most intense orgasms I've had in my life while whispering Wyatt's name—I'm not sure I can look the man in the face. At least not without turning as red as the tomato I was slicing for our sandwiches.

When we get to the lake, he isn't there.

I'll admit—to myself, anyways—that there was a touch of disappointment. Jesus, I'm so fucked up over this whole thing. One minute I don't want to see him and the next I'm let down he isn't around.

"He's on a run," Mia says as I'm unloading the car.

"Who?"

She just gives me a look that says *Don't even try to play games with me, sister,* but she doesn't comment further.

It was an amazing day in the sun—fishing, watching Colby get excited then scared when Knox tried to get him to unhook the fish he caught, and sitting under a giant shade tree with my friends, enjoying lunch and homemade lemonade. Even if it did seem like something was missing. That something being the six-four biker who's probably having a good time riding to God knows where, doing God knows what, with God knows who. Not that I'd know what they actually do on a run.

But whatever it is, he's perfectly entitled. He's not tied down—he doesn't answer to me or anyone else.

I manage to keep him out of my thoughts for the three nights I'm off work. I don't pull out my toy or think about him before I go to sleep. Okay, that last one isn't entirely true, but I don't act on any of my fantasies. If I'm going to get over the idea of him, I need to stop considering him as an option, and that's certainly not going to happen if I pretend he's with me while I get myself off.

Tuesday night rolls around, and I'm back at work. It was nice having a few days to myself without being surrounded by all things Wyatt. It gave me some perspective that I think I desperately needed.

That perspective flies right out the window about an hour before we close and he comes strolling in. I'm beginning to think that talking to the girls about it wasn't the best idea. I never had this kind of trouble tamping down my desire for the biker who just walked through the door. Before I admitted anything to my friends, I was able to pretend they were crazy for thinking it was anything more than friendship. Now, the idea of something happening between us consumes me. I thought I had a handle on it, but I was clearly wrong. So, so wrong.

"Hey," he says, giving me his usual warm smile. It isn't forced like the one he wore the last time I saw him. It's natural, comfortable, and just as infuriatingly kissable as usual.

Wyatt and his damn smile.

"Hey, yourself," I say, attempting to sound light and carefree. I'm not sure it lands. "Heard you were out of town."

"Got back a few hours ago. Thought I'd come check on you."

"Me?" I cock my head to the side in question. "Why?"

He shrugs as I set a beer in front of him. "No real reason. Just haven't seen you in a few days."

"Oh, I'm good. Went to the lake and took Colby fishing." I smile, remembering the way he nearly dropped the fish while he was gingerly trying to unhook it.

"I wish I could have seen that. I've been telling him I'd take him. I feel kind of bad that I wasn't there," he says, returning my smile with a soft one of his own. "If it's okay with you, maybe I can take him out later this week."

"You don't have to do that. He knows you had to work."

"Maizie, I want to. Plus, Pepper told me he missed him, and I hate to disappoint Colby *and* my dog." He releases a light chuckle.

I slowly shake my head back and forth. "There he goes having all kinds of conversations when we're not around."

Wyatt's lips kick up in the corner. "I told you, he's shy."

"Mm-hmm," I hum and turn to refill drinks for the group sitting at the end of the bar. I grab a few things from the back to start restocking before it's time to close. When I walk back over to Wyatt, he's nearly finished with his first beer.

"Another?" I ask, pointing to the bottle.

He nods, and I place a longneck in front of him.

"So, have you had another date with that guy? What was his name?" His tone is meant to be casual, but I catch a hint of tension in it.

"I don't think I ever told you his name, but it's Steven," I answer. "We have one set up for this Saturday, actually. He's coming to town, and we're going to have dinner at the new steak house that opened last month."

Wyatt nods. "Nice. I've been meaning to try that place out myself."

"I'll let you know how it is."

It's not often Shine gets anything new in the way of restaurants, and the variety is seriously lacking. Either that, or I've just eaten everywhere around here about a thousand times already.

Wyatt doesn't say anything else on the subject as he sips his beer. The mood seems to have shifted a bit, the air a bit thicker. It's probably my imagination, but Wyatt looks to be gripping his beer bottle a little tighter than necessary.

But that's crazy, right? He's the one who asked me about Steven.

I go about my business and finally cash out the last of my customers. Well, except Wyatt, but the brothers aren't expected to pay. One of the perks of being an MC member, I guess.

Wyatt stands from his seat and starts putting chairs up on the tables. I grab the key from the register and make my way over to the door to lock it.

"This damn door needs to be fixed," I say, pulling it as hard as I can so the lock can line up correctly while simultaneously turning the key.

"Here, let me help." Wyatt comes to stand behind me and grabs the handle, tugging it a bit harder, and I'm finally able to slide the dead bolt in place.

I expect him to move when it's locked.

But he doesn't.

Slowly, I turn around, my body between the door and Wyatt's wide body. His hand stays on the handle and it brushes against the small bit of exposed skin between my tank top and jeans. A shiver travels down my spine, and the nerve endings on that small patch of skin light up.

Wyatt's other hand reaches up, and I feel the soft brush of his fingertips against my cheek as he swipes a piece of hair that's come loose from my ponytail. He tucks it behind my ear, and as if on instinct, my head tilts into his touch. He doesn't drop his hand. Instead, he allows his thumb to brush my lower lip. He's studying my face as though he's never been this close to me before—and he hasn't. Wyatt has always kept a respectable distance, but he sure as hell isn't now. He's intently watching his thumb slide back and forth. My breath hitches, and his gaze collides with mine.

CHAPTER NINE
WYATT

"I can't."

Those two words are like a bucket of ice water thrown over the charged moment between us.

My hand lowers from her face, and my arm drops from the door handle. I take a step back, and it feels as though the foot of space I put between us stretches as wide as the Grand Canyon.

Stupid move, Wyatt.

"I'm sorry," she says the same time I start to apologize.

"No, let me get this out," she starts. "I work for the club, and I need this job. Colby depends on me to keep a roof over his head. We're friends, and you're friends with my kid. I can't do anything that would jeopardize that. No matter how much I want to."

Well, that makes me feel marginally better. At least I'm not imagining this insane attraction between us that we've been dancing around.

"Really, Maizie. It's fine. I totally get it." I have no idea what I'm supposed to say in this situation, seeing as nothing like this has ever happened to me before. Being part of the Black Roses hasn't exactly made women run away from me. "I would never want you to feel uncomfortable." I laugh, trying to dispel the tension between us. "It's been a hell of a long day. Cash wanted to get back to Shine, so we rode for nearly twelve hours straight. My head is"—I shake it as if to demonstrate—"not in the right place."

She gives me a smile. "No harm, no foul," she says in an overly bright voice. "I should probably finish up here. Get home so Cece can have the rest of her night to herself."

I nod. "Okay, let's finish up."

"You don't have to—"

I take another step back and grab a chair, flipping it over and setting it on the table. "Four hands are better than two."

She's still standing against the door, and I swear, there's nothing I want more in this moment than to press her against it with the length of my body and show her we're more than friends. But I don't. Instead, I grab another chair and flip it over.

"Thanks," she says and picks up the broom to start sweeping.

When we're finished with closing duties, I walk her to her car. I open her door—because I'm a fucking gentleman—but I don't allow there to be less than three feet of space between us the entire time. When she sits in the driver's seat, I shut it for her and she starts the engine. I step back and she gives me a wave before pulling out.

It's awkward as fuck.

There's a strain that's been gnawing at my gut for the last twenty minutes it took us to close down Thorn and Thistle. I hate that it's there, and even more, that I'm the one responsible for putting it there.

I watch her turn right toward her house and stand next to my bike for a few minutes, collecting my thoughts. My hands fist the side of my hair as I let out a frustrated breath through my teeth.

"Fuck," I say to an empty alleyway. "That definitely could have gone better, dumbass." But it could have gone worse, too.

No matter how much I want to. That's what she said.

I'm not about to force myself into her life as more than a friend, but it's obvious to me that she needs some reassurance that her job and our friendship are safe. I don't want to be just friends. I want more. And I don't just want it for the here and now. I want it for always. If she'll have me. There's nothing about the woman that I couldn't fall in love with. No part of her that I don't see and already feel...something more than friendship.

And she feels it, too. This isn't some fleeting attraction. Not anymore. Talking with Knox, overhearing the girls' conversation the other night, and having hours riding to Michigan and back have given me plenty of time to think. Plenty of time to get my head on straight and out of my fucked-up past.

She's it for me.

Now I have to figure out how to get her to come to terms with that. It's time we stop running from our feelings.

A couple days later, Knox is having people over, or rather, Mia wanted to invite us over for a family dinner. Linc and Charlie show up, followed by Jude and Lucy. Even Cece shows up with Colby.

"Pepper!" Colby exclaims when he runs through the door to where we're all sitting around on Knox's patio furniture. For not being one who likes people in his space, he's got a pretty nice area for entertaining.

Pepper's ears perk up, and as soon as he sees Colby, he hops up from where he was lying next to me and starts jumping around the boy.

"Pepper, sit," I command.

He does, but I can tell he's waiting on pins and needles to be released from his command.

"He wasn't hurting me or nothing, Wyatt. I'm big," Colby complains.

"I know, but remember what I said about not wanting any trips to the ER while your mom's at work?"

He nods.

"Oh, come on. Let the poor thing go," Lucy tells me with a smile on her face. "You can't get in the way of a boy and his dog having a good time."

I wish Pepper were Colby's dog. That would mean I'd be a permanent fixture—not friend-zoned by the boy's mom like I currently am.

"Okay," I say, releasing Pepper, and he charges into the grass, running around and bending low on his front paws, waiting for Colby to go down there with him. It takes less than five seconds before the two of them are running around the backyard.

I look over at Knox, who is eyeing me much like he was at Maizie's the other night. He doesn't say anything, but there's sure to be a follow-up conversation to the one we had previously. That's fine with me. I have a clear view of the future I want.

When we went on our run to the Iron Disciples clubhouse in Michigan earlier this week to drop off a shipment from the Monaghans—since we're now the go-between for the Irish mob family and the MC—I had a lot of time to think while I was on my bike. That's the real reason I showed up at the bar. I wanted to see the woman who is going to be mine. It's just a matter of time.

We eat our weight in BBQ ribs, and I marvel at how messy one five-year-old kid can get. I pretend I don't see him sneaking the dog bits of meat here and there. Cece takes him home not long after dessert with a promise from me that we're going to go fishing as soon as his mom has time in her schedule. Obviously it won't be Saturday, considering she has her last date with Steven that night.

Jude and Lucy are next to take off, followed closely by Linc and Charlie, and then it's only Knox and I left on his back deck, enjoying a cool evening.

"It was something seeing you with Colby," Knox says over the rim of his whiskey glass.

"Is that good or bad?" I ask.

"It's good, brother. You seem to take to him like a duck to water."

"He's a good kid. Easy."

"Nah," he says. "It's more than that. After our conversation the other night, I got the distinct impression that you didn't think you were father material. That's what you'll have to be if you want to be with Maizie, you know?"

I nod. "I know."

"And you've worked out the bullshit that was in your head?"

"You mean my shitty childhood and worrying that I was too much like my old man to be trusted with a woman as spectacular as Maizie and her kid?"

Knox arches his brow. "Yeah, that shit."

I chuckle. "I won't lie and say the thought of turning out to be anything like my old man doesn't scare me. I think any sane man would be worried about that. But I'm not going to let it stand in my way anymore. She's scared, though."

He nods with a thoughtful look on his face. "That's understandable. She's been doing it on her own for a long time. As far as I know, Colby's dad has never been in the picture. When she came back to town, she refused to tell anyone who it was. He must have been a real piece of shit."

The idea that any man would let her go, especially at such a vulnerable time, skyrockets my blood pressure.

I take a calming breath before continuing. "It's more than that, though. She's worried about her job. And she's worried that if things don't work out, I'll ditch her kid, too.

"Well, to her first point, that's crazy. She's the best damn bartender we've ever had. Ozzy was just talking about giving her a raise. Hell, I think if anything were to go south between you two, he's more likely to strip your patch than fire her," he says, chuckling at his own joke.

"You're probably not that far off, brother," I grumble as I sip from my rocks glass.

"And to her second point. Would you stop being a part of Colby's life if it didn't work out between you guys?"

"Fuck no," I reply. "One, he's a great kid. I'd never ditch him or his mom if she decided she didn't want to be with me. Because that's what it would take. Her bailing on me. This isn't some flash in the pan for me. I've never been the love 'em and leave 'em type. Shit, I've never been the love 'em at all type."

"You saying you love her?"

"I'm saying that I'm sick of not spending every night with her. I'm sick of leaving her house with my dog in the truck to go back to the clubhouse because my place isn't in her bed. Yet."

Knox's brows lift in surprise and maybe a little shock. "Damn, Wyatt. You're coming in a little hot. You sure you're ready for that?"

"Brother," I say, looking him dead in the eye, "I've never been more sure of anything in my life."

CHAPTER TEN
MAIZIE

It's Friday night, and I'm working—as usual—but at least the girls are here to keep me company. Not that I've had a lot of downtime. It seems like just about everyone in town is starting their weekend at Thorn and Thistle tonight. Lucy even offered to hop behind the bar and help me out for a minute, but I thrive in the chaos. This is easy for me. I can get in the zone and work like a well-oiled machine. Plus, it helps keep my mind off what happened in this very bar just a few nights ago.

"So you have another date with Steven tomorrow?" Lucy says, eyeing me over her glass.

"Yup. He's taking me to dinner," I say when I'm finally able to stop and catch my breath for a minute.

"He's coming to Shine?" Charlie asks.

"Yeah. He's never been here, not that there's much to see, but he didn't want me to have to drive to meet him this time."

"That's thoughtful," Charlie says.

"He seems to be that." Once again, when I think about Steven, there's not even a hint of...anything.

We've talked over text messages a couple times this week—normal run-of-the-mill stuff. Nothing like *hey, one of my bosses almost kissed me the other night, and I really wanted him to, but I'm scared shitless of losing him as a friend, but I also can't stop thinking about him, so we should probably not see each other again.*

I *should* cancel the date, but I told myself I would give Steven a shot. Whatever happened between Wyatt and me the other night doesn't change that. It's not like anything *really* happened anyway. We maybe *almost* kissed. But we didn't. Because I stopped it. Because I'm an idiot. *Knock it off, Maizie. You were being responsible.*

"You don't seem particularly excited," Charlie points out.

"I am. It's just a busy night, and I didn't sleep well last night."

I don't tell her it's because I've been tossing and turning in bed the last few nights, thinking about the kiss that never happened with the man I want in said bed next to me. And his name does not start with an S.

I've thought about pulling out my toy and seeing if getting some physical relief would help. But I swore to myself I wouldn't do that while thinking about Wyatt again. It muddles my brain and my boundaries too much. Since he's all I've been thinking about lately, I'm not even willing to try.

"I don't get it, sister," Lucy says, placing her drink on the bar and folding her arms before she rests them on the bar. "I'm not saying don't go out with Steven again, but we all know he does nothing to tickle your fancy."

Charlie snorts. "*Tickle her fancy*? I see Jude's been rubbing off on you."

Lucy rolls her eyes in Charlie's direction then turns back to me. "As I was saying, I don't get why you're so adamant about giving a guy who you're not excited about a shot. There's a guy who does give you butterflies, who lives in Shine, and you don't have to convince yourself to go out with him. You actually *want* to. Are you afraid he doesn't feel the same way? Because if that's the case, you are as blind as a damn bat, my friend."

"No, I know he's attracted," I reply, looking to the side and thinking of the other night.

"Oh-ho-ho," Lucy says, sitting back and pointing at me. "There's a story there that you haven't shared. Spill it."

Blowing out a breath, I look at Charlie, but I can tell from the excited look on her face that she's not going to be any help.

"We may have...had a moment. The other night. In this bar," I confess.

"Tell us everything right now!" Lucy exclaims, jumping around in her seat.

"Nothing happened. I stopped it, and he blew it off like it was no big deal. Said something about being on a long ride and his head not being right. I don't know, I kind of freaked out and was more than willing to drop it."

"That's why you haven't been sleeping. I know you, and the only thing that keeps you from dreamland is when something is bothering you," Lucy says.

I love my friends like sisters. But damn, I really wish they didn't read me so well.

"Where's Mia tonight?" I ask, not wanting to talk about the *why* behind how tired I am.

"At her grandmother's for dinner. Jude and Linc are working on the bike. Wyatt was on his way over when I grabbed Lucy to come get a drink. And don't try to change the subject. You aren't smooth about it at all," Charlie answers. *See? Absolutely no help.*

So Wyatt's at Linc's and not partying on a Friday night at the clubhouse or at Midnight Rose. That shouldn't make me feel as good as it does. Not that he doesn't have every right to do whatever he wants. He's single without any commitments, least of all to me.

I look over, and people are lining up at the bar again. This I can do. Pouring drinks and talking to customers comes a lot more naturally to me than one would think, seeing as I was raised in such a religious household. But I like being friendly, I like seeing familiar faces and sharing a laugh. Not that we get much more than familiar faces here. That's one of the things I hated about Shine when I was young, but absolutely love now. I feel safe here. This is my town—my people.

"Sorry, sister. Duty calls," I say to the girls.

"Don't think this conversation is over. We'll drop it for now, but be prepared for a night of wine and spilling your guts," Lucy calls as I head over to the other side of the bar to get back to work.

The next day at Colby's T-ball game, the club shows up again, and again I'm hit with so much appreciation for my friends who have become the closest thing to family I could hope for. The girls made T-shirts with Colby's number on the back and our last name. He got a big kick out of that one. Of course, I teared up and my son was confused.

"Happy tears, buddy," I reassure him.

He studies me for a moment. "I don't cry when I'm happy," he says in confusion.

"You might someday."

He shakes his little head. "Girls are weird."

A laugh escapes me. "Yeah, we can be sometimes."

Even Wyatt is here, which I was unsure of, considering I haven't seen him since our *almost something* didn't happen. He's his usual friendly self, not even a hint of discomfort or awkwardness coming from him. I should be happy about that, and I am. But it stings a touch that he seems to have forgotten the moment between us and is acting like everything is normal. Maybe to him it is. I'm probably the only one blowing the entire encounter out of proportion.

Even though we don't keep score for the teams at this age, every time one of Colby's teammates runs home—spoiler alert, they all do—the club and all of the people who came out to see Colby cheer as though the kids are T-ball phenoms. I love it.

Gramps and Elaine come to say hello since she didn't ask me to pick her up this morning.

"The boy has good form," Arthur says, watching Colby swing his bat, knocking the ball off the T.

"I told you, Arthur. He's a natural," Elaine says then turns to me. "Mia tells me you've been seeing a young man you met on one of those dating apps."

"I don't know if *seeing* is the correct term. It's only our second date tonight," I say.

"In my day, it didn't take more than a few dates to know if there was enough there to build on," she says.

"Kids these days are different, Elaine. Always waiting to see if there's a more attractive fish in the sea before they settle," Gramps says, shaking his head.

It always cracks me up when Gramps refers to any of us as kids. I may be young, but I feel ten times older than the typical person my age.

"Are there?" Elaine asks me.

"Are there what?"

"More attractive fish in the sea," she answers.

As though my eyes have a mind of their own, my gaze drifts to Wyatt. Yeah, one in particular. He must feel my unintended stare because he turns to me, giving me that half smile that causes all kinds of fluttery things to happen in my chest.

When I take too long to answer, Elaine's eyes travel to where I'm staring. "Hmm. Well, I guess that answers that."

I turn my head and meet her gaze. "I'm not sure what you mean."

She doesn't comment, just gives me one of those knowing smiles I see from her from time to time. "Whatever you say, dear."

When the game ends and everyone is saying their goodbyes, Colby asks Wyatt if he's going to bring Pepper over tonight.

"No, can't tonight, buddy." He sees the disappointment on my son's face, and it's clear to me that it pains him. "How about we go fishing tomorrow? I heard you're practically a pro now."

I have to stifle my laugh, remembering the look on his face when the fish was flopping all over as Knox tried to show Colby how to unhook it.

"Can we, Mommy?" my son asks with pleading eyes.

I look at Wyatt, who is wearing a similar imploring expression. "Sure, monkey," I concede with a chuckle.

Colby turns to Wyatt and gives him a high five as though their master plan came to fruition. He runs over to where he left his bag and grabs it, being stopped by one of the kids on the team. I watch them laugh at some joke, and Colby waves goodbye as he makes his way back to us.

Before he reaches where we're standing, Wyatt asks, "Is that okay? I didn't mean to put you on the spot, but when he looked at me with those disappointed eyes, I couldn't..." He shakes his head.

"Trust me, I get it. And it's completely fine. I like that you have a hard time disappointing him, if that makes sense."

Wyatt shoots me a soft smile. "It does."

Colby is back a second later. "See you tomorrow, Wyatt," he says.

"Can't wait," Wyatt replies, then looks at me. "See you later." He's doing that half-smirk thing again. He means tomorrow. He'll see me tomorrow. Because tonight I have plans with another man.

When Colby and I get home, I fix him a snack. Cece texts and confirms that she'll be here tonight. She's only missed one babysitting gig, but she still feels guilty about it, even though I've told her about a hundred times that it happens and not to stress about it. Since then, she's been confirming every afternoon any time she's set to watch Colby.

I look at my outfit for tonight before laying it down on my chair in the corner. I decided to go with a dress. Nothing fancy, but I feel like getting a little dressed up. It's a white spaghetti-strap peasant midi dress that I plan to pair with a belt and cowboy boots. Seems fitting for the western-themed steak house we're going to.

Plus, it's rare I'm in anything other than jeans or shorts paired with a loose T-shirt.

I'm also hoping getting dressed up will improve my mood and get me a little excited to be going out tonight. I don't have the same nerves as last time, which is good. Or bad, depending on how you look at it, I guess. There are no flutters of excitement at the thought of seeing Steven. I don't dread it by any means, but there's no eager anticipation.

Okay, that's it. If I don't at least feel one flap of a butterfly wing, I'm not going out with him again. This isn't fair, especially seeing as I had an entire kaleidoscope of them in my stomach at Colby's game today when Wyatt smiled at me.

With that decision made, I already feel better about tonight. As though there's less pressure. I'm not going to stress about trying to make something work with someone I don't feel a spark toward with the hopes it will come. I'm going to enjoy a nice dinner out with a perfectly nice man and probably not go for a third date. It's not as though either of us is emotionally invested at this point. Plus, this will give him the opportunity to find someone who lights up every time he's in the room.

After a few hours of cleaning and paying bills—all the fun life stuff—I'm ready to head out. There's a knock on the door, and Cece stands on the porch holding a container of something I'm sure is delicious.

"I don't know what that is, but if you save me some, I'll give you an extra ten bucks," I say, moving out of the way so she can enter.

She walks to the kitchen, and Colby runs up to her with a piece of paper waving in his hand. "Look what I made you."

Cece takes the picture from his hand and examines the drawing with a smile on her face. "This is the best one yet," she says, and he beams.

He jumps and runs out of the room, most likely to work on another drawing.

"I've been meaning to bring this up, but I felt kind of weird about it," Cece starts. "Colby showed me the painting he did with him, me, and Cash at the park. I hope it's okay with you that he sometimes meets us there."

"It's totally fine with me," I say, sensing that she wants to say something else.

"It's not like something's going on between us or anything. He's just...easy to talk to when I'm having a hard time. It never interferes with my time with Colby, though," she rushes out.

"I know it wouldn't. Colby loves you. Trust me, if he didn't, I would know about it. That kid has no filter." I absolutely love that about him. He's a terrible liar, not that he ever really tries. I'm raising him to be a hundred-percent honest, and he knows he can tell me anything, no matter how small. I think that's part of the reason showing me a picture with Cash and Cece didn't seem at all strange to him.

"Right. And nothing's going on anyway, so there's nothing to worry about."

"You already said that," I say.

I think the lady doth protest too much.

"He's too old for me. Plus, he's a brother, and Lucy would have a shit fit if she ever thought I was getting involved with him. Not that she can talk, but she has a different set of rules for herself than she does for me."

I sense a bit of irritation coming from Cece over that fact.

"Lucy has a different set of rules for the world," I say, and Cece chuckles.

"That she does."

"If you feel like there's stuff you can't tell your sister or want to talk to someone other than Cash, I'm here for you, too."

Cece sends me a small smile. She really is strikingly beautiful with long blonde hair and eyes so big and blue she almost looks like a doll. But there's pain behind those eyes, pain I don't have the first clue about.

"Thanks. That really means a lot," she says. She walks into the living room with Colby. Maybe one day she'll be comfortable enough to talk about everything she holds inside. But that day is not today.

I grab my purse and head into the living room, finding Cece and Colby sitting on the floor in front of the coffee table, each with a crayon in their hand and paper in front of them.

"Okay, kids. I'm taking off. There's money on the counter for dinner, which you have to eat before you have whatever Cece brought over," I say, giving my son that look that tells him I mean business.

"Okay, Mommy." He jumps up from the floor before walking over and wrapping his arms around my waist. I bend and kiss the top of his head.

"Love you, buddy."

"I love you, too."

He lets me hug him for a beat longer before he's squirming out of my arms, ready to work on his next masterpiece.

The restaurant is pretty busy for a Saturday night, but Steven made reservations, so we don't have to wait for a table. He looks nice tonight in a collared shirt and a pair of slacks with his dark hair swept to the side. Perfectly respectable and looking every inch the accountant that he is. And just like last week, there is zero spark. Not even a flicker of something.

Steven is handsome in the classic sense. Good bone structure and nice hair. He's got a friendly smile, but when he turns it in my direction, I feel nothing. Zip, zilch, nada. That doesn't mean I'm going to have a terrible time, though. In fact, I'm having a perfectly nice evening with someone with whom I have as much chemistry as I would with my cousin—which is to say, none.

"I like this little town here. It's like an unknown gem," he says as we eat our spinach and artichoke dip appetizer.

"You wouldn't be saying that if you grew up here," I reply with a chuckle. "It's small and everyone knows everyone. You can't really get away with anything without someone telling someone who tells your parents or grandparents."

"I don't know." He tilts his head to the side. "That seems kind of nice to me."

I lean back and take a sip of my wine. "I like it more as an adult than I did when I was younger. At least I know my kid won't be able to get away with anything."

Just then, the server brings over a glass of wine and another beer. I look at her with confusion in my gaze.

"From the two guys at the bar," she says, seeing my unasked question.

I look around her, and sitting at the bar with smiles on their faces and beers in their hands are Wyatt and Barrett. Wyatt tips his beer bottle in my direction, and I turn back to Steven.

"Who's that?" he asks.

"One of my bosses," I tell him. "Perks of a small town." I try to smile as though it's no big deal, but I seriously doubt I'm pulling it off. And those butterflies I was talking about earlier? Yeah, they decided to try to migrate out of my belly. Unfortunately, not toward the man currently sitting across from me.

"That guy's your boss?" Steven asks, probably noticing the MC cuts Wyatt and Barrett are wearing.

"Yup, they own the bar I work at. Good guys," I say and pour the remnants of my wine into the glass that Wyatt sent over before taking a healthy swig.

"I didn't realize you worked in a biker bar," he says, and immediately my hackles rise.

"It's not some sort of trashy place." *Like your tone suggests*, even if I don't say it. "They run a clean place. And they're all great guys. A few of my girlfriends are dating some guys in the club, and Colby loves all the brothers."

His head rears back. "You raise your kid around bikers?"

Okay, this conversation is taking a very judgmental turn, and I am not impressed, nor am I feeling as though I want to spend my evening defending my parenting choices to a man I've gone out with all of twice.

"I don't know what you think you know about bikers, but it's probably completely off base." It probably isn't too far away from the truth, but that shit stays away from me and Colby. Plus, I really don't like what he's implying. "Those bikers were there for me when my grandma passed and have made Colby feel loved and supported for no other reason than we're a family of our own making. Exactly like all the brothers are family." I think back to the game and seeing everyone show up for my kid, back to last weekend we spent at the lake, Knox teaching my son to fish.

"Sorry, it's just not something I've ever been around. Accountant, remember? I don't exactly run with that type of crowd." He must see the annoyed scowl on my face because he's quick to add, "Not that there's anything wrong with people who do. I just...I just don't know if I'd be comfortable with it. No judgment."

I give him a flat smile. If it wasn't obvious before, this clinches it. There will be no third date.

Steven excuses himself from the table before our entrées arrive, and I lean back in my seat, letting out a long breath. Well, at least I'll get a decent meal out of the evening. That has to count for something. Steven is perfectly nice. He tried to clean up the mess he was getting himself into when he put his foot in his mouth about me working for—and hanging out with—the MC, but it was too late. I'm pretty sure he sensed that he'd stepped in it when he asked about me raising my kid around bikers. I grew up surrounded by people who were judgmental assholes. I don't need to put up with it now, especially because I live my life and raise my kid to be the exact opposite.

"This seat taken?" Barrett asks, sliding into the booth before I have a chance to answer.

"My date is going to be back any minute," I say, looking toward the bathroom then around the bar area of the restaurant. "Where's Wyatt?"

Barrett shrugs. "He had a phone call or something. Thought I'd come over and say hi. Having fun?"

It's my turn to shrug. "Sure."

"You don't really sound like it." He's eyeing me like he's waiting for me to admit something, which is odd. I'm not particularly close with Barrett, though he's been known to make me laugh when he comes into the bar with jokes and tall tales. If there's one person in the club who has Wyatt beat in the totally free and unmoored way of life, it's the man sitting across from me.

"I'm having a perfectly fine time. Why wouldn't I? It's a nice restaurant, good food—"

"You're on a date with a dentist," he interjects, cutting me off.

"Steven is an accountant," I inform him.

"Huh," he says, tilting his head to the side. "He looks like a dentist to me."

"Well, he's not, and he's going to be back any second."

Barrett shrugs and points to the dip. "You mind?"

"Go for it," I reply and notice he's looking pretty much anywhere other than me.

Studying the man in front of me, the way he's trying to play it a little too casual, I get the sneaking suspicion that Barrett and Wyatt didn't just happen to show up at the same restaurant as me and Steven by chance.

And I also know a distraction when I see one.

"Mmm, this is good," he says around a mouthful of the creamy dip.

"Glad you like it." I lean across the table. "Now tell me, where the hell is your partner in crime?"

CHAPTER ELEVEN
WYATT

As soon as I see Maizie's date, *Steven*, get up from the table, I get up from my stool.

Barrett shoots me a look, his brow arching. "I hope you know what you're doing, brother."

"I'm not doing anything," I reply, and he rolls his eyes.

"If you say so."

"Why don't you go keep Maizie company until I get back," I suggest, nodding to the gorgeous woman sitting by herself.

"You mean until her date gets back," he says.

I shrug. "Sure."

Walking into the hallway where the bathrooms are located, I find Steven washing his hands. When he sees me in the mirror, every muscle in his body immediately tenses. I'm pretty fucking adept at reading body language, and his is screaming uneasiness.

"Hey, man," I say, the door shutting behind me. "You're here with Maizie."

"Uh, yeah. Thanks for the beer you sent over, by the way."

"Sure, sure," I reply with a false casualness to my tone. I don't need him more on edge. I'm not here to necessarily scare the guy, just to let him know the score, if you will. To make sure that he understands this will be the last date he has with the woman I plan on making mine.

"This is your first time in Shine, right?" I ask.

He nods as he finishes rinsing his hands, then grabs a paper towel from the dispenser next to him.

"I don't think you should come back," I say, studying his reaction.

He jolts in surprise, and he turns to face me. "Come again?"

"See, that's exactly what you're *not* going to do. Come to Shine again." I move out of the way of the door and lean against the wall with my arms crossed over my chest. My stance is moderately laid back, and I'm keeping my tone casual—but it's fake, and the guy in front of me knows it.

"Maizie isn't going out on another date with you," I inform him.

He straightens to his full height, even though he's still a few inches shorter than I am, and tilts his head to the side. "Well, I think that's between her and me."

I huff out a chuckle and a small grin appears on my face. Guy's growing a pair right in front of me. Only thing is, mine are bigger.

"No, it's not between you and her. This conversation is between you and me. I'm telling you, you're going to walk out this door and make your way to the parking lot. Then you're going to get in your car and drive back to your apartment—alone." I shoot him a sharp smile. "And you're going to lose Maizie's number and block her on that stupid fucking app. Do whatever you have to do so you don't speak to her again. I'll make sure she gets home safe. Thanks for playing, but you lose."

He crosses his arms over his chest and scoffs. "Is this some small-town biker bullshit? You see another guy who's smarter and better off than you, and you don't want me encroaching on your turf or something?"

At that I really do laugh. "One, I doubt you're better off than me, whatever the fuck that means. And that's not what Maizie's about to begin with. Two, I definitely know you aren't smarter than me because a smart man would have left the second I told him to—instead of trying to swing his dick around. Not smart of you at all."

"I'm not scared of you," he says, but the slight shake of his voice tells a different story.

My arms drop to my sides, and I straighten from the wall, taking a step toward him. "Sure about that?"

Steven looks at me for a beat, trying—and failing—to stare me down. "I don't need this shit. You want her? She's yours. I'm out of here."

He walks past me, making sure not to accidentally brush against me as he squeezes between me and the sink to my left.

Steven has one thing right.

She *is* mine.

When I walk back to the table, I hear Maizie ask Barrett where the hell I am. Well, she uses the term *partner in crime*. No crime has been committed. Not saying that assault wasn't necessarily off the table if Steven hadn't made his exit rather than run his mouth, which I could tell he wanted to do. He left, so maybe the man is a little smarter than I gave him credit for.

"Hey, Maizie," I say, sliding next to her in the booth.

"Look, if you guys want to meet Steven, I'll be happy to introduce you, but you're kind of crashing my date here," she says, scooting over so I can fit in next to her.

"Yeah, about that." I smile at Maizie, and she bites her bottom lip. The urge to swipe my thumb over the abused flesh is nearly overwhelming. "We met. In the bathroom. I don't think he's coming back to the table."

Her lip falls from her teeth as her brows dip in confusion. "What did you—" She shakes her head. "You chased him off?" she asks, her voice a couple octaves higher than normal.

Looking over at Barrett, I notice he's having a hard time containing his smirk. Actually, as his eyes dart between me and Maizie, he gives up the fight and sits back, ready to enjoy the show.

"I may have...suggested he leave, yes," I answer.

The waitress comes over with two plates. One is a steak with garlic butter melting on top and all the fixings to go along with it. She sets it in front of Maizie. The other is half a chicken and a double side of vegetables. Who goes to a steak house and orders chicken?

"Chicken at a steak house?" Barrett asks, mirroring the same question I have. He shakes his head then looks at the waitress. "Can I have some BBQ sauce?" Apparently, he isn't going to let a plate of food go to waste on his watch.

"I can't believe you would do that, Wyatt. It's not like you and I—"

"Not like we what?" I ask, cutting her off.

Her eyes dart to Barrett, obviously not wanting to have this conversation in front of him.

"You can't just run my dates out of town," she says, changing course. "The man did nothing to you."

"You weren't having a good time. Plus, I saw the way you stiffened up after we sent over a couple drinks." I point to her wineglass. "You're welcome, by the way." She shoots me an unamused look.

"How do you know I wasn't having a good time? I could have just had a back cramp or something. Maybe I didn't like the spinach and artichoke dip," she challenges. Fuck, I love her fire.

"First of all, I know for a fact that you love spinach and artichoke dip. Every time Tanya makes a bowl of it, she makes extra to send home with you. Secondly, there isn't anything I don't notice about you, Maiz. I thought you would have figured that out by now."

She lets out a deep breath. "Wyatt..."

"Eat your steak, sweetheart. Enjoy your new date," I say, waving a hand over my body.

"Wait, does that mean I'm a third wheel?" Barrett asks around a mouthful of chicken.

"Yes," I answer at the same time as Maizie says no.

His eyes look between us, but he just shrugs, swallows, then takes another bite.

"I'm still mad at you," Maizie says.

"That's fine. But can I have a bite of your steak? It looks amazing." I shoot her a charming smile.

Maizie stares at me for several beats, her mouth opening and closing a couple times as though she's going to say something, changes her mind, then wants to say something again. Finally, she waves her hand in front of her plate. "Go for it. I'm sticking you with the bill either way."

I let out a laugh and wave down the waitress. "Would you mind bringing us another set of silverware and an extra plate? Oh, and can I order another baked potato with everything on it?"

"Of course. Anything else?"

"Another round of drinks," Maizie says before taking a long sip of her red wine.

The next hour goes by with only a moderate amount of irritation radiating off the woman next to me. Barrett and I discuss Linc's new build, and of course, the fucker orders dessert. We talk about how much fun it's been having the club at Colby's T-ball games. That's about the only time I feel anything other than frustration from Maizie. It's like old times, according to Trick and Tanya, when everyone used to gather for whatever game Linc, Knox, or Ozzy were playing.

Barrett tells us his parents signed him up for T-ball when he was a kid. He played a couple of years but had more fun playing pranks on the coach and making an ass of himself on the field than actually playing the game.

"I think I was the first and only kid in history to be asked not to come back after my third year," he says with a smile on his face. Guess he was born a natural outlaw.

Maizie is in stitches next to me, and it's a welcome change. When the check comes, I throw several bills on it.

"I was kidding earlier. I can pay for mine," she says.

"Not in this lifetime," I reply.

"Wyatt—"

"Maizie," I say, turning to her, "you aren't paying for anything when I'm around. Ever. End of."

She takes a breath through her nose and stares at me, but I'm unmoving in my resolve. Finally, she nods and looks at Barrett, who is looking everywhere but at us.

"Thank you," she says, turning back to me, though her tone doesn't come across as particularly grateful. Understandable, considering I hijacked her date after I got rid of the guy she was here with.

"This was fun, kids, but I promised a certain someone I would pay them a visit tonight, so I need to skedaddle."

"I didn't know you were seeing someone, Barrett," Maizie says.

"I'm not," Barrett replies.

The man is never seeing anyone, but that doesn't mean he doesn't see plenty of beds belonging to various women.

"Okay then," she says. "Time to go."

I move out of the way so she can stand, and this is the first look I get at what she's wearing. It's a pretty white dress that fits tightly around her spectacular breasts with a layered skirt. And she has on a pair of dark-brown leather cowboy boots.

I've seen Maizie in just about every kind of out-fit—but never this. She looks feminine, sweet, and sexy all at the same time. The last thing I want is to watch her leave. I want to take her out, take her dancing, show her off. Okay, maybe not the dancing part since I don't actually know how, but the showing off part? Definitely. It seems like a waste to go home so early on a Saturday night.

"Want to go get a nightcap at Thorn and Thistle?" I offer.

Maizie shakes her head. "I'm pretty beat. And you promised to take us fishing tomorrow, remember?"

"Of course I do," I reply, slightly offended she thinks I would forget. "I'd never disappoint your kid by bailing, Maiz." My statement has two meanings. One about fishing and the other referring to the worries she expressed the other night.

I don't wait for her to comment; instead, I hold out my arm, indicating that we're leaving. She walks in front of me, and I follow her with Barrett walking out behind me. We head to her car as Barrett walks over to the bikes.

"Thanks for dinner," she says. "Even though you kind of owed me after the stunt you pulled."

"I'd say I'm sorry, but..." I let the sentence trail off. She knows me well enough to know I'm not sorry in the least.

She wants to say more. Probably wants to tell me—again—why this is all a bad idea. But rather than hear her list of concerns again, I open her car door. She slides into her seat, and I smile down at her.

"Night, Maiz. Drive safe."

Her eyes narrow, and she shakes her head before tinkling laughter falls from her full lips. "Night, Wyatt."

I close the door, stepping back as she starts her car and pulls out of her spot.

When I walk back to where we parked the bikes earlier, Barrett is standing there with his hands in his pockets.

"Wanna tell me what all that was about?" he asks.

Barrett is a good brother. He had no idea what was going on, but he didn't ask questions. Just followed my lead and had a good time doing it.

"Nothing to tell. Not yet, anyways," I say, watching Maizie's taillights disappear around the corner.

"I think there's a lot to tell, actually. Namely, that you have the hots for our favorite bartender, and she's into you, but something is holding her back."

I turn my head and look at him. "Sounds like you're caught up, then."

Barrett looks off into the distance and nods a few times. "You know, if you hurt her, Ozzy will probably knock your teeth out. So will just about every other brother."

"That include you?"

He shakes his head and scrunches his nose. "Nah. But I will break that pretty nose of yours."

"You think I'm pretty?"

"Won't be when I get through with you."

He says it as a joke, but I know he'd have no problem knocking me the fuck out if I made Maizie cry. And I love him more for it. She may be an employee of the club, but she's family. Her and Colby. And we look out for our own.

We get back to the clubhouse and find the prospect on the couch, watching some MMA fight on television with Pepper asleep at his feet. Have to admit, it's nice having a built-in puppy sitter for when I'm not around.

"Hey, man. Good night?" I ask, walking over to give Pepper some ear scratches.

"Yeah," he replies. "Quiet."

Barrett, who pulled up behind me, is already at the pool tables with Cash and Braxton. I stand straight, and

Pepper lifts his head, but he stretches then curls up on his bed, content to stay where he is.

"Wanna play?" Cash calls to me.

"Nah, think I'll just grab a beer."

Instead of bothering the prospect, I go behind the bar and grab a longneck from the cooler. I'm feeling uneasy and restless, which is unusual after just having gotten back from a ride. Granted, it wasn't a long one; the restaurant is only about ten minutes from the clubhouse.

I walk over to the pool table, where Barrett is regaling the small group with the story of our evening.

"She was so pissed. You guys should have seen the look on Maizie's face when Wyatt asked for a bite of her steak. Of course, I was stuck eating her date's chicken. Not bad," he says, patting his stomach. "But who the hell orders chicken at a place like that?"

"How are you still concerned with what that asshole ordered?" I ask, remembering he made the same comment at the restaurant.

"I just can't wrap my head around it, man," he says, shaking his head back and forth. "It's practically the same as being a vegetarian and going to a steak house for dinner."

I bark out a laugh. "It's not the same at all."

Cash is giving me a skeptical look, while Braxton is eyeing the pool table, searching for a good shot.

"Spit it out," I tell our treasurer.

"I knew you had a bit of a crush on the bartender, but wasn't running her date off a bit much?" Cash asks.

"Nope." I take a pull from my beer, but it's not tasting right to me. I'm not getting the usual calm feeling of shooting the shit with my brothers, playing pool, and drinking a few beers.

"Man. I wish I would have been a fly on the wall in that bathroom," Braxton says after making his shot.

Shrugging, I tell him, "It wasn't much. He tried some dick-swinging bluster, but even a dumbass like him realized pretty quick that he was outmatched."

Braxton and Cash resume their game, dropping the subject and moving on to shit-talking, which is pretty on par when the guys play each other.

Still, that restless feeling in my gut won't fucking quit.

I look at my phone and wonder if Maizie made it home okay. I'm sure she did, but there's this incessant, gnawing urge to check. Or an urge to see her face one more time tonight. Setting the beer on the table next to me, I stand from my chair.

"I'm going for a ride," I tell the small group.

"Want some company?" Barrett offers.

"Nah. Just need to get out a bit. See you fuckers later," I say and walk toward the couches. Pepper lifts his head. "I'm taking off for a while." My dog wags his tail but doesn't get up. He's probably hopeful that I'll take him with me, but I'm taking my bike. Regardless of how many pictures Colby has drawn with Pepper on my motorcycle with me, that shit isn't happening.

"Cool, man. We're good here," the prospect says.

I give him a nod and head back out.

These solitary late-night rides are something I've been doing for years. I love being out on my bike after dark, hitting the city limits and rolling through the country roads. The stars are brighter out here, and the moon is high in the sky tonight. It's the perfect kind of night to shut off my brain and let the road lead me where it will.

Where it takes me tonight is no surprise.

I pull up to Maizie's house and stare at the darkened front. It's after ten. She's been home for over an hour and is probably in bed. Shit, I should be too, considering I have a fishing date with two of my favorite people tomorrow. But I can't make myself leave just yet. Being this close to her, even though she has no idea I'm out here, is already settling that restless feeling I had at the clubhouse.

It's so fucking weird. I've never even kissed the woman, yet I can't get her out of my mind. Can't stop picturing what it would be like to have her in my arms, in my bed.

The front porch light turns on, and my gaze flies to her front door. She opens it wearing an oversized T-shirt and a pair of sleep shorts that peek out the bottom.

"You gonna sit out here all night? My neighbors might get the wrong idea and call the cops to report a stalker," she calls.

I huff out a laugh and lower my kickstand, getting off the bike.

"Thought you'd be in bed," I say as I walk to her front porch.

She closes the door behind her and steps toward the two rocking chairs, taking a seat in one. "Couldn't sleep."

The corner of my mouth ticks up a bit. "Me neither."

Walking up her steps, I have a seat in the other rocking chair.

"Tonight was..." she starts, but I can sense she doesn't exactly know how to finish.

"I had fun. Good food, good company, once I got rid of the asswipe." My attempt at a joke doesn't land, and Maizie purses her lips.

"You can't do that, Wyatt. It might not have been the right match with Steven, but that doesn't mean there won't be someone else."

"I know that. I'm just trying to stack the odds in my favor that the next guy is me."

Maizie groans and gets up from her chair, walking to the railing of her front porch and looking out on the quiet neighborhood.

She turns to face me. "I still have the same reasons for not wanting to start something as I did the other night," she says, leaning against the wood.

"Yeah, about that. I don't like your reasons, so I've decided to overrule you."

Her brows shot up her forehead. "I'm sorry. What now?"

"Maizie, all your reasons were based on fear." I lean forward and rest my elbows on my knees. "None of them were valid. At least not to me."

"You're going to have to explain that a little further, Wyatt. From where I'm sitting, it sounds like you're trying to barrel yourself into my life with no regard for my feelings, and I'm not sure I'm a fan."

"I am thinking about your feelings. And mine. I've spent a lot of time these last few weeks—hell, years if I'm really being honest with myself—thinking about your feelings and Colby's. I get that you're scared. I was scared too. I get that you have a no-biker rule. But here's the thing. I'm a biker, and I don't follow rules."

"Wyatt—"

"Not finished yet, sweetheart," I say, getting up from my chair to stand in front of her. "I'm not just some biker, Maizie. I'm the man who will stand between you and the rest of the world to protect you from everyone who would do you harm or make you sad. I'm the man who will protect your son because he's the most important thing in your life, and I happen to love that kid. Your job will never be in jeopardy, and neither will your heart. Or Colby's. The only way I would leave either of you is if you told me to. If under no uncertain terms you don't want this. If you don't feel the same, then tell me to leave, Maizie. It will kill me, make no mistake about that, but if you can stand there and tell me you don't feel this"—I wave my hand between us—"tell me to go," I finish in a whisper.

We stand facing each other, both of us breathing hard, staring into the other's eyes.

"I can't," she says.

In the next breath, my chest is pressed against hers with my hand cupping the side of her face as I pull her lips to mine, taking her mouth in a fierce kiss.

CHAPTER TWELVE
MAIZIE

Wyatt's kiss is so sudden, it stuns me for a beat before my arms wrap around his waist and I pull him tighter against me. This is crazy and reckless and all the things I swore to myself I wouldn't be when Colby was born.

But, oh God—this is exactly what I want. What I've been craving. His hand that's cupping my cheek slides into my thick, dark hair as he grasps the back of my head. When his mouth opens, his tongue slips against mine, tangling and twirling. Kissing him is everything I imagined—decadent and passionate, and so, so right.

When his other arm bands around me, his hand glides under the oversized nightshirt I'm wearing. His touch is needy as he presses his hand against my heated skin. He runs his palm over my back and lets out a quiet growl into my mouth when he realizes I'm not wearing a bra.

Wyatt breaks the kiss and presses his forehead against mine. "Fuck, I'm not going to be able to stop in a second, and I'd rather not give your neighbors a show."

"We should go inside, then," I say, my voice breathy and quiet.

He pulls his head back and stares into my eyes. The desire and question I see in his gaze mirror the feelings swirling through me. "You sure?"

"You trying to talk me out of it? After that whole speech?"

God, that was a good speech. Wyatt touched on everything I was afraid of. My job, my kid. When he said we were safe with him, all of my doubts fell away. I could see the sincerity in his eyes, hear the promise in his words. And instead of denying it, denying him, I'm choosing us.

He doesn't answer with words. He grabs the back of my thighs and lifts me effortlessly, my legs locking around him. I yelp in surprise, but Wyatt swallows the sound with a kiss, his tongue sliding into my mouth like he owns it. My fingers knot in his hair as he spins us toward the front door. I grip tighter when he opens it one-handed and carries me over the threshold—our mouths still fused.

He kicks the door closed, and both of us still, our lips breaking apart as we listen for any signs of life from Colby.

"Shit, sorry," he whispers, then starts trailing his lips down the column of my neck.

"We should probably go to my room," I say, my hips writhing against him.

He pulls his head back. "Are you sure?"

"Why do you keep asking me that? You're going to give me a complex or some shit. I'll be fucking pissed if

I have to pull out my vibrator and finish the job myself tonight."

His mouth opens and closes a few times as though he can't form words, then he nods. "Okay, we'll be revisiting that at a later time."

I dip my head into his neck and stick out my tongue, tasting his skin.

"Fuuuck," he groans out. "I have so many ideas for that."

"Me too," I whisper in his ear, then suck the lobe into my mouth, gently biting down.

The growl that escapes Wyatt is anything but quiet.

"We really need to go to my room," I say.

This time, he doesn't question me. He silently makes his way down the hall and walks into my room as my lips continue the exploration of his neck. When we step through the doorway, I drop my legs from his waist.

"Hold on one second," I say and step out of my room and walk to Colby's. As gently as possible, I turn his doorknob and dip my head inside. My son is sound asleep, wrapped in a light blanket. Shutting his door, I make my way back to my room and close my door behind me.

Wyatt is sitting on my bed, leaning forward with his elbows resting on his knees.

Sweet Jesus. He looks fucking good in here, waiting for me, his eyes dark with need.

"Come here," he says as he sits straight, his gaze tracking every step I take.

I walk to the lamp that I left on earlier to shut it off.

"What are you doing?" he asks, reaching out to grab my hand.

"Shutting the light off," I reply.

"Fuck no, you're not."

I've never been naked with someone with the lights on, and he must see the sudden onset of self-consciousness flit across my face.

"Maizie, I've been waiting a hell of a long time to be here with you. I plan on taking in my fill, which includes seeing every inch of your gorgeous body."

He pulls me between his legs and his hands slip under my loose shirt and wrap around my waist.

"I've never let anyone see me with lights on before," I whisper, my fingers running through his thick waves.

"I'm not anyone." Wyatt leans in and presses his mouth against my covered stomach. "I'm yours."

"Getting a little ahead of yourself, aren't you?" I joke in a lame attempt to dispel the fear I feel at the idea of him seeing me for the first time in a bright room with no clothes on.

Wyatt's grip tightens at my waist. "Let's get one thing perfectly clear, sweetheart. When I sink into you tonight, I'm claiming you. We can figure out the particulars as we go. We can take it as fast or as slow as you need to wrap your pretty head around that, but you're mine, regardless. That means this body is mine to worship. Every inch of it."

He holds my gaze as his hands travel up and over my ribs, the shirt nearing the bottom of my breasts.

"Arms up, baby," he says, and he whips the shirt over my head, letting it fall to the ground next to my feet.

Wyatt releases a slow breath. And that breath speaks volumes. He's staring at my naked body with reverence in his brown gaze. A look that says all of his waiting, his yearning, is finally being sated by seeing me like this for the first time. His fingers skate over my ribs as he looks from my eyes to my body and back to my eyes again.

"Fuck, baby. You're everything I imagined. And I did a lot of imagining." The smirk that I love plays across his mouth.

I bite down on my lower lip, loving the way he's looking at me, but feeling so exposed. "Sorry, this is kind of hard for me. I'm not perfect. My body isn't the same as before Colby was born."

My hand goes to my lower belly, where I have stretch marks that have faded but have never gone away completely. I'm not like the other girls Wyatt has been with, with tight ab muscles and smooth skin that has never been stretched to oblivion.

Wyatt moves my hand and kisses the faint lines. "You're everything I dreamed of, Maizie," he says when he pulls his lips away. His gentle touch traces over the marks. "This is proof that you carried that precious little boy—who happens to be one of my favorite people on the planet—inside of you, loving him and taking care of him before he came into the world." He kisses my skin again. "These marks are beautiful." Another kiss. "You're amazing." Another kiss. "And fuck, I must have been a saint in a previous life, because you're mine."

He grips the waist of my shorts and slowly pulls them down my legs. When he skates his fingers up my legs, I'm on the verge of melting into a puddle before him. He grips the back of one thigh with his hand while the other glides over my center, his finger dipping in just the slightest bit.

"You're soaked for me," he breathes out, and I nod.

Wyatt slides his finger between the lips of my pussy, gathering the wetness on the digit before putting his finger in his mouth. The groan that leaves his throat is fucking ravenous.

"Goddamn, baby. Better than I could have imagined."

He stands suddenly and captures my mouth in a searing kiss.

"I swear to God, I'm going to take my time with you," he says breathlessly when he pulls his mouth away. "But right now, I need to eat that sweet fucking pussy."

I nod as he wraps his arm around my waist and spins us so that the back of my knees hit the bed. I sit on the edge and lean back on my arms, spreading my thighs apart as he kneels between them.

"You're so fucking perfect," he says, leaning forward and swiping his tongue through my center as though he can't wait another second to taste me. "Mmm," he hums, then lifts his head, straightening his body and grabbing the back of my neck before he pulls me in for another soul-shattering kiss. "You're so goddamn sweet. I could spend the night right here and not need another single fucking thing."

My hands slip under his shirt, and I wrap my arms around his back, exploring the taut muscles with the tips of my fingers. "You'd better make good on your promise, Wyatt."

He tilts his head to the side, a question in his dark stare.

"You said that when you sink inside me, you're going to claim me."

"Oh, baby. You're mine no matter what. But I haven't had my fill of your pretty cunt yet."

He lowers himself, and my fingers grip his dark strands. He begins licking at me as though he's a man who has been deprived of his last ten meals. His licks are slow, then fast. Long, then short. He takes me to the edge over and over, pulling back right before I'm ready to fall. Then he does it all over again. My hands are tugging at his hair. No matter how much I beg him to make me come, my pleas fall on deaf ears.

When he adds two fingers to my soaked channel, there's no stopping the wave that washes over me. It starts in the center then bursts through my arms and legs, this feeling of euphoria. I have to cover my mouth so I don't cry out and wake the entire neighborhood with my screams. I pulse around his fingers, completely soaking his face as the orgasm washes through me.

When I've finally settled, Wyatt looks up at me with a giant wet grin. "Fucking perfect."

He stands from the floor as I'm still trying to catch my breath and shrugs off his cut, laying it on the chair in the corner of my room. Next, he grabs the collar of his shirt and pulls it over his head. This is the first time I've seen Wyatt without a shirt. It's also the first time I've felt the intense urge to run my tongue over his washboard abs and trace his tattoos with my lips. An intricate black rose wrapped in thorns adorns the muscle over his heart. He rubs the spot as he stares at me, naked in front of him, as though he's keeping his heart from bursting out of his chest.

I sit forward, holding his gaze as my hands grab his belt buckle and slide the leather from the metal. Then my fingers find the button of his jeans, and I pop it open. Wyatt's eyes don't stray from mine as I lean in and kiss the spot right below his belly button. Our gazes stay locked as I slide the zipper of his jeans down. The tip of his hard cock pokes out of his black boxer briefs. When I lick the bead of precum, he hisses through his teeth, his head falling back before he snaps it forward when I wrap my lips around the soft head of his shaft.

"You're going to fucking kill me, baby," he says, grabbing the back of my head and squeezing. He steps back and pulls his pants the rest of the way off, stroking himself as his eyes drink me in. "I don't want anything between us. I just had a physical, and I'm clear."

"I had an IUD put in after I had Colby." When things started heating up with the guy from out of town, I went to my doctor. No way was I going to have any more unexpected surprises. "And I haven't been with anyone since my last checkup." Hell, in the last several years, but I don't say that.

Wyatt smiles and stalks toward the bed. I scoot to the center, and he leans over me, pressing me into the mattress before he takes my mouth in a bruising kiss. Guess he likes the idea of being inside me with nothing separating us. His arm slides under me, and before I can register what's happening, he's flipped us over so I'm lying on top of him.

"I want to watch you ride me. Fuck, I've had dreams about it." He groans, then takes my mouth in another breath-stealing kiss.

His hands knead the flesh of my ass as I writhe on top of him, his hard cock between our bodies. When I sit up, he takes one of my breasts in his palm and squeezes while his other hand grips my hip. His fingers twist my peaked nipple, and I let out a hiss of pleasure, like I would when I was using my toy but imagining it was Wyatt's hands on me.

"You like that?" he asks and does it again.

"Fuuuuck," I moan out, feeling like there is a direct line from my nipple to my clit.

I can't wait anymore. I need to feel him inside me. My hips lift from him, and I grab the base of his cock as I sink down onto him.

I let out a long breath, and Wyatt releases a hiss of pleasure.

"Holy shit, Maizie, you feel so fucking good," he grits out as I lower myself even more, taking him deeper.

As soon as I'm fully seated, Wyatt leans up and kisses me senseless. Tongues lash and teeth nip as I begin moving, my hips lifting then lowering at a slow pace as I get used to being stretched wide by him.

"God, I'm so full," I say on a moan, moving a touch faster.

"Can you take a little more?" he asks and I nod, though I'm not sure what he means by that.

He leans back, his head resting on the pillow as he holds my hips and plants his feet on the bed behind me. He holds me up a bit, then slams into me from the bottom. I let out a cry. I've never done this, and the change in position and intensity is like nothing I could have imagined.

"Oh fuck," I say through clenched teeth as Wyatt pistons his hips up and down, holding my hips as he fucks me.

I topple forward, catching myself with my arms before I crash into his chest.

"I'm going to come," I say, my arms shaky as I brace myself.

Wyatt lifts me fully off of him and flips me onto my back before lifting one of my legs over his shoulder, then he fills me again.

"You're so fucking tight, Maizie. Fuck, I need you to get there. I'm about to fill you up, baby," he says.

The hand he has gripping my hip finds my clit, and he starts rubbing furiously as sweat drips down his chest. This isn't slow, and it's not particularly gentle, but it's everything I hoped it would be and sure as hell everything I need right now. It's wild and desperate, the years of yearning and desire curling tight right here and now.

Then it explodes.

My pussy spasms, squeezing around him as I come undone. He keeps pumping into me, keeps stroking my clit through every clenching pulse.

"Jesus," he grits out. "That's it. Fuck, your pussy is made for me."

I feel him swell inside of me as his jaw tightens so hard I'm worried he's going to crack a molar. His cock jerks as he comes on a low moan, trying to stay quiet so he doesn't wake my son. "Goddamn," he breathes out when he finally stills.

Wyatt turns his head and kisses my ankle before lowering my leg to the bed. Then he leans down and takes my mouth in a soothing kiss filled with gratitude and something else I don't want to look too closely at—at least, not yet.

When he pulls out, we both let out a small moan. He lies next to me and gathers me in his arms.

"Never in my life have I found a woman so fucking right for me, Maizie," he says, running his fingers over my sweat-slicked back. "I never thought there was one out there for me. Then I met you, and fuck, I've never been happier to be wrong," he finishes on a whisper.

I tilt my head up, meeting his thoughtful gaze. "I felt it, too."

Wyatt smiles softly before inclining his head and placing a gentle kiss on my lips. "Give me fifteen minutes, and I'll prove it to you again."

"Prove what?"

"That you're mine."

I smile and nestle into his chest. "Okay. But listen, I know this is probably a terrible time to bring it up, but you can't stay the night." I angle my head toward his. "It's just that Colby has never seen a man in the house, and we should talk to him about it before he sees you coming out of my room or something."

He kisses my forehead. "You don't have to explain, baby. We take this at your pace, remember?"

God, so much emotion feels like it's going to burst from me. How did I get so lucky to have a man like Wyatt who understands what I need without getting bent out of shape? Someone who understands that this is all new, and it's going to take me a second to catch my breath and make sure I explain this properly to my kid.

"Just with Colby. With me, though?" The corner of my lips tips up. "We could probably turn it up a couple notches."

"Jesus, woman," he huffs out. "That was some of my best work, and you want me to turn it up?"

"Thought you liked a challenge."

Wyatt rolls me onto my back, his strong body hovering over mine. "You trying to kill me?" he asks, then buries his face in my neck, growling and nibbling at the damp skin there. I feel his cock start to harden between our bodies as he peppers my throat with love bites and tongue lashings.

"Thought you said fifteen minutes?" I ask, giggling while he nibbles.

"Who said that? It certainly wasn't me. Not when I have you underneath me, naked and practically begging for me."

"I wasn't begging."

He lifts his head and gives me that damn smirk. "Not yet. But I plan on changing that."

Chapter Thirteen
Wyatt

The warm body wrapped around me is the first thing that registers before I open my eyes. After the third time being inside of Maizie with her on all fours as I sunk deep inside her heat while she bit down on a pillow when she came hard around my cock, we collapsed onto the bed. My eyes closed on their own volition, exhausted from how hard I came. I remember telling her that I wouldn't fall asleep. I was just resting my eyes as she caught her breath, her own eyes shutting.

Guess I fucked that up. Not that I mind. Waking up like this is one of my fantasies come to life. I roll over and see light peeking through the blinds.

"Shit," I say and check my phone. It's just after six in the morning.

Maizie stirs next to me.

"Baby," I whisper, moving her dark hair from her face. "We fell asleep."

Her eyes pop open in an instant. "Fuck, what time is it?"

"Just after six."

She relaxes. "Colby is never up this early."

A devious grin stretches across my mouth. "In that case," I say, leaning down to brush my mouth against her kiss-swollen lips.

"Not so fast," she says, pressing her hand to my chest. "That doesn't mean he's not going to be up in the next hour."

"I'll be quick," I reply, following her mouth when she backs away.

"Just what every girl longs to hear," she says, gently pushing me away. "I don't want to test our luck."

I groan, but allow her to put some distance between us. "Fine," I say with a little pout, which only serves to make her laugh. Perfectly fine with me. I love the breathy giggles that come out of her, especially last night when I found a particularly ticklish spot on the inside of her thigh...fuck, I need to stop thinking like that—otherwise I'm going to have a very uncomfortable ride back to the clubhouse.

I rise off the bed, and Maizie sits up, throwing her legs to the side. "Don't you dare." I find my jeans lying in a heap on the floor, and my boots are lying haphazardly next to them. "You need your sleep, sweetheart." I pull my jeans up my legs, and Maizie's eyes track my movements as she lies back down.

Sitting on the edge of the bed, I put my boots back on and grab my T-shirt from the floor. "I'll be back in two hours with Pepper and my truck so we can go to the lake. Or would nine be better?" I wore my woman the fuck out last night. Shit, I'm feeling pretty tired myself, but energized at the same time, if that makes sense.

My woman.

"Two hours should be plenty of time," she says with a sleepy smile, her eyes already starting to droop. I lean over and kiss her before standing. I grab my cut from the chair and walk out of her room, then gently shut the door behind me. As I make my way down the hall, I slide my arms through my cut, a grin on my face the entire time. I'm so distracted by this ecstatic feeling in my chest that I don't clock the little boy sitting in the living room as I'm about to pass it to sneak out.

"Hi, Wyatt," Colby's cheery voice says from the couch. "What are you doing here? Where's Pepper? When can we go fishing?"

"Hey, buddy. You're up early," I say a little louder than I normally talk, hoping that Maizie hears me and comes to handle this with me. I'm totally fine with acting like me spending the night is perfectly normal, but I know she had some reservations.

"'Cause when I opened my eyes this morning, I re-membered we were going to go fishing, and I got so excited I couldn't close them. Then I had to go pee real bad, so I got out of bed. And look"—he points to the TV—"I put my movie in and turned it on all by myself."

"Great job, buddy," I say loudly again.

Maizie comes running down the hall wearing the sleep shirt and shorts I peeled off her last night. "Colby, you're up early," she says, a little out of breath.

"Morning, Mommy. I put my movie in," he tells her, obviously proud of his accomplishment. "Are we leaving soon to go fishing?"

"Uh. Not quite yet. Wyatt just came over to..." she starts, then stumbles.

"Fix your mom's sink in her bathroom. It was leaking," I finish for her.

"Oh, okay. When can we go?"

It seems we were a little more worried than necessary about Colby seeing me this morning. That kid has one thing on his brain, and it has nothing to do with figuring out that I spent the night here.

"I'll go get Pepper and my fishing gear and come right back, yeah?"

"Okay. See you soon," Colby answers.

"Alright," Maizie says, clapping her hands together. "How about breakfast, bud?"

"French toast?"

Maizie nods, and I step toward her. I'm about to kiss her goodbye on instinct, then realize there are little eyes watching us, so I pull back and move closer to the door instead. "See you in a few."

"Wait," Colby chimes in. "Mommy, you have to say thank you. Remember? You always tell me when someone helps you with something, you make sure to say thank you. Tell Wyatt thank you for coming over and fixing your broken pipes."

Jesus fucking Christ. It takes every ounce of willpower I have to not burst into a bellowing laugh.

Maizie's wide eyes turn to me. "Thank you for fixing my pipes this morning," she says, and I can tell it's absolutely killing her inside.

I shoot her a half smile. "Anytime."

Thirty minutes later, I'm back at Maizie's house with an excited dog in the truck next to me. We really need to make it clear to Colby that I'm going to be spending the night here on occasion. I hate leaving Pepper with the prospect. Not that he isn't well taken care of at the clubhouse when I'm not around—I've even caught Ozzy sneaking him bits of bacon in the morning—but I still feel guilty about leaving him there.

When I pull up, Colby is waiting on the front porch. As soon as he sees Pepper jump out of the truck, he runs over and rubs his ears, the dog lapping at his face.

"Where's your mom?"

"Inside, making sandwiches and stuff. Come on, Pepper, I have your rope in the backyard."

Colby bounds up the steps and turns into the kitchen, running past his mom through the back door. Maizie has a smile on her face, watching him, then goes back to putting some turkey sandwiches into a bag.

"Hey, baby," I say and walk up behind her, caging her against the counter with my arms on either side of her as I press a kiss to the side of her neck.

"Wyatt, Colby might see you," she says, giggling when I give her a gentle love bite.

"He's playing out back with Pepper. Trust me, the only things that kid cares about are his dog and when we're going to leave for the lake. Actually, now that I think about it, I'm starting to feel a little tossed to the side like yesterday's trash. He used to get excited to play with me, not Pepper."

"Sorry, honey. Since Pepper came around, all of us have taken a back seat to the dog." She turns around and plays with the hem of my shirt. "You said his dog just now."

I tilt my head to the side in question.

"You said Colby only cares about *his* dog."

"I mean, he did name him." I shrug. "Hell, pretty sure Pepper loves Colby more than me. It's fitting."

She has a soft look in her gaze before her eyes dart to the backyard. Colby's back is facing us as he throws the rope toy for Pepper.

Maizie rises on her tip-toes and presses an all too brief kiss against my lips.

"I'm all done here. Let me grab a swimsuit and I'll be right back," she says.

"You know, I should really check that pipe. Make sure no problems have come up since I screwed it in tighter."

Maizie groans and rests her forehead against my chest for a moment. "This is one of those stories I'm going to tell Colby's girlfriend when he's older. Let him deal with a quarter of the embarrassment that we had to this morning."

"I thought it was fucking great," I say on a laugh.

"Of course you do," she mumbles then steps around me.

Naturally, I follow her into the bedroom, and she starts rummaging around one of the drawers of her dresser on the opposite wall from the door. She pulls out a black one-piece and I walk over to see what else she has in there. A bright-pink two-piece bikini catches my eye. Pulling it out of the drawer, I hold up both pieces.

"How about this one?" I suggest.

Maizie groans. "Lucy bought that for me last year. I've never worn it. It's just so...revealing," she finishes, her hand waving over her flat stomach and shaking her head.

"Obviously I didn't get my point across to you last night," I say, throwing the suit on the bed and gathering her in my arms. She drapes her hands over my shoulders and looks at me with an adorably scrunched-up nose. "You are fucking gorgeous. Every single inch of you. As far as I'm concerned, you're perfect. And if anyone were to ever say otherwise, I'd have no problem telling them to shut the hell up. Even you, sweetheart."

"Are you telling me to shut up?" She arches her brow and I get the distinct feeling that is not a phrase she likes to hear.

"Uh...no. I'm telling you you're beautiful, and I don't like you talking or feeling bad about yourself."

Maizie smiles. "I may need a little more convincing."

"That I can definitely do," I say and lean down, pressing my lips to hers. She opens immediately, and my tongue tastes hers, the sweetness of the maple syrup she had with her waffles and Maizie exploding in my mouth. My hands slide down her waist to the curve of her delicious ass and I squeeze, pressing her into my ever-hardening erection.

Then we hear a door slam.

"Moooom," Colby calls. "Can we go soon?"

"Damn," I mumble as she breaks the kiss and steps back. "Cockblocked by a five-year-old."

Maizie huffs out a laugh. "Welcome to dating a single mom." She turns toward the bed with both suits lying on it. "You better go out there. I need to change."

I press a kiss to her cheek then walk toward the door. "Hey, Maiz?"

She looks over at me with raised brows.

"I wouldn't have it any other way."

She smiles. It's one of her shy ones that says she's not used to this kind of attention, but loves it just the same.

"Mooom, where are you?" Colby yells down the hall.

I dip my head and walk out, seeing Colby making his way to her room before I close the door behind me.

"What are you doing?" he asks. "Is Mommy in there? Pepper and me are ready to go."

"I was just making sure everything was fixed still," I say. "Your mom's going to change, then we'll hit the road, yeah?"

Colby nods and turns around, walking back to the front of the house.

"Hey, I could use your muscles to help me load the truck, what do you say?" I ask.

He holds up both of his arms and curves them, flexing his nonexistent biceps. "Let's do it."

I chuckle and run my hand through his sandy hair a few times, ruffling it before walking into the kitchen. There's a cooler sitting on the small wooden table, and I look in the freezer, finding a couple of ice packs. I hand them to Colby, and he sets them in the bottom of the cooler. Then I gather the sandwiches.

"What should we bring for drinks?" I ask, opening the fridge.

"Soda!" he yells.

Of course he would say that.

I grab a few out of the fridge and several waters, putting them on top of the ice packs then laying the sandwiches over them.

"What about towels and stuff?"

We're going to fish, but it's not like we can't jump in the lake when it gets too hot under the summer sun.

Colby runs down the hall and comes back less than a minute later with three beach towels.

"You're a big help, buddy. I wouldn't be able to do it without you," I say, and he beams.

"That's because I'm big now. I help Mommy with stuff all the time."

"It's important for men to help people they love, buddy. I bet she really appreciates it too."

He nods enthusiastically. "Is that why you help her with stuff? Because you love her too?"

Holy fuck. The air is knocked from my lungs for a split second, but in the next breath, his words settle over me. And they feel right.

"Yup. I love both of you guys," I say.

"And Pepper," Colby says, bending to give the dog a kiss on the head as the mischievous fur ball sniffs at the cooler sitting on the table.

"And Pepper," I agree.

"Here, like this," I say to Colby, bending down on one knee to help him tie the worm to the hook on his fishing line.

"Ew," he says, giggling as I stab the center of the worm with the hook.

"It's not that gross. And the worm doesn't feel anything," I say, and the boy gives me a dubious look.

Shit, I don't know what worms feel, but I seem to remember hearing that somewhere.

"Look over here, guys," Maizie calls. She holds her phone up and takes a picture. When she lowers it, I see her examine the photo with a wide smile on her face. "Perfect," she says, and I return my attention to the worm and the hook.

"Now, you want to make sure you always know where your hook is. The last thing you want to happen is for you to hook your finger. We would definitely feel it and probably have to go to the ER so they could take it out. And what's my number one rule?"

"Don't do anything that means we have to make an ER trip," Colby replies solemnly.

"That's right." I lean his pole against the fish cooler I brought in case we catch any big enough to eat. "You wanna do mine?"

He shakes his head. "No...I think I need to watch again."

A light chuckle escapes me. I wasn't a fan of hooking the worms at his age either. My dad used to take me fishing when I was younger. Before he lost his job and everything started going to shit. He eventually found work, but it was less pay, and by that time he and my mom were on a slippery slope straight down.

Once I have my line ready, I hand Colby his pole. "Okay, what do you know about casting?"

"Knox showed me, but I don't remember exactly," he answers.

"That's okay. Here." I bend and show him what to do with the reel when he casts his line. "Okay. You go first," I say. He launches his hook into the water at an almost perfect arch. "Wow, buddy, that was great," I tell him and he looks up at me with a beaming smile.

I do the same, and we spend the next hour casting and reeling. Colby caught one tiny fish that he decided should go back to grow some more, and I agreed. When I reeled in a medium-sized fish, Colby thought it should go back as well. I think I'm picking up on a pattern with this kid.

"Have you ever eaten the fish that you catch?" I ask.

"No. I don't really like fish," he says, watching his line for a bite.

I let out a booming laugh and turn toward Maizie. When we got here, she'd laid down a blanket and set up three camping chairs and an umbrella to keep the sun off of us. She's been sitting in a chair with a book in her hand, wearing the pink bikini and a pair of shorts. I thought my tongue was going to fall out of my mouth when she took her T-shirt off and I saw the bright-pink material underneath. Fuck, my woman is stunning.

"You could have told me he didn't like fish," I call to her with laughter lacing my words.

She laughs. "He likes fishing, though," she yells back.

"Do I have to eat it?" Colby asks, looking at me with a touch of worry creasing his brow.

"No, buddy. You don't have to," I say, smiling down at the boy.

"You guys getting hungry?" Maizie calls.

"What do you think?" I ask Colby.

"I want a soda," he says.

"Do you have to eat lunch first?"

"I'm hungry for lunch," he calls to his mom.

I'm sure he is.

We reel in our lines, and I set them aside before we make our way over to Maizie.

This was probably one of the best afternoons I've spent in a long time. How could it not be? I get to spend time with my woman and her amazing kid. The only thing that would make it better is if I could wrap her in my arms and kiss her like I've been tempted to do so many times. But we haven't had that conversation with Colby yet, and it wouldn't be fair of me to spring it on him without Maizie and me talking and deciding how we're going to discuss it first.

After lunch, Colby is done fishing and insists on playing in the water. I grab the ball I brought with us and throw it in the lake over and over so the dog can swim out and grab it. To Colby, this is the funniest thing he's seen all day, and he even tries to race Pepper to get the ball while Maizie takes a ton of pictures. When we're done with swimming, Colby and Pepper lie out on the huge blanket and fall asleep, both tired from two hours of playing in the lake.

"Shit, I forgot my sunscreen," Maizie says, rummaging through the bag. "I think I left it in the truck. Be right back." She hops up, and I watch the way her ass sways in those denim cutoff shorts.

Never let it be said that I'm one to let opportunities go to waste.

I get up from my chair, and Pepper raises his head. "Lie down," I tell him, and his head rests on his paws next to Colby, who is still sound asleep.

Jogging to the truck, I arrive just as Maizie closes the passenger door, her sunscreen in hand. She yelps when she turns and finds me behind her, but I cut it off by pressing my mouth to hers.

"Fuck, I've wanted to do that all day," I tell her, trailing my mouth down her sun-warmed skin.

"Mmm, I know the feeling," she says. "But we can't. Not yet."

"I know, baby. But I wasn't about to let this chance pass me by." I grab the lotion from her hand, and we start walking back toward our little setup. "You get my back and I'll get yours?" I ask, waving the bottle with a salacious grin on my face.

"Deal."

We get back to the house just before dinnertime, and I can tell Maizie is exhausted. I have to admit, I'm pretty beat too, but honestly, I'm not ready for the day to end.

"Pizza?" I ask after getting a very tired kid and all of our stuff in the house.

She lets out a relieved breath. "That sounds perfect," she says.

"How about you go take a shower, and I'll order it. Mushroom and sausage okay?"

Her adorable nose scrunches much in the same way Colby's did when I suggested the same pizza a couple weeks ago. "Yes to the sausage, no to the mushrooms."

I laugh and grab my phone from my pocket. "I'll get you both to like mushrooms one of these days."

It's such a nice night, we decide to eat dinner outside. Maizie and Colby have sun-kissed skin and smiles as we devour the pizza in front of us.

"That was the best day ever!" Colby exclaims with sauce all over his face. "Can we do it again next weekend?"

I smile at the little guy and nod. "If it's okay with your mom, absolutely."

He turns to Maizie and looks at her with pleading eyes, and I do the same.

Maizie laughs, taking a sip of her water. "Jeez, between the two of you, how could I say no?"

Later that night, as I'm lying in bed, that restless feeling I had last night comes back. Pepper is asleep in his bed on the floor and I feel bad about what I'm about to do, but...

I grab my phone to text Maizie.

Me: *Colby asleep?*

Maizie: *Knocked out cold.*

Me: *I really don't like this, baby.*

Maizie: *What?*

Me: *Being in a bed without you.*

Maizie: *I'm not a fan either.*

Maizie: *If you promise not to fall asleep, maybe you would want to come over?*

Me: *On my way.*

I get up from my bed and throw my jeans, T-shirt and cut back on.

"Come on, Pepper," I say, and he rises from his bed and follows me out of my room. When I walk into the main area of the clubhouse, the prospect is cleaning up behind the bar while a few brothers play darts.

"I'm going out for a while. You got Pepper?"

"Of course," the prospect says.

"Go lie down," I tell the dog, and he trudges over to the bed Knox bought him between the couches and the TV and lies down.

I walk outside and get on my bike. If I get my way, I won't have to leave the clubhouse late at night much longer—Maizie and I will be sharing a bed under the same roof.

Chapter Fourteen
Maizie

I wanted to ask Wyatt to stay. So bad. But we haven't talked with Colby, and aside from him claiming me as his last night, we haven't really spoken about where this is going. It's so strange, feeling like we're starting something new in the middle of something we already have. I guess that's what it means when you finally let down your walls with your friend whom you've had feelings for and discover he feels the same. It's new, but not. Exciting yet comfortable, while at the same time all-consuming.

At least that's how I felt all day. Watching him with Colby at the lake, the kiss at the truck, the fact that he saw how tired I was and took it upon himself to order dinner and give me a break to shower the lake off me, it meant everything to me. Though that last thing he would have done even if we hadn't spent the night tangled with each other, because that's who Wyatt is. He sees what needs to be handled and takes it upon himself to do it.

When he left before Colby went to bed, I wanted to grab him, kiss him, and tell him to stay. Stay with me.

Stay with us. Considering I was so scared just a day ago about starting something with the biker, and now I can't imagine not having him here, this is a new and strange feeling. But that's what Wyatt does for me. He takes my fear and soothes it. Listens to my doubts and reassures me.

And when he texted and said he didn't like being in bed alone, the decision was easy to ask him to come back.

He pulls up on his bike, and I'm waiting for him on the front porch so he doesn't have to knock. I don't think for a second that he would wake Colby—I'm not sure a meteor hitting the neighborhood could at this point—but I didn't want to chance it.

In a few long strides, Wyatt crosses the driveway to the porch, taking the steps two at a time. He grabs me around the waist and pulls me against him, kissing me so thoroughly it feels like we haven't seen each other in weeks instead of just hours.

"God, I have been dying to do that all day," he says, breaking the kiss and pulling me upright from where I was bent slightly backward.

I slide my hands under his shirt and grab his belt buckle before I take a step back and pull him toward the house. "You have no idea how hard it was to keep my hands off you today." I remember the way my mouth watered when he took his shirt off and was wearing nothing but a pair of dark-blue swim trunks when he got in the lake to play with Colby. The shorts fell low on his hips, and I kept imagining running my tongue over the line of muscle that pointed to his cock.

"I want to taste you tonight," I tell him and watch his expression darken with lust.

We walk through the door, and he grabs my wrist, yanking my body to his and taking my mouth in another deep kiss. "Fuck, baby. I can't get enough of your mouth. You want it filled with my cock?"

"Yes," I hiss out. This isn't something I ever craved to do with any other man other than Wyatt. Not to say I haven't given a blow job before, but it was more of a tit-for-tat thing. But with Wyatt, I'm desperate to have my mouth stretch around his hard length. I need to bring him to the point of blinding pleasure like he did to me last night, over and over.

He grabs my tits in his hands, squeezing and molding my flesh. "I want to fuck your tits, baby. And I want you to lick the head of my dick while I do."

I moan, rubbing myself against him as he pinches my nipples through my thin shirt.

We hurry to the bedroom, and as soon as I close the door, Wyatt presses against my back, trapping me between his body and the wood. His hand dives into my panties and instantly finds my clit, rubbing tight circles around the swollen bud.

"Fuck, you're so wet thinking about my cock in your mouth, aren't you?"

I whimper in response.

"I'm going to fill your tight pussy and make you come so fucking hard you'll feel me for days."

Another whimper is followed by a long moan when he fills me with two of his thick fingers.

"But first," he says, pulling away and ripping my panties down my legs, "you're going to get on your bed and kneel." I shakily lift one foot, then the other, so he can free them from my body. He spins me around and yanks the shirt over my head. Wyatt steps back and removes his cut, laying it on my chair, then toes off his boots before pulling his own shirt off.

"Get on the bed, Maizie," he commands, and a shiver runs down my spine.

When I walk to the edge of the mattress, I lean over and start to crawl to the head of the bed. Wyatt grabs my hips, stopping me, and buries his face in my pussy from behind. I throw my head back, desperately wanting to cry out. But I keep as quiet as possible, which is no easy feat when his tongue circles the tight pucker that no one has ever touched.

"Fuck, baby, every part of you is delicious." His tongue circles me a few more times, and my arms strain while trying to keep myself upright.

He stands, and I turn to watch him undo his belt. His pants drop to the floor, followed by his boxers.

"Where are you supposed to be?" he asks, jolting me out of my momentary daze while I watch him stroke his hard length.

I crawl to the head of my bed and face him, kneeling before him like he asked. His knees meet the mattress facing me, then he turns around and lies back. "Come here." He grabs the back of my thighs and guides me until I'm kneeling over his mouth. "Sit."

"Wh-what?" I ask, slightly confused.

"Sit on my face. I'm going to eat this perfect pussy while you lean forward and swallow my cock."

Holy shit, this man's mouth is absolutely sinful, and I love it.

I lower myself an inch, afraid to put too much weight on him. But that's not good enough for Wyatt.

"I said sit, Maizie." He grabs my hips and pulls me down, taking the choice away from me. His face is buried underneath me, and he starts to fucking feast. His tongue slides into me and swirls before finding my clit. He grazes it with his teeth, then sucks, slow and deliberate. Every nerve ending in my body is lit up as I lean forward and lift his heavy length from where it rests against his stomach. My mouth slides over the head and Wyatt groans, the vibrations running over my clit. Jesus, he's so much better than any toy I've ever used.

I slide his hardness deeper into my mouth and begin bobbing my head up and down, taking him as far to the back of my throat as I can manage. My hand is tight around the base, and I pop my mouth off him so I can run my tongue over his length, swirling it around the head a few times, then put him back in my mouth and repeat the motions all over again. Wyatt never ceases his licks, and I can't help but rock my hips back and forth over his supremely talented mouth.

I lift my head. "Fuck, I'm going to come," I say, stroking him as his arms band around my waist and he pulls me tighter against his mouth. When he sucks on my clit once again and moans, I fucking detonate. The orgasm is so intense I nearly collapse, but Wyatt keeps me steady as I come on his face, lapping at every last drop as though he isn't willing to waste a single thing.

I fall over, a satiated mess of limbs, and Wyatt sits up, grabbing my thighs and spreading me wide. "I'm not done with you yet." He aligns himself with my entrance, and in one deep thrust, he's seated fully inside of me. My back arches off the bed as Wyatt begins pumping into me with my legs draped over his arms.

"Goddamn, your pussy is so good. I'm never going to get enough of this." Sweat drips down his brow as he moans words of praise. "Just like that," he says. "Your cunt was made for me. You take me so fucking good, baby."

He thrusts—over and over. His eyes dart between where we're connected and my own stare.

"Play with your tits, baby. Show me what you like."

I take my breasts in my hands and pinch my nipples, making them harden into tight points.

"Fuck," he breathes out. "You look good like that."

"I'm going to come," I cry, the sensations of my fingers and his cock so goddamn deep making it too much to hold back any longer.

My pussy clamps down around Wyatt's shaft, and I feel him jerk inside of me, both of us reaching this intense climax together. He fills me as I tighten around him over and over again, each pulse sending fireworks shooting through my entire body.

When each of us is spent, Wyatt leans down and kisses me, his tongue gliding into my mouth, gently playing with mine. He breaks the kiss and presses his forehead to mine.

"I'm thoroughly addicted to you, Maizie. Every part of me belongs to you."

"Me or my pussy?"

He kisses the tip of my nose. "Smart-ass."

He lifts up and removes himself from me, both of us groaning when he does.

"We're a mess," I say, looking at the sweat glistening across his chest and face. I'm sure I'm no better off as my damp skin begins to cool.

"Come on," he says, standing from the bed and holding out his hand. "Let's get cleaned up."

I slide my palm into his, and he leads me into the bathroom, turning on the faucet for the tub. He dips his fingers beneath the stream to check the temperature, then presses the drain stopper so the tub can fill.

"Wow, I get all the special treatment today, don't I?" I ask and shoot him a smile.

"You deserve nothing less, baby. You spend all your time taking care of one of my favorite people; it's time someone takes care of you."

He holds my hand as I step into the bath and sit down in the center. Wyatt climbs in behind me, and when he's situated in the water, he pulls me against his chest before using his foot to turn off the water. I don't know why seeing our legs tangled like this is making my chest feel light, but it is. I relax back into him and rest my head against his shoulder.

"We haven't talked about what we're going to tell people yet," he says, his hand resting on my stomach as though he wants to make sure I don't bolt out of this tub.

Not that it's necessary. I doubt I could move right now.

"I'm not sure we should say anything yet. It's early and..."

"It's really not though, is it?" he asks.

His question mirrors the thoughts I had before he came back tonight.

"I guess not," I say in a breathy chuckle. "Our friends never met the guy I dated. I mean, Lucy and Charlie weren't even around then, and when he would come into the bar, none of you were there."

"Well, I've never really dated anyone, so they've never seen me in a relationship either."

He doesn't have to elaborate. Wyatt has never struck me as a person who's made commitments to a woman—or anyone other than his brothers, for that matter. And if I'm honest with myself, that scares me a little. Does he really understand what he's getting himself into? Answering to another person? Taking someone else's feelings into consideration?

"I can practically see the steam coming out of your ears, baby. What's going on in that head of yours?" he asks, burying his face in my hair.

"You've never done this," I blurt. "Been in a committed relationship."

"Not since my first and only girlfriend in high school, no."

"Why did it end?"

The chuckle that rumbles through his chest vibrates into my back. "Um, because we were seventeen. I didn't much care for being tied down, and she went away to college. It was no big love affair and no big loss."

It's not as though I have much experience with relationships either. Colby's father and I were never together, and the only other guy I'd been with didn't even live in town.

"Yeah, I've never been with someone who, if I lost them, I would be devastated either," I say.

I remember back to the time that the guy I was seeing on occasion told me that his territory had changed and he wouldn't be making his way through Shine anymore. I never felt a sense of loss. Mild disappointment was about as deep as my feelings went.

"What about Colby's father?" Wyatt asks.

The mention of Nolan instantly has my muscles tensing, and Wyatt clearly feels the shift. His hands move to my shoulders, and he begins rubbing small circles in my suddenly tight muscles.

"You don't have to talk about him, Maizie. If it's too painful."

It is, but it isn't. I could so easily come clean about what I found out about Nolan a few weeks ago. Wyatt would understand. Probably. But I've spent years keeping quiet about him, never even saying his name out loud in front of anyone.

No one knows the circumstances around the night I conceived Colby. No one knows that his father is a member of the Bone Breakers. Shit, I didn't even know what that meant until last year when Ozzy asked us to keep an eye out and report to him if we saw any of them around town. Until then, as far as I knew, he was just some biker who lived in Arizona. There was no reason to suspect the clubs were somehow involved or that they didn't get along. And once I found that out, I was determined more than ever to keep my secret. I couldn't jeopardize my job or Colby's safety.

When I open my mouth to speak, I give him as much of the truth as I'm willing to divulge. At least right now. "It was a one-night stand. I was out with friends at a bar celebrating my birthday, and I met a guy. We partied and he took me back to his motel. I hardly even remember the night; I was so drunk. Then, he left the next morning, and that was that. Found out I was pregnant a few weeks later and moved back to Shine."

It's all true. Not one lie was spoken, only a few details left out. But it's more than I've ever told anyone else. When my parents asked, I clammed up, refusing to disclose even that much. My grandmother simply asked if I wanted to talk about it, and when I shook my head no, she never brought it up again.

"You're the only person who knows that he was conceived from a one-night stand. I've never told anyone else," I say in a quiet voice. "I don't know. I was raised in an extremely religious household, and I guess I carried around some shame from that for a while. Not that I was ashamed to have a baby, but the way it came about."

"You have nothing to be ashamed of, baby. So it wasn't exactly like you probably imagined having your first kid, so what? That boy is fucking awesome, and nothing can ever take away from that. You did that. You cared for and have made that boy's life what it is. Trust me when I tell you, not every parent is as committed to raising a kick-ass kid like you are."

A breathy laugh escapes my throat. "He is pretty cool, huh?"

"The coolest. And his mom is pretty spectacular, too."

"Oh yeah?"

Wyatt chuckles. "Well, I happen to think so, and since no one else is around, mine is the only opinion that matters. Actually," he starts, and I turn to see him lift a brow. "Even if anyone else was around, my opinion on the subject would still be the only one that mattered."

"You're awfully full of yourself."

"I'd rather you be full of me."

I let out a groan laced with a chuckle. "You need to work on your jokes."

Wyatt's fingers go to the side of my ribs, and he starts tickling me. I thrash in the tub, water splashing over the side. "Stop," I wheeze out, trying to contain my laughter. "We're going to wake up Colby."

He slides his hands around my waist and pulls me tighter to him, growling into the side of my neck.

"You think I'm hysterical, don't deny it. You love my jokes. Admit it or we're not getting out of this tub."

"I like this tub."

"Admit it or I'm not going to take you to your bed and make you come two more times before I leave," he says, nipping at my bare shoulder.

"I have a vibrator that will do the trick in a pinch."

He growls again. "Don't think I've forgotten about that and all my ideas for using it on you. How I'm going to hold it over your clit while I have my tongue in your pussy. Or how I want to fuck you with the toy as I slide my cock between your tits and come over this pretty throat." He accentuates his point by biting down on the spot where my neck meets my shoulder.

Instead of laughing, a moan escapes, and I feel his cock growing hard behind me. My body is on fire, and it isn't from the temperature of the water.

"You like that, don't you? Hearing all the things I want to do to you? I could go on, tell you how hard I would come just from watching you get yourself off. How I'd watch you take yourself to the brink, then just before you fall over, I'll sink inside you so you come around me and not some toy. How I'd keep going, taking you over again and again."

I'm squirming in his hold as he slides his hand over my pussy and slips a finger inside of me.

"Yeah, I'd say you definitely like that idea," he says, pumping one finger in and out of me tortuously slow.

"Please don't make me beg," I moan.

"But you do it so well."

"Fuuuck," I breathe out. "You're killing me."

"No, baby. I'm bringing you back to life," he whispers, and I whimper.

In an instant, he pulls his finger from me and stands, stepping out of the bath and holding out his hand. I slide my palm in his, and he helps me from the tub before leading me to the bedroom.

We spend the next couple of hours acting out Wyatt's fantasies. We even come up with a couple new ones. And when he leaves me sleepy and sated, he kisses the hell out of me, promising to come back tomorrow night and do it all over again.

CHAPTER FIFTEEN
WYATT

We've spent the last two weeks sneaking around. I don't know how many more things I can come up with to "fix" around the house. There are no runs scheduled for a while, so I've been able to hang out with Maizie and Colby every day. If she's at work and I'm not watching Colby—which I've been doing more often lately, because he's a great kid and I genuinely enjoy hanging out with him—I come over after Cece leaves and stay until the early morning hours. Even when I'm there, I stay until just before dawn, not wanting to leave my woman a second sooner than I have to.

Today, Maizie has the day off, and we're at the park with Colby and Pepper.

"Lucy and Mia want to stop by. Said they grabbed some treats and coffee from Cool Beans for me and Colby," Maizie tells me as she sets her phone back down between us.

"What about me?" I ask.

"You want me to text her back and have her get you one of the caramel drinks I like? Something with extra whipped cream?" Maizie asks with a smirk.

Last week, before I came to watch Colby, I stopped by the coffee shop and grabbed one of Maizie's favorite drinks with extra whipped cream for her and a couple things for Colby. While he was out back playing with the dog, I pulled Maizie into her bathroom and added the whipped cream to her already sweet pussy. Then I licked it all off before she had to tend bar for the rest of the night.

"Nah, I'll just taste yours." Fuck. I want to lean over and press my lips to hers. So damn bad. "Baby, we need to tell people. I can't keep pretending we're just friends. I want to kiss you where I want, when I want. I want everyone to know you're mine."

She lets out a long breath. "I know. You're right. God, Lucy is going to gloat so hard," she says.

I think part of Maizie has been waiting for the other shoe to drop, even though she would deny it. I'm starting to regret telling her she can take the lead, and we can announce it on her time. But I also understand the caution behind it. It's not just Maizie, it's her son too.

"Do you trust me?" I ask, and she whips her head toward me.

"Of course."

"Do you trust me with Colby?"

Her brows dip. "You know I do."

"Then what's the problem?"

She huffs out a laugh. "There isn't one. Honestly, at this point, I've built it up in my head so much I've probably made it a bigger deal than it actually is."

"I don't know, I think I'm a pretty big deal," I say and shoot her a smirk, to which she rolls her eyes.

"So cocky."

My smirk turns into a wicked grin. "I'll show you what I can do with my co—"

"Hey kids," Lucy calls, walking up to the bench we're sitting at. She waves to Colby and holds up a bag with a big smile on her face.

"How are you guys?" Mia asks, giving Maizie a hug and sitting on the other side of her.

"Great, thank you for this," Maizie replies, taking the drink from Mia's hand, and I eye the whipped cream.

Fuck, I think to myself and adjust the way I'm sitting before anyone notices the quickly developing situation going on in my pants.

Colby comes running over, and Lucy cackles as he jumps for the bag she's holding over his head. Pepper starts jumping, too, thinking they're playing a game.

"Does Pepper get a treat, too?" Colby asks when Lucy finally takes pity on the poor kid and hands him a cake pop.

"They don't have doggy treats at Cool Beans, bud. Sorry," Lucy says.

"Oh, I picked some up on our way here. I'll run and grab them," Maizie says, standing from her seat. She takes a long drink of her froufrou coffee and shoots me a meaningful look. Or maybe I just understand the meaning since we were both remembering the other day with the whipped cream.

When she's out of earshot, Lucy turns her attention to me and narrows her eyes.

"What?" I ask.

She quirks a brow.

"Is this how you get Jude to spill all his secrets?" I ask as her questioning gaze pierces into me. Fuck, she could probably get all of my bank account information out of me if she keeps this up.

She tilts her head. "Do you have secrets, Wyatt?"

"Nope." At least I'd rather not.

"Maizie's buying treats for your dog," Lucy says.

"That's what she said," I shoot back and look at Colby, who is happily munching away on his treat while Pepper stands next to him wagging his tail and waiting for any crumb to fall.

"I think I need to have a conversation with my friend," Lucy tells me, and I look at her.

"I think you do, too," I agree.

She wears a self-satisfied grin on her face while Mia's gaze ping-pongs between us.

Maizie comes back and shakes the bag in her hands to get Pepper's attention.

"I should get going," I say, and Maizie's brows dip a bit, causing a tiny line to appear.

"I thought you didn't have church for a couple hours," she says.

"I don't, but I have some errands. Is it okay if you watch Pepper for me? I'll swing by later and pick him up when you get home from work."

"Yes," Colby answers for her, and she laughs.

"Sounds good," Maizie replies, and I head to my truck.

I drive away but park my truck a couple blocks from the playground and pull out my phone to text Maizie.

Me: *Pretty sure Lucy knows.*

Maizie: *Is that why she has a weird look on her face?*

Me: *I have no idea. The only woman I pay attention to is you.*

Me: *I'm telling the guys at church today. I'm tired of leaving you and not being able to kiss you goodbye when people are around. If you want to wait for me to tell Colby, I'd love to be there.*

I doubt Colby would have a problem with anything, but just in case he does, I want to reassure him that I'm here for him and his mom. Make sure he understands man-to-man—or man to five-year-old boy—what that means.

Maizie: *Divide and conquer?*

Me: *We're not going into battle, baby. Just letting our friends know that you scored the hottest biker in Shine.*

Maizie: *Jude might disagree with that statement.*

Me: *As long as you don't.*

Maizie: *I don't. And I'll talk to them before we leave the park.*

Me: *Okay. I'll see you tonight.*

I want to tell her I love her. That seems like what couples do. And I do. I love Maizie, and I have a strong feeling she loves me too. And now that we're making everything public, I plan to show her what that love is going to look like—every possible second—for the rest of her life.

"Any other business, or can we get the hell out of here?" Ozzy says before slamming the gavel down to adjourn the meeting.

I raise my hand. "Right here."

"This isn't second grade, Wyatt. You don't have to raise your hand," Knox says.

"Fuck off," I tell my VP, but there isn't any heat behind my words. "I wanted to let everyone know that Maizie and I are together. She's my woman."

I look around the table at my brothers. No one bats an eye. Not that I necessarily thought they would, but not a single raised brow or curious stare?

"Any other business?" Ozzy asks, and I give him an incredulous look. He was the one who told me to stay away. I thought if anyone would have something to say, it would've been him.

"What?" he asks, meeting my gaze. "Do you want me to throw a party to memorialize the occasion that you finally pulled your head out of your ass?"

"I mean, I'm always up for a party. But you were the one who warned me away from her."

"That was right after she had a baby and was taking care of her sick grandma. I didn't want anyone fucking

with her head, least of all one of the brothers. You fucking with her head, Wyatt?" His tone is both questioning
and threatening.

"Not at all. I'm claiming her. She's mine and I'm hers.
End of."

"End of?" Ozzy asks.

I give him a decisive nod. "Yes."

"Good then. Now that we can put Wyatt's love life to
bed, can we fucking get out of here? It's a gorgeous day,
and I want to take my woman out on my bike." Ozzy
slams the gavel down, and we all get up to file out of
the room.

Barrett comes up behind me and slaps me on the
back. "Did you really think we didn't know?"

I shoot him a surprised look. "You didn't say anything."

At that, he laughs. "What should we have done? Made
some tea and had a chat like a bunch of old biddies? I
knew you would claim her sooner rather than later. It's
not like I wasn't there when you chased off her date a
couple weeks ago. Or that I've missed the fact that you
haven't gone with us to Midnight Rose in months. Or
that you've been out late every night, but have a spring
in your step every morning. Only one thing has that
effect on a man, and it's good p—"

"Finish that sentence and I'll knock your teeth down
your throat," I tell him, my tone leaving no question that
I mean it.

"Hell yeah," he says with a wide smile. "If you're
threatening me, then I know you mean it."

"I've never meant anything more." My commitment to Maizie and my threat to punch him in the face.

"Happy for you, man. Now there're more women left for me."

I scoff. "I think you've been with nearly every single woman in Shine and the surrounding towns."

A devious grin spreads across Barrett's mouth. "Most. But not all."

I shake my head, and bellowing laughter bursts from him. "I'm going to head to the shop and help the guys out. This weather has everyone around here taking out their motorcycles and old cars for Sunday drives. They've been swamped getting cars ready or fixing them after some dumbass drives it too hard after having it sit for eight months."

The club owns the only shop worth a damn when it comes to motorcycles and classic cars in a fifty-mile radius. They stay pretty busy throughout the year, working on various makes and models of all cars, but summer sees a huge influx of cars people only take out when the roads are clear.

"I'll come help out for a few hours, too."

We've hired some of the best mechanics around who do top-notch work at a fast pace, but usually around this time, there's one or two brothers in there to help pick up the extra work we get. Plus, I've got nothing better to do until later, and spending time with my brother—elbows deep in something—sounds like a fan-fucking-tastic way to spend the rest of my afternoon.

I pull up to Thorn and Thistle and spot my brother's bikes. Jude, Linc and Knox are here, which means their women are probably here, too. I haven't heard from Maizie since I saw her this afternoon, but I hope like hell she talked to the girls. Otherwise my greeting is going to shock the hell out of them. I'm sick to death of seeing my woman and not being able to kiss her, to touch her like I want, when people are around.

When I pull the door open, Maizie looks up from where she's standing behind the bar. My mind registers that there are other people here, but the only person I have eyes for is her.

My steps are sure and quick as my legs carry me inside, and I walk behind the bar, grab her around the waist and crash my mouth to hers in one fluid motion. Her hands immediately slide across my shoulders, and she pulls herself tighter to me as our tongues dance in a deep and powerful kiss. Her lips curve in a smile against mine before I break it. After making sure she's steady on her feet, I press my forehead to hers.

"Hi," I whisper. "I missed you."

"Hi yourself. Did you make your point?" she asks in a breathless laugh.

I shake my head and claim her mouth again, my hand tangling in her hair.

"I think I just got pregnant," I hear Lucy say with a chuckle somewhere on the other side of the bar.

Maizie pulls away and giggles, and I turn my head toward my brothers and their women.

"Now that that's settled, can I get another beer?" Knox asks.

That makes Maizie laugh harder as she grabs a long-neck and sets it in front of Knox.

"You want a beer?" she asks me and I nod. "You gonna go sit down so I can get back to work?"

I tilt my head back and forth as though I'm considering her question.

She rolls her eyes. "Wyatt, I do have a job to do."

"And you look damn good doing it," I say and shoot her a wink.

My woman giggles again. I love that sound. "Go." She pushes me out from behind the bar.

"I fucking knew it," Lucy says, sitting next to Mia with Jude on the other side. "You tried to play it off, but I saw the way you looked at our gorgeous friend over here." She nods toward my Maizie.

"Yes, yes, Lucifer. You're all-knowing. Must be a by-product of those demon powers," Jude jokes and leans over to give Lucy a kiss on the cheek as I sit down on the other side of my brother.

Maizie shoots me a smile and sets a beer in front of me.

"So what was all that shit with the dating app thing, then?" I ask.

"Oh, it was my way of giving you a little push, and it worked," she replies, waving her hand between Maizie and me.

"Lucy, that could have gone horribly wrong," Charlie admonishes.

"But it didn't," Lucy replies with a knowing smile. "See? I'm a genius."

Last night, after making it known to everyone in the bar that Maizie is mine, I took her home and spent hours worshipping her delectable body. I didn't spend the night though. We decided that we would tell Colby together that we're...well...together.

"Why am I so nervous?" I ask Pepper as we park in front of Maizie's house.

I look over at my dog, and he's happily wagging his tail as he looks out the window, knowing exactly where we are.

Knox came by earlier and dropped off some cookies that Mia made, saying she thought cookies would sweeten the boy up to the idea that there was a man in his mom's life now. Until that moment, I didn't give it much thought. Colby and I get along great. Why wouldn't he be happy I'm going to be around more? And yet, here I am, second-guessing the confidence I had that this would go smoothly. All because of some damn cookies.

The door opens, and Colby comes bounding down the stairs. I swear, every time he sees this dog, it's like reuniting with his best friend. Hopefully, if nothing else, he'll be happy that Pepper will be around more.

"Hey, buddy. Look what Mia gave me to give you," I say, holding up the bag of treats as I open the door so Pepper can jump out.

"Cookies!" He jumps up and down. Pepper just as excited as he runs around the yard.

"You can have these after lunch, yeah?" I say when Colby comes over, making silly, grabby-hand gestures. "Mommy is finishing up now, but she said I could open the door for you guys. Come on, Pepper, she made extra bacon for you, too."

I hand Colby the bag of cookies, and the dog follows him into the house.

Maizie is in the kitchen, finishing up some BLT sandwiches for us.

"Mommy, look what Mia gave me," Colby says, handing her the bag.

"You gonna share those, son?" she asks.

His mouth twists in concentration as though he really has to think about it, then he starts laughing. "Of course. Those are way too many for me to eat by myself."

Maizie laughs. "Okay, buddy. Go wash your hands, then we'll have lunch."

The kid spins on his heels and rushes to the bathroom.

"Everything is at warp speed with that one, huh?" I ask, smiling as Colby speeds past me.

"Pretty much. I'm told it's a boy thing, but I have a feeling it might be a Colby thing," she says.

"I certainly never ran to wash my hands. Though I wasn't promised dessert after lunch, so that might have something to do with it."

Colby comes running back into the kitchen, and Maizie hands him a plate with a sandwich and a few chips. "Go sit at the table."

He carries the plate with intense concentration to make sure the sandwich doesn't fall over. She hands me one next, and I smile. "Thank you, baby." I want to kiss her. It was so easy and natural last night around all of our friends, just like I knew it would be. I want to be able to do that all the time, even around Colby.

She and I walk over to the table, and I pull out the chair for her beside her son.

"Dig in, guys," Maizie says and lifts her own sandwich to her mouth. When I taste mine, the salty richness of the bacon explodes over my tongue.

"Holy sh—wow," I say, looking at Colby then back to Maizie. I should probably start watching my swearing around the kid. You know, be a positive influence and all that. "This is delicious."

"It's really good, Mommy," Colby agrees.

We sit at the table, and Colby practically inhales his sandwich. "Can I have a cookie now?" he asks.

Maizie chuckles and nods toward the counter. "Why don't you bring the bag over here, bud. I wanted to talk to you about something."

He hops up and grabs the bag, then sits back down at the table with us.

"Wyatt and I wanted to talk to you about him spending more time with us. He's become someone very important to me, and I know you like him a lot, too."

Colby shrugs. "Sure."

"We've decided that he's going to be my boyfriend. If you're okay with it," she says.

"Okay," he says, nodding.

"Do you know what that means, bud?" I ask.

"Yeah, you guys will hold hands, and you'll let her kiss you even though I think kissing is gross. Amy Watson from my school tried to kiss me last year at the swing set and I almost threw up." He gags overdramatically.

"And you're fine with that?" Maizie asks, trying to stifle her laughter.

"Are you going to sleep in Mommy's room like Auntie Mia and Knox share a room?"

"Sometimes," I answer honestly. No use lying about it.

"Does that mean Pepper is going to sleep in my room?"

"He can, sure," Maizie answers.

"Can they have a sleepover tonight?" Colby asks Maizie with hopeful eyes.

This time, Maizie can't control the laughter that bursts from her. "Sounds good to me."

"Yes," Wyatt says, pumping his little fist and looking down at the dog. "We get to have a sleepover, Pepper." He looks at the bag on the table. "Can I have a cookie now?"

Mia nods with a smile and watches as Colby reaches in and pulls out a chocolate chip cookie, hopping up from his chair and running outside with it.

She turns to me with relief and a touch of surprise in her eyes. "Was it seriously just that easy?"

"You promised him sleepovers with Pepper. Of course it was that easy." I smile and grab the seat of her chair, pulling her closer to me. "Now I can do this whenever I want." I lean over and press my lips to hers. "Oh, and look, I don't even want to throw up."

Maizie bursts out laughing, and my heart swells.

I might not be who she imagined herself falling for, but I'll be damned if I ever let her go.

Chapter Sixteen
Maizie

"Can I just say how much I love seeing you here with Wyatt. It's like you guys always belonged together, and now you finally are," Lucy comments as we're sitting on the back patio of the clubhouse.

The guys have a giant waterslide set up behind the clubhouse and we've all been enjoying having some fun on the thing. Wyatt walked us out to the backyard, and Colby's eyes went as wide as saucers when he saw the giant blue-and-yellow monstrosity set up in the back. He thought it was someone's birthday, not just a regular Sunday afternoon. But that's Wyatt. He loves being able to do things like this just to see Colby's reaction. I told him he was setting the bar so high that by the time his birthday actually rolled around, he'd be expecting a trip to the Magic Kingdom. Wyatt simply shrugged and told me that was actually a good idea.

"You haven't missed an opportunity yet, why start now?" Charlie says next to Lucy and Mia.

"Shut it, sister. You're just as thrilled as I am," Lucy tells Charlie.

"And you never miss an opportunity to gloat like you were single-handedly responsible for our friend finally letting her guard down and admitting to her feelings," Mia adds, and I laugh.

"Where would I be without you?" I ask Lucy in an overly sweet tone.

"Bored and at home without the glowing skin of someone who's getting that good dick on the regular," she says with a knowing smirk.

"Jesus," Charlie breathes out. "I thought you were bad when you beat everyone at pool or darts, but we're never going to hear the end of this one, are we?"

Lucy shrugs but doesn't comment.

Gramps comes walking out of the clubhouse with Elaine on his arm.

"I didn't know your grandma was coming," Charlie says to Mia. "Those two have been seeing an awful lot of each other." She nods at the couple as Gramps leads Elaine to where we're sitting.

"Hello, dears. Mind if this old lady joins you?"

"If this is what old looks like, then sign me up," Lucy says. "How are you, Elaine?"

"Oh, lovely. It's a beautiful day to spend time with family and friends, and Arthur promised me some delicious BBQ, even though I told him Americans hold the blue ribbon for best BBQ, not the Brits."

Gramps laughs as Elaine takes a seat next to me.

"Wait until you taste my ribs, Elaine. You'll be eating those words." Gramps smiles and nods at us in greeting.

"I'm going to go supervise my son and grandson," he says and walks to where Ozzy and Trick are manning the grill.

Freya walks out moments later with a bottle of chilled wine, followed by Tanya with a giant charcuterie board.

"Good Lord, have the guys been hogging the slide?" Freya asks, watching Barrett climb up and topple down, followed closely by Cash.

"They've been sharing like good little boys," I tell her. "Colby is just taking a break." I look over and find him and Wyatt standing a bit farther from the crowd with Pepper. Wyatt has been trying to get the dog to train with Colby so that he listens to my son just as well as he does with Wyatt. It's been...slow going. Mainly because all Colby wants to do is run around and play with him—the dog, not Wyatt. Though sometimes Wyatt, too.

We talk about Freya's workload and how that's going with the wedding planning.

"Honestly," she starts, staring at her ring. "We aren't in a hurry. I don't have much family other than my parents. My dad still isn't a hundred percent on board. He thinks I threw away my career by moving back to Shine and opening a family law practice."

Freya was a US attorney who put one of the worst mob bosses on the East Coast in prison. When her life was being threatened before the trial, the Black Roses were tasked with protecting her. She'd grown up here and was actually shot in this very clubhouse when she was still in high school. The hit was ordered by the boss she put away, and she spent the next fifteen years working toward her goal of prosecuting the worst of the worst. But when she and Ozzy reconnected, there was no stopping them from falling in love again, and she decided to lay her roots back in Shine.

"Well, I for one am glad to have you back," Mia says. "And I know a few women who are, too."

Freya has become one of the best family law attorneys this town has ever seen. Many of the cases she takes are pro bono, and she's helped several women get themselves and their kids out from under horrible situations here and in surrounding towns.

My phone dings with a text, and I grab it from the table.

Unknown Number: *Hey.*

My brows dip. Who...

Unknown Number: *It's Nolan.*

What the fuck?

Nolan: *Hear you've been fucking one of the Black Roses.*

Me: *What do you want?*

The noises around me fade into the distance, and the only thing I hear is blood rushing to my head and the way my heart sounds like it's going to pump out of my chest.

Nolan: *To make a deal with you. My kid for information.*

Me: *I told you he's mine.*

I swallow and look around. The only person who seems to notice that I'm in distress is Elaine. But she doesn't talk to Nolan, so it's not like she would have told him anything.

Nolan: *We can let the courts decide that. I don't think they look too favorably on a mother who kept the existence of a child from the father for six years.*

Me: *You fucking asshole. You knew I was pregnant.*

Nolan: *Did I? Can you prove it?*

What the fuck was I supposed to do? Send him a certified letter? When Nolan told me to get rid of it, I took that as he didn't care one way or the other what the hell I did.

Nolan: *Your friends haven't been very nice to mine. In fact, a few of my brothers went missing a while back. Then they burned down our most lucrative business when one of their women was taken back to her family. We want answers, and you're going to get them for me.*

Me: *I don't know anything about that.*

Nolan: *But you're going to find out. If you don't, I go to the courts and take my son. You aren't the only one with connections in that town. My parents are loaded and will do whatever they can to get their grandson where he belongs.*

I stand abruptly, my chair toppling backward.

"Maizie?" Lucy asks, staring at me. But I can't answer her. My breaths are coming too fast, shallow and erratic.

Oh fuck, oh fuck, oh fuck.

"Wyatt," someone calls, and he races over as I'm in the midst of a full-blown panic attack.

"Baby?" he says, coming straight to my side as the tears begin to fall down my face.

"He's going to take him," I say between panting breaths.

"Who? What are you talking about?" Wyatt says, turning me toward him and holding me by the arms. Good thing, too, because I'm about to sink to the ground.

"His father. Nolan Dawson."

I feel like absolute shit. I've never had a panic attack before. Sure, I've been scared and felt helpless at times in my life, but that was on a whole other level.

Wyatt whisked me away to his room in the clubhouse and left me there, promising to be right back. When he walks into his room again, he has a glass of water and hands it to me.

"Trick and Tanya took Colby to their place with Pepper. Said they were going to have a sleepover."

"Good. That's good. Colby loves Tanya," I reply woodenly.

"Do you think you can tell me what's going on now?"

I blow out a deep breath, but don't answer.

"Maizie. I need you to tell me what's going on. I know you're scared, and I know you've kept this from everyone for so long, but it's time you came clean. About all of it."

Wyatt stands on the other side of the room, leaning against the dresser. His arms are crossed over his chest, and though his words aren't angry, per se, they sure as hell aren't warm.

"Are Elaine and Mia still here?" I ask, and Wyatt nods. "I need to tell this story, but I need Elaine and Mia to hear it, too. It involves all of us."

Wyatt nods again and opens the door, extending his arm to signal that he's following me out.

When we emerge from the hallway, everyone is gathered in the main room of the clubhouse. Mia and Charlie are sitting on the couch next to Elaine, Ozzy stands behind Freya—who has taken a seat on one of the bar stools next to Gramps—and the rest of the brothers are scattered around the space. None of them has looks of anger or disgust on their faces, so I guess that's a good start. My friends look at me with worry in their eyes, along with Elaine, which makes me feel even more awful for having kept this from them.

Lucy walks up to me with a glass of amber liquid. "Here, sister, looks like you need this."

I give her a nod in thanks and toss back the whiskey. "I don't know where to start," I say to the room.

"Do you want me to get rid of the guys?" Ozzy asks. Not him, just the other brothers. This involves his club, and he takes that responsibility very seriously.

I shake my head. "No. It needs to come out. I've lied to you all for long enough."

Wyatt leads me over to one of the barstools, and I take a seat with him standing next to me.

And I begin my story.

"I saw Nolan in a bar in Boston when I was out celebrating with some girlfriends. He remembered me, and I always had the biggest crush on him in high school." I look at Mia. "Sorry I never told you."

She shakes her head. "It's okay."

"We had a night together," I continue. "A few weeks later, I found out I was pregnant. I knew I couldn't take care of a baby, go to school, and afford to live in Boston, so I came home. My parents kicked me out when I came home pregnant and unwed, refusing to tell them 'who ruined their daughter's life,' and I went to live with my grandmother. I didn't want her to have to support me and Colby any more than she already was, so I got a job at Thorn and Thistle. I never told anyone who Colby's father was because when I told him I was pregnant, he wanted me to get rid of it and I...I didn't want to."

"You have every right to do what you want with your body and make the choices that are right for you," Freya says.

"That's fucking right," Lucy agrees.

"I didn't bother to tell him I was keeping the pregnancy. Honestly, I didn't think he would care as long as I didn't try to go after him for money." I turn to Ozzy. "I swear to you, I had no idea that the Bone Breakers were an enemy of the club."

"They weren't when you were hired, sweetheart. They were barely even on our radar," Ozzy says.

"After you asked everyone to keep an eye out, I was scared to come clean. By that time, Colby and I were already so enmeshed with the club, and I was afraid you would turn your backs on me—on him—if you knew who his father was."

I look around the room and see varying degrees of pity mixed with anger on the brothers' faces. Wyatt's hand stays on my shoulder as I tell my story. The constant protector, making sure everyone in this room knows I have his support, just in case they need the reminder. It's so much more than I deserve.

"That never would have happened," Barrett says, unusually serious. "You're family, Maizie. You and your kid."

"I...I couldn't be sure. But I knew I couldn't lose my job, and I didn't want to lose you guys. That's why I kept my secret. I was scared to death." I turn my gaze to Elaine. "I'm so sorry I never told you that you have a great-grandson. It was unfair to keep that from you."

Elaine gives me a soft smile and shakes her head. "You think I didn't know, dear?"

Uh, what now?

"Did you know dimples are genetic? Nolan has the same one on his cheek as Colby. I also happened to know that Nolan was in Boston that weekend. It was one of the few times he stopped by my house. Of course, it was only to try to get money out of me on his way back to Arizona. He said he ran into you the night before and wanted to know if Mia still talked to you. When you came home pregnant and refused to tell anyone who the father was, I had my suspicions. About two years ago, when I ran into you and Colby was a little older, I put two and two together."

A lump grows in my throat. "I...I don't know what to say. How do you not hate me?"

"Because I know my grandson," she says, shaking her head in disappointment. Not at me, but at the fact Nolan turned out to be the way he is. "And I knew you had your reasons for not telling anyone. I wasn't going to call you out for it before you were ready. I also wasn't going to *not* get to know my great-grandson or not be a part of his life."

It all makes sense now. Why Elaine took such a liking to Colby, why she would call me to spend time with my son, invite us over, or go with us to Colby's T-ball games. She wanted to be a part of his life even though I hadn't been honest with her about who his father was. To her, it didn't matter. He was—*is*—her blood.

"What did his text message say?" Ozzy asks.

I blow out a breath. "He knows the club had something to do with the missing Bone Breakers." I see Lucy give Jude a meaningful look. Guess Nolan was right about that. "He wants me to spy on the club, get proof of what happened to them. He says if I refuse, he'll get money from his parents for a lawyer to take Colby away from me."

"Over my dead body," Freya says. "You are now my client, and like hell is that man getting anywhere near even a supervised visit with Colby."

"Nolan always thought his parents were rich. He thought that meant he could have whatever he wanted. Not saying my son and his wife aren't well off, but I have pockets that run far deeper than theirs. And connections. He won't get within a hundred feet of your son, Maizie," Elaine assures me.

Tears prick my eyes. "Thank you. Both of you."

"Sounds like the Bone Breakers want a war," Cash says, and Ozzy's jaw tenses.

"Sounds like," he replies.

"What are we going to do?" Wyatt asks.

Ozzy thinks on it for a few moments. "Not entirely sure yet. Did Nolan say when he wanted his information by?"

I shake my head. "No. I haven't received any other messages from him. Not since the one telling me he was going to take my son."

Ozzy nods. "Okay. For now, we're going to play it by ear. We'll see what he says when he reaches out again."

"I'm so sorry, Ozzy. I brought this to your doorstep," I say to the MC president.

"No, you didn't. This has been a long time coming. They obviously didn't get the message when their brothers went missing—no one fucks with us. We'll be sending a stronger one this time."

I look at Mia and Elaine, neither batting an eye at what Ozzy just said.

"There's nothing we can do right now," Ozzy starts. "And I'm not letting all this food go to waste. Let's eat. I'll sit with this for a bit, and we'll talk about it at church tomorrow, yeah?"

The rest of the guys nod, but the mood has definitely shifted as everyone gets up and goes outside. Lucy, Charlie, and Mia come up to me and give me a hug. They don't offer any words of comfort, but I don't need any. Just by them being here and not screaming at me, I know they support me.

When Elaine walks over, I can't help but apologize to her again for not saying anything all this time.

"Now you listen to me, dear. I don't care that you didn't tell me. I knew in my heart that boy was family. That *you* are family. My grandson made his bed, and I accepted it a long time ago. All I care about is that you and Colby are safe." She leans in to hug me, and when she pulls away, she has a mischievous glint in her eyes, and it strikes me that I often see the same one in my son. "Besides, now I can really spoil him, and you can't tell me no. Great-grandmother's rights and all that."

I laugh and she walks outside, followed by Gramps, leaving Ozzy and Freya as the last in the clubhouse with Wyatt and me.

"No matter what happens, Maizie, Colby is safe with you, and I'll make sure it stays that way," Freya says. "The last thing Nolan's going to want is a spotlight on why he's unfit. I still have contacts in the US attorney's office here and in Arizona. A couple phone calls is all it will take for an investigation into the Bone Breakers. If it comes to that."

"It won't," Wyatt replies and Ozzy nods. This isn't going to be handled by the law.

Freya shrugs. "That works for me, too."

"You guys staying?" Ozzy asks, and I shake my head.

"I'd like to go get Colby and head home. I'm pretty beat after that." Pretty beat is an understatement. Feeling like I've been run over by a semi-truck is probably a more accurate description.

Ozzy nods and looks at Wyatt. "Go get your kid and take your woman home. Take care of your family, brother."

"I plan on it," Wyatt replies.

When Ozzy leaves, Wyatt comes to stand in front of me. "You sure you want to get Colby, or do you want him to spend the night at Trick and Tanya's? Let you wrap your head around everything."

"No, I need to hold him," I say.

"That makes sense. I'll grab my truck keys, and we'll head out." He's saying what I want to hear, but his voice is still a little off.

"I'll understand if you don't want to stay with me tonight. I sort of threw a bomb at you and the club."

"Maizie, I'm in shock. Not gonna lie. I'm a little heart-broken you weren't honest with me. That you didn't trust me enough with your truth." I open my mouth to argue and tell him it had nothing to do with how I feel about him, but he holds up a hand. "No, listen. I'm upset and have some shit to sort through, but I'll be doing it at your house, with your kid, in your bed tonight. That is one thing that your revelation hasn't changed. Never will change. Understand?"

I nod, and he holds out his hand.

"Okay, good. Let's go home."

Chapter Seventeen
Wyatt

After getting back from picking up Colby, Maizie was exhausted. I've never been more scared in my life than when I saw her having a panic attack at the clubhouse. Her eyes had glazed over, and she wasn't focused on anything. Her body was shaking so hard, it terrified the hell out of me.

Trick and Tanya had made burgers, so they packed up a couple plates for us since we left before we ate at the clubhouse, and Tanya wrapped Maizie in her arms, whispering words of comfort that I couldn't hear. Tanya knows a thing or two about having an ex who threatens kids. The club took care of it back then, just as we're going to now.

Maizie barely touched her food. I ate my burger and tried to have a conversation with Colby to make things as normal as possible, but the meat tasted like ash in my mouth. Colby ate and chatted with me, but he wasn't as animated as usual. Kids sense when things aren't right with their parents. He kept glancing at Maizie, who tried to smile, but it was forced. At bedtime, she had lain in his bed with him, read him three books, and held him as he slept.

When I peeked my head in the room, she met my gaze with glassy eyes.

"Come on, baby. Let's get some sleep," I said, and she rose from Colby's bed and followed me into the bedroom.

Silently, she went into her en suite and brushed her teeth as I undressed and crawled under the covers. When she emerged from her bathroom, I held out my arms, and she came to lie next to me. We didn't say anything. Hell, I was still a mess about what all of us learned, but she finally settled, and we both fell asleep.

"Thanks, man," I say to Knox and hang up the phone just as Maizie slips out the back door and meets me on the deck with a cup of coffee in her hand.

She looks beautiful as always, with her hair mussed from sleep and her breathing deepening after that first sip of morning coffee.

"You're up early," she says and sits on the chair across from me. I know she's putting distance between us. She's scared of my reaction this morning since I didn't give her much of anything last night.

I don't know how to do this. How to navigate this conversation. I've never let anyone in like I have with

Maizie. And up until yesterday, I didn't have the slightest worry about it. But today? Today, I'm worried that she doesn't feel the same way about me as I feel about her. That she doesn't trust me with her secrets or her heart.

"I made Colby some eggs and toast," I say and take a sip from the coffee I have resting on the knee that's crossed over my leg. "Knox and Mia are going to come pick him up. I haven't had a chance to get you a helmet or a jacket yet, so Mia is bringing hers over for you to borrow."

Her brows dip low in question. "Why?"

"Because I need to clear my head, and a ride always helps with that. But I don't want to let you out of my sight, so you're coming with me."

Maizie nods and doesn't argue. "I'll go get Colby ready." She stands from her seat and walks back into the house, and I finish my coffee then head inside to get ready as well.

Twenty minutes later, Mia and Knox are in the kitchen, pouring coffee into mugs from the pot I made earlier. Mia hands Maizie the jacket and helmet Knox bought for her a few months back when they started dating.

"The helmet should fit you fine," Mia says. "The jacket might be a little short."

Mia barely reaches five-foot-four, and Maizie is five-foot-ten. She slips it over her tank top and smiles. "Thanks for this," Maizie says.

"You doing okay this morning, sister?" Mia asks.

Maizie huffs out a laugh. "Not really. But I'm getting there."

"How about you, brother?" Knox asks.

"Same," is the only reply I give.

He nods in understanding.

Colby comes bounding into the kitchen with Pepper and a few dog toys. "I'm ready, Aunt Mia."

When he calls her *aunt*, I can visibly see her getting choked up. Mia has always treated Colby as family, along with everyone else, but now she knows he really is her nephew.

She clears her throat and smiles. "Okay, monkey. Let's hit it."

They're taking him to the park, then over to Mia's grandmother's house. Knox said Elaine called Mia this morning because she didn't want to bother Maizie after yesterday. When Mia told her they were going to take Colby for a few hours, Elaine insisted they come pay her a visit.

Maizie leans down and wraps her son in her arms. "Have fun and be good for Knox and Mia, okay, buddy?"

"Of course. Me and Pepper will be on our best behavior."

Maizie stands and smiles proudly at her son. "You always are."

They walk out the door, and it's just Maizie and me left in the house.

"Ready?" I ask.

"Let's go."

My bike is parked in front of her house, where it's been for the last couple of weeks. Since telling everyone Maizie and I are together, I haven't spent a night away. This is the first time I'm taking her out on it, though. Why didn't I do this sooner? Why is our first ride when we're both feeling untethered? I hate this feeling, but there was no way I was going to leave her here. I'm upset, I have questions, but I still feel the same intense pull toward her I've always felt. Actually, that's not true. It's gotten stronger as the days and weeks have passed.

I get on my bike and show her how to get on behind me—where to put her feet and also where to steer clear of so she doesn't burn herself on the pipes. When I start my bike and settle into the seat, her arms wrap around my waist, and she presses herself to my back. Feeling her so close is as comforting as much as it is painful.

Why didn't she trust me?

We head away from her house and out of Shine's city limits. I drive around for about half an hour before deciding where we're going to go to have the talk we need to have. Ten minutes later, I'm driving slowly down the dirt road that leads to the small lake we've taken Colby fishing at. It's secluded enough that we can yell, scream, or cry if we need to. I didn't want to be around a bunch of people and have to temper—or have Maizie have to temper—any emotion that arises.

When I park, I let her off first and then dismount, taking my helmet and cut off as she does the same. She hands me the helmet and jacket, and I lay them next to mine on my bike.

"I've always loved this place. I kind of wish you hadn't taken me out here for this conversation. It's like we're bringing our baggage to one of my favorite places," she says, looking around.

"I wanted privacy," is all I say.

She wraps her arms around her middle as though she's protecting herself from what I'm going to say next.

"Okay." She closes her sad eyes for a moment, then opens them, meeting my gaze. "Let me have it. I deserve it."

"Maizie, I'm not going to yell at you. And you wouldn't deserve it if I did," I say. "I just want to know why you don't trust me. Why didn't you think you could be honest with me about who Colby's father is?"

"Because it doesn't matter who his father is. I'm his mother, and Nolan Dawson has no right to him." I can sense her hackles rising. I don't want to fight with her, but it sounds like this is a point she's had to make before.

"That doesn't mean you shouldn't have told me. I get the rest of the club, but I've been *your* friend for a long time, and now I'm *your* man. I'm the one who takes everything inside of you, all your secrets, and holds them close to my chest."

"You're also a brother, Wyatt," she says, her voice pleading for me to understand where she's coming from. "There's no way you wouldn't have been able to not tell Ozzy."

"Don't you get it, Maizie? You're my woman now. That comes before everything. Means everything to me. Would the club know eventually? Sure, but we would have figured out a way to tell them together. Instead, I had to watch you break down in front of everyone, and they all found out when I did. That wasn't fair to me."

"I'm sorry," she says softly. "I've spent so much time being the only one who knew. I thought if no one ever found out then it wouldn't matter. It was dumb. Never in a million years did I think Nolan would try to use my son against me to try to get information from the club. I don't even know how he found out about us."

That's something that's plagued my thoughts as well.

"I should have known that secrets don't stay buried," she says.

"Did you see him after the park with Mia when he was in town?"

She presses her lips together and nods. "He found me at Thorn and Thistle. When I was taking out the trash that night, he was waiting in the alley for me."

"I was there that night, and you didn't tell me?" I'm trying to be understanding, but fuck. The fact he cornered her behind the bar is ratcheting my blood pressure to dangerous levels.

"I was scared, Wyatt. He wanted to know if Colby was his, and I told him the same thing I tell everyone. He's mine. He seemed to take it in stride and said he didn't want a kid anyways."

"Is that why you were so tired that week? Because you were afraid he was going to come looking for you?"

She nods again. "I didn't sleep. I would lie on my couch with my gun in the safe next to me, loaded and ready to go if Nolan somehow found out where I lived and tried something. That's how I knew about the family of raccoons living in my backyard." Her lips tipped up in a smile that I didn't return.

My woman was lying on her couch every night, not sleeping and scared that her one-night stand was going to come take her kid. That makes me fucking furious.

"I never intended for it to come out—to anyone. I was going to take it to my grave, to be honest. But I'd been living with the secret for so long, it didn't matter to me anymore. If I thought it was going to come back and hurt the club—"

"Fuck that. It hurts me," I say a little louder than intended. "It kills me that you feel like you ever have to keep secrets from me. Good or bad. I don't think you understand what it means to be claimed by me. It means that you don't keep anything from me. That I protect you no matter what, and if anyone in my club would have had a problem with who Colby's biological father is, then they can talk to me and have their teeth knocked down their throat for saying he's anything other than mine. You and Colby are mine, Maizie."

I stomp toward her and take her mouth in a bruising kiss—proof that the words I'm saying are true and that I've never meant anything more. Her arms wrap around my middle as my hands hold the side of her face, and I plunge my tongue into her mouth. I lick the inside of her mouth, tasting her minty toothpaste.

"I can't protect you if I don't know what I'm protecting you from," I say when I break the kiss. "No more secrets."

She shakes her head. "No more."

My hands grip the back of her thighs, and I lift her in my arms, wrapping her long legs around my waist. She finds my mouth again and kisses me hard as I walk us back to my bike. When I set her down, I turn her around and she places her hands on the seat of my bike, her arms locked so she can stay upright.

"I hated not being inside you last night. But you needed rest, and I needed to get my head straight. Today though?" My fingers find the button of her tight jeans, and I pop it open. "I'm not wasting a second alone with you," I say as my hand dives into her panties, and I find her center. "You're mine. Your heart—" I begin to strum her clit. "Your body." I dip my finger into her center and pump a few times, feeling the wetness coat me before pulling my hand free and bringing my finger to my mouth, sucking her flavor off. "And this delicious fucking cunt," I say on a moan.

"Please, Wyatt," she groans.

"Please what, baby? Make you come with my fingers, or would you rather I yank your pants down and sink inside of you?"

She nods frantically. "Yes. All of it, yes."

I step back and tear her jeans, along with her black panties, down her legs. Kneeling behind her, I lean forward and bury my face in her ass, licking that tight pucker. "One of these days, I'm going to claim this, too, but we'll have to work up to that. Get you good and stretched out so I can fit inside your tight little asshole."

A shiver runs through her body at my promise. I lick my way to her center and spear my tongue into her opening. My hand finds her clit, and I begin rubbing it in small, tight circles at a furious pace. I need her there as fast as possible, otherwise I'm going to have a mess in my pants on the ride home.

She releases a keening wail as her pussy tightens around my tongue, and a rush of wetness explodes in my mouth. I pull my face away, but don't stop rubbing her clit as I thrust three fingers into her. She's in the middle of her orgasm, and I draw out her pleasure until she's begging me to have mercy on her.

I stand behind her and undo my buckle, then my zipper, reaching in to free my cock. I don't bother pulling my pants down, too desperate to feel her from the inside.

I thrust in—hard—seating myself in her tight heat.

"Can you give me another one, baby? My cock missed the feeling of your pussy strangling it last night."

I begin pumping in and out of her as sweat drips down my brows and into my eyes. But I don't stop. I don't think anything could tear me away from her right now. It's never been like this with anyone else. I've never had sex without a condom, but I knew from the second that Maizie kissed me there was no way in hell I wanted anything between us. I needed to feel every inch of her. I needed to come inside her and make her mine. Because no matter what she does, what she keeps from me, what she doesn't say, that's exactly what she is.

Mine.

My mouth presses against her ear. "Are you going to trust me now? With everything?"

"Yes, fuck, I promise. With everything."

"Even with your heart?" I ask as I continue pumping. When she doesn't answer, I stop my motion. It fucking kills me to do it, but I need an answer. "Maizie?"

"Yes, Wyatt, even with my heart."

I press my lips to the back of her head. "You're such a good fucking girl, taking what I'm giving you," I say as I resume my thrusts. "I need you to come again, baby."

Seconds later, the walls of her pussy squeeze around my cock as I bury myself inside of her as deep as I've ever been and bellow out my release. Maizie cries out as she falls with me, her beautiful cunt clenching my dick. A flock of birds takes off, squawking their disapproval at being disturbed. I'm not the least bit sorry.

I lean over her for a moment to catch my breath. When I pull out of her pussy, I bend and pull her jeans back up her legs. Before pulling them over her ass, I place a kiss on each of her cheeks, and she giggles. She turns and zips her jeans as I'm tucking myself back into my own.

"Wyatt, I just want to say again that I'm sorry for not telling you about everything."

"Shh, baby," I say, taking her in my arms. "It's sorted. I know where you stand and you know where I stand. And I know it won't happen again."

"Never," she says, her tone solemn with the promise.

I smile at her and kiss the tip of her nose. "That's all that matters then."

We stand next to my bike for a few minutes, me with my arms wrapped around her and her with her head resting against my chest right over my heart.

"Should we go get Colby? I feel kind of bad for sticking him with Mia and Knox on short notice."

I chuckle. "Hell no. It's a beautiful day, and I have my woman with me. We're going to take a ride, then I'm going to take you home and make you come on my face again. Then you can call Mia and get Colby."

"You're the boss," she says, and I hear the smile in her voice.

"I'm really not, baby. You've always been in charge. I'm just the lucky son of a bitch who gets to take a little bit off of your plate sometimes."

Luckiest man in the world.

I make good on my promise to Maizie before heading into church. We're all sitting around the table, discussing the situation with the Bone Breakers. This is the first time I've been around my brothers since finding out about that fuckwit, Nolan. I won't lie and say I wasn't a little cautious before walking into this room. Secrets aren't something my brothers take lightly, but they're also understanding of circumstances. We've had to be. The Bone Breakers have been a problem for a while, one that it's time we take care of.

"Alright, then. Brute force it is," Ozzy says.

We landed on taking the fight to them. They threatened my woman—tried to make her a rat. It's time we cut them off at the knees.

"Jude, get a hold of your brother. I'd like to get some images of their compound in Arizona so we have a plan going in," Ozzy says, and Jude nods. "Once we have an idea of what we're dealing with, we can figure out exactly how we're going to do this."

"Something like when we rescued Lucy?" Jude asks.

"That's what I'm thinking," Ozzy replies. "You good with that, brother?" he asks me.

"Sounds like a fucking plan to me. The sooner we get rid of those fucks, the better I'll sleep."

And the sooner my woman and her kid are safe once and for all from that asshole Nolan Dawson.

Chapter Eighteen
Maizie

It's been four days since I got the text from Nolan and my entire world imploded. I was so afraid that Wyatt would turn his back on me. That's why I didn't tell him in the first place. I thought if anyone found out, they would look at me with suspicion in their gaze, thinking I was somehow in cahoots with a rival club.

Wyatt made sure to put those fears to rest. But there's no getting rid of the cloud that's hanging over all of us. He hasn't told me exactly what course of action the club is going to take. Not that he doesn't trust me, he said. He just wants to protect me from the darker parts of this life. It doesn't take a genius to figure out what that means, though.

I've been around long enough to know that the likelihood that Nolan is going to survive this is slim to none. He fucked up when he tried to use my kid in this fight, and I'll have no problem making peace with whatever happens to him. No one fucks with my son or threatens him in any way and gets away with it.

It's been a slow night at the bar, and for that, I'm grateful. I know the guys are taking off soon to handle business, and I want to spend as much time with Wyatt as possible before he leaves. He's at the clubhouse tonight, working out the logistics of their trip. What that means, I'm not sure, but it makes me feel better that they're planning everything up to the smallest detail. Cece even mentioned that Jude's brother, Liam, is coming to town and staying for a couple of days. I wonder if that means he's going with the guys or if he's staying to keep an eye on things.

It takes me hardly any time at all to close the bar and lock up. When the prospect tasked with keeping an eye on the bar while I'm here walks me to my car then shuts the door for me, I pull out my phone.

Me: *Headed home. You going to be home soon, too?*

Last week, before shit went down with the text messages, I'd started moving my things around and making room for Wyatt in my house. Since the day following my panic attack—when he took me to the lake and fucked me senseless against his bike—neither of us has been keeping up any sort of pretense that he doesn't live with me and Colby now. And I wouldn't change that for the world. The circumstances surrounding him moving the rest of his things into our house? Sure. But not the outcome. Never that.

Wyatt: *Almost finished here, baby. I'll be thirty minutes, tops.*

Me: *Okay. See you soon.*

The urge to text him that I love him is strong, but I haven't actually said those words to him yet. I don't think the first time should be through text. But holy hell, I'm completely in love with Wyatt Davis. I know he loves me too. And what's even more spectacular about the man that I've been sharing a bed with for these last few weeks is that he loves my kid.

Starting my car, I put it in drive and head home. I think a glass of wine after the long day I've had is in order. Usually if I make it to the house before Wyatt, he has one waiting for me—like the night when he watched Colby for the first time. It brings a smile to my face every time I walk through the door and he's on the couch, pats his knees, and I place my feet in his lap so he can rub them while I sip on my wine and we talk about our day. It's nothing I ever expected to have in my life, but I can't imagine it without him now. When we were at the lake, it was as though the last of the walls I'd been hiding behind crumbled around my feet. I'm all in, and so is he.

After parking my car, I walk up the steps and put my key in the dead bolt, but it's already unlocked. That's weird. Cece is usually really good about keeping the house locked up. Shine is a safe town, most people probably don't even bother locking their doors at night, but that isn't me. And it's not usually Cece, either.

I open the door and step over the threshold. The first thing I notice is how quiet it is in the house. It's late, so it's not as though I expected Colby to still be up, but usually Cece is on the couch reading a book or watching some baking show on TV. But there's no sound. And it's pitch black inside. Not even the light I leave on over the sink is lit up. As though the power is out.

"Colby? Cece?"

No answer.

I try the light switch next to the front door and nothing happens. I look out onto the street and see that my neighbor's front porch light is on.

"Colby!" I yell through the house while I grab my phone from my purse and use it as a flashlight. I take a step into the hallway, and my boot crunches on something. Pointing the light to the ground, I find a broken picture frame with shards of glass all over the place. I direct the light to the wall where the picture of me and Colby was hanging and find them all a little skewed. A couple of them are cracked as though there was a struggle in the hallway and they were knocked around.

"Colby!" I scream, praying that I'll hear his little voice call back to me, but there's nothing as I run into his room.

Empty.

I throw open the bathroom door and look behind the shower curtain.

Nothing.

When I rush into my room, a whimper hits my ears, but it's not human. I run to the other side of the bed, and lying on the floor is Pepper. He barely lifts his head, and another whimper escapes as he looks at me with terrified eyes. I fall to my knees, checking for signs of injury, but I'm not a fucking vet.

"I'll be right back, I promise. Okay, buddy? You're going to be just fine."

Jumping up, I run down the hallway, into the kitchen, out the back door, and into the backyard.

"Colby," I call again, hoping he's hiding somewhere outside. I run around the house but don't see any signs of him or anyone else. As I run back inside the house to get Pepper, I call Wyatt.

"Hey, baby, I'm just abou—"

"Colby's missing. So is Cece, and Pepper is hurt," I rush out. "I can't find him, Wyatt. I can't find him."

"Slow down, baby. Where are you?"

"I'm at home. Someone cut the power, and there's broken glass. Colby and Cece aren't here. Pepper's hurt bad. He won't move."

"Okay, this is what you're going to do. I want you to pick up the dog and get out of the house. Start heading toward the clubhouse."

"Okay."

"I'm going to jump on my bike and meet you on the road, baby. But I don't want you in that house alone."

I'm nodding, though he can't see me. "Okay. Will you stay on the phone with me?"

"Absolutely."

I hear him yell to someone that shit's going down and to call the vet, then moments later, he connects the call to the Bluetooth in his helmet.

"Okay, I'm going to pick him up," I say.

I slide the phone into my back pocket and kneel next to Pepper as the sound of more than one bike starting filters through the phone.

"I'm so sorry about this, buddy." My hands slide under his shoulder, then his hips. He lets out a yelp of pain, but otherwise, he doesn't struggle when I lift him from the floor. I walk/run out of the house, trying not to jostle the injured dog too much. I position him in my back seat, then haul ass out of my driveway. Less than three minutes later, four bikes pass me and quickly turn around. I recognize Wyatt's motorcycle immediately, thankful that he and the brothers are hauling ass to get to me while I drive the rest of the way to the clubhouse.

He jumps out before I have a chance to turn my car off and rushes over to my door, flinging it open and pulling me from the car. I'm a mess of shaking limbs and panting breaths.

"It's okay, baby. We'll figure this out. Nothing is going to happen to Colby."

"Something already has, Wyatt," I cry into his chest.

"Shhh, I know. But we're going to find him safe and sound, baby." Though I appreciate his attempts to reassure me, my mind is going in a million different directions—none of them good.

Pepper whimpers in the back as Barrett and Linc open the back door of my car and gently lift the injured dog from the seat.

Lucy rushes out of the clubhouse with a man in scrubs right behind her. "Where is he hurt?" the vet asks.

"Uh, I think his hip. When I touched him there, he cried," I say.

"Where's your phone?" Wyatt asks, and I pull it from my back pocket, disconnecting our call from earlier. "We want to make sure it stays charged, okay?"

I nod, and he leads us into the clubhouse, followed by Lucy.

We pass the rest of the brothers and the girls as we rush into one of the guest rooms where a vet tech is finishing setting up a metal table and has several vials sitting on the dresser.

That's when I see his red-stained muzzle.

"I don't know where the blood is from," the vet says as Barrett and Linc set him on the table and the man immediately starts looking for injuries. "He isn't bleeding anywhere."

"I do," I whisper and look at Wyatt. "He was protecting my son."

Wyatt's jaw is tense as the tech puts a line in Pepper's uninjured leg. Within seconds, the dog closes his eyes and his breathing starts to even out.

"Seeing as I don't see any injuries that need emergency attention, I need to take him to my office and get some X-rays so I can assess him properly. As best I can tell right now, it's a broken leg—but I won't know the extent until I have the images back," the vet tells us.

"Whatever you need to do," Wyatt tells the man.

The vet nods and he and the tech quickly gather their things and wheel the metal table out the door with Pepper lying still on top.

I turn toward Wyatt, and he wraps me in his arms as tears trail down my face. "I'm so scared, Wyatt. Some monster has my son, and we don't know who or where. Oh, God. What if they..." I can't bring myself to voice the fear that I may never see my child again.

"Baby, I promise you I will do whatever it takes to bring that boy home to you safe and sound. No one will be safe from me until he's home."

A hand is pressed against my back, and I turn my head to see Lucy standing behind me. "We'll get him and Cece back," she reassures me.

"Oh God, Lucy. Your sister—"

"Is going to be fine. She didn't survive the hell we grew up in to have it all fall apart now."

I nod, and she looks at Wyatt. "I'll meet you guys out there," she says, nodding toward the doorway.

"We're going to walk out of this room and figure out a plan. All the brothers are here to do whatever needs to be done to get Colby and Cece back where they belong. And make no mistake—they will be coming home, baby."

It's everything I can do to take a deep breath and let those words in as truth. They have to be. I won't survive any other possibility.

Just as we're about to walk out of the small room, my phone dings with a text.

Nolan: *Change of plans. We want a meet with the Black Roses. Make it happen if you want Colby and Cece back. I'll be in touch.*

"Motherfucker!" I yell, throwing my phone on the bed and grabbing my hair at the roots. My eyes squeeze shut as a feral scream pours out of me. "I'm going to fucking kill him." I have never meant anything more in my life. He's a dead man walking.

"What is it?" Wyatt asks, grabbing my arms with a look of confusion and fear swirling in his eyes.

I point to the phone, and he picks it up, his eyes blazing with fury as he reads the text from Nolan.

"Let's go," he says, grabbing my hand and rushing out of the room.

We head through the hallway, and every eye in the room is on us when we enter the main area of the clubhouse..

"It's Nolan Dawson. He has Colby and Cece," Wyatt announces.

Cash stands from the table he's at and throws a beer bottle against the wall, the glass shattering in an explosion. "What the fuck?"

Jude is staring at Wyatt as though he's ready to burst out of his skin. "What do you know?"

"Someone broke into the house and cut the power," I say. "There was no sign of Cece or Colby, but Pepper was hurt really badly. I think he bit the hell out of whoever was there because he had blood all over his face."

"Braxton," Ozzy says in a voice I've never heard him use, but if I had to guess, it's the *do not question me and follow my orders* voice he uses in situations like these. "You and Linc go check any pharmacy or drugstore within a twenty-mile radius. Ask questions and see if there're any signs of the Bone Breakers. Maybe whoever got bitten needed medical supplies. I want to know how many of them we're dealing with, and it might give us a clue as to where they are."

"He wants to meet. Nolan. He texted Maizie and said he wants a meeting with us or we'll never see Cece or Colby again," Wyatt says.

"Where?" Ozzy asks.

"I don't know. He didn't tell me. Said he'll be in touch," I reply.

My phone buzzes again, and I lift it to see another text from Nolan.

When I open the photo he sent me, my blood runs cold.

It's a picture of Colby and Cece. She has a gash over her eyebrow and a bruising eye. Her arms are wrapped protectively around Colby, but I see his little face. Tear marks are tracked down his cheeks, but he's staring into the camera with a look of pure defiance.

"Oh God," I cry, nearly dropping the phone.

Wyatt grabs it from my hand, pulling me tightly to him so I don't collapse.

He looks at the picture, and I can tell it's taking every ounce of willpower not to throw the phone across the room.

"He's dead," Wyatt says as Ozzy comes and takes the phone.

Ozzy grabs Wyatt by the shoulder and squeezes. "No doubt about that, brother. We just need to find him first."

"Please, Ozzy. He has Colby. I know you want him dead. And believe me when I say I want the same thing. But please make sure my baby is safe before you go in guns blazing. If he gets caught in the cross fire…"

"There is no reality where me or any of the guys would let that happen, Maizie. Colby will be safe and in your arms by morning. Trust me on that," Ozzy assures me.

"I'm going. Wherever those fuckers want to meet, I'll be there," Jude says, tightening his hold around Lucy before kissing the top of her head. "We'll get them back, love."

"Me too," Cash says. He sat back down after his outburst, and now his legs are spread in front of him with his hands clasped between his knees. "They have Cece and Colby. I'll make sure they're safe first, but those assholes don't live through the night."

Ozzy nods and studies the picture on my phone. "They have to be somewhere local. Or at least fairly close. Do you have any idea how long Colby and Cece have been missing?"

"I talked to Colby about two hours ago. He wanted to tell me good night. I told him he needed to stop conning Cece into letting him stay up late, and he laughed." My voice is shaky and it cracks at the end, remembering Colby's boyish laughter.

"Okay, so they were home two hours ago. That means we're looking for somewhere that takes less than that to get to. I just wish I knew if they were in a house or a hotel. But they're close. That's good."

Barrett walks over to Ozzy and looks at the picture, his eyes squinting as he takes the phone from his hand. "I know where they are." He points to the wall that they're leaning against. "I recognize the wallpaper and that god-awful carpeting. It's a little motel just off the highway, a bit off the beaten path."

I don't ask how he knows, but I could kiss him right now for the fact that he recognizes the small amount of the room that's in the picture.

"Alright, boys." Ozzy looks at Knox. "Call your brother and have him come back. We're going to load up and go get your kid back," he promises when he finds my gaze.

Wyatt is still hanging on to me, his body tight with simmering rage. I turn into him fully and wrap my arms around his waist.

"I'll make sure he's safe, baby. Our boy will be home soon."

CHAPTER NINETEEN
WYATT

Maizie is a mess. Though she's not screaming and crying or sitting in a corner rocking back and forth, I can practically taste the fear emanating from her. Shit, from everyone. Those assholes thought they could come into our town and take the people we love. We're going to show them what a deadly mistake that was.

Knox, Linc, Barrett, and Ozzy are in the basement gathering all the weapons we'll be taking with us. We were actually in the process of doing just that when I got the call from Maizie. Our plan was to head out to Arizona in two days and take those fucks by surprise. Now they've moved up the timeline. Stupid assholes.

Jude and I are standing by the van with our women as Braxton takes off through the gate.

"Where is he going?" Maizie asks.

"To Knox and Mia's. Charlie was over there when you called me. We don't know how many Bone Breakers are in town or who they might be keeping tabs on. We don't want to be spread thin, so Mia and Charlie are going to stay together, and Braxton is going to be their shadow."

I'd much prefer Maizie and Lucy to stay with them as well, but when I brought it up, Maizie let me know that, under no uncertain terms, she was going to be there when we got Colby back. Lucy is an ace shot and has been working with Maizie at the shooting range. It goes against every fiber of my being to have her with us when we hit the motel, but I also know she's more than capable with a gun if the need arises. And I know when not to argue—especially with a mother who's as fierce as Maizie.

"Wyatt, I'm so scared," Maizie whispers. "I finally have someone I love who I know loves me back and loves my kid, and now you could be taken away from me."

She buries her head in my chest, and I feel her body shudder with the tears she's trying to hold back. This isn't the way I wanted her to tell me that she loves me, but it's not as though I didn't already know that. Hell, she knows damn well how I feel about her, but I would have preferred we not be in this situation when we said those words to each other for the first time. Things don't always go as planned, though, and I'm not walking away from her tonight without her knowing for a fact that I feel the same way.

"I love you, Maizie, and I'll be damned if I have that taken away just when we're getting started. The only outcome I'll accept is walking out of that motel room with our kid and growing old and gray with tons of grandbabies running around our house. You get me?"

She looks up and nods.

"This is forever. You, me, Colby and any more babies you let me put in you. No one is taking that from us."

"I love you. So much," she says as tears run down her cheeks.

When my brothers emerge from the clubhouse, each carrying a black duffel bag loaded with weapons and extra ammo, Linc walks up to Lucy and hands her a gun.

"I believe this is your favorite," he says.

She nods, checks the barrel to make sure it's loaded and the safety is on, then tucks it in the holster she's wearing. "Thank you."

Ozzy comes over to us and hands Maizie a gun as well. "I've seen you shoot. You're damn good. If anyone other than one of us comes out of the motel, don't hesitate. Protect yourself and Colby."

"Got it," she replies.

Ozzy turns to the group. "Let's roll out."

He gets in the driver's side of the van, and Knox sits in the front with him while Cash and Barrett load the bags into the back. The rest of us get in, taking our places on the bench seats that line the wall of the van.

Ozzy enters the location of the motel into the GPS. "Forty-five minutes," he tells us.

The ride is quiet, each of us thinking about what's going to happen when we get there. At least that's what's going through my head as we make our way down the highway.

This is what I do every time we head out on any mission like this or run for the Monaghan family. I visualize how it's going to go down, imagine the plan going smoothly, and then I think about being home or going to Thorn and Thistle to see Maizie after everyone is safe and back in Shine. It helps center me to imagine being on the other side of whatever we're doing. Maizie didn't even know she was my center every time I walked into Thorn and Thistle, but she was, and she always will be.

We pull up to the motel and park the van across the street from the one-story building. It's your typical nondescript building with a neon-red sign over the office and a light from somewhere in the back, illuminated through the glass that reaches from the ground to the roof. There are two cars parked in the lot in front of the rooms, but we don't see any bikes.

"The owner works most nights by himself," Barrett says. "Met him a couple times. Nice guy. I'll go have a chat with him."

He gets out of the van and jogs to the office. We watch Barrett talk to a man behind the desk. He nods, and as Barrett is walking out of the office door, the office sign above him goes dark and the NO is illuminated next to the vacancy sign.

Barrett gets back in the van and closes the door behind him. "They're here. Rooms five and six. He said there were three Bone Breakers here, but he didn't see anyone else with them. Those are their cars," he says, pointing to the two late-model sedans. "He turned the security cameras off for the night and is heading home."

"You trust him?" Cash asks.

"I trust that he knows what will happen if he goes to the police or anyone else about us being here. The grand I slid his way didn't seem to hurt any, either. I also promised that we would have everything cleaned up by morning. It'll be as though nothing happened."

This isn't the first time we've had to do a cleanup after a night like this.

"The farmer know we'll be making a stop at his place tonight?" Linc asks, and Knox nods. The pigs will be eating well tonight.

The door to room five opens, and out walks one of the assholes. He's got a bloody bandage wrapped around his arm and seems to be limping, too. *Good dog*, I think to myself. We watch as he opens the door to room six and shuts it behind him. Moments later, room five's door is opened again, and out steps Nolan Dawson. He heads to one of the vehicles and backs out of the parking lot, driving in the opposite direction of where we're parked.

"Okay. Jude, Linc and Knox, you're room six. Wyatt and Cash, you're with me in room five. Barrett, you're staying in the van with Lucy and Maizie."

"Got it, Prez," Barrett says.

Ozzy looks at my woman and Lucy. "Have the guns ready. Remember what I said. If anyone comes out of those rooms who isn't us, take them out."

Maizie removes her gun from the back of her jeans and holds it in her lap.

Ozzy opens the driver's side door, and Barrett climbs up to have a seat behind the wheel, just in case we need to make a quick getaway.

"I love you, baby. Colby will be in your arms before you know it," I tell Maizie and take her face in my hands, bringing her lips to mine for a soft kiss.

"I love you, too, Wyatt. Go get our son."

I stare into her deep whiskey-colored eyes, hoping she can see the promise in mine.

Linc opens the door, and we all quietly pile out the back. Lucy moves to shut the van door behind us.

"Hey, Lucifer," Jude says, looking at his woman before she shuts it all the way. "I fucking love you."

Lucy smiles. "I love your cocky English ass, too." She smiles and latches the back door of the van.

"You guys are fucking weird," Linc says.

"I know. Ain't it grand?" Jude says with a smile tilting his lips.

We make our way across the darkened street, our eyes never leaving the front of the hotel rooms. Linc, Jude and Knox step to the side of the door at room six and we do the same in front of room five.

Ozzy and Knox lock eyes, and Ozzy holds up three fingers, using them to silently count down.

Three.

Two.

One.

Ozzy's boot crashes into the door at the same time as Knox's, and we step into the room.

What I see makes my stomach turn.

On the bed, one of the Bone Breakers has Cece pinned to the mattress on her back, her shorts halfway pulled down her hips. She screams when we burst through the door, and the fat fuck on top of her turns his head. His eyes widen in shock as he lets go of one of her wrists and reaches for the gun on the nightstand next to the bed. Before he can grab it, Cash fires two rounds, one hitting him in the shoulder, the other in his neck. He partially collapses on top of Cece, and Cash takes two long strides, shoving him off of her. She rolls off the mattress, between the bed and the wall. Cash points his gun at the dying man's head and puts a bullet in the back of it, finishing the job that his first two bullets didn't.

"Colby's in the bathroom," Cece yells.

I run to the door, but it's locked.

"Colby, it's Wyatt. Stand back."

I use my shoulder to break down the flimsy door. The bathroom is small, but I don't see Colby. Then I hear crying coming from the other side of the shower. Ripping open the curtain, my heart breaks at the sight. Sitting in the tub with his knees against his chest and his hands clutching his ears is a hysterical five-year-old boy.

I kneel and wrap my hands around his small wrists.

"Buddy, it's me. You're safe."

He opens his eyes, and as soon as it registers that it's me in front of him, he launches himself into my arms.

My arms wrap around him and I hold him tightly to my chest, his little body trembling against me. "Shh, I got you. You're safe, buddy. You're safe."

I don't know who I'm trying to convince, the terrified boy in my arms or myself.

"Where's Mommy?" he asks, his eyes darting to the doorway behind me. "The mean man said she was going to be here, but he's a liar."

"She's waiting for you right outside, buddy. I'm going to take you to her now." I stand with Colby wrapped tightly around me. "I need you to do something for me when we walk out of here, okay? I need you to squeeze your eyes shut real tight and keep your face on my shoulder, okay? Don't open your eyes until I tell you to. Can you do that?"

Colby nods and he closes his eyes, burying his tearstained face in my neck. I haul ass out of the room with my hand protectively gripping the back of Colby's head to make sure he doesn't move it. I don't want him seeing the gore that covers the walls of the dingy hotel room.

When we get outside, the back door of the van swings open and Maizie runs toward us.

"Okay, buddy, you can open them now," I say just as Maizie reaches us and wraps her arms around the two of us.

"Mommy," Colby cries and wiggles from my grasp right into her arms, clinging to her as though he's never going to let her go.

I wrap them both in an embrace and look at Maizie, who has tears running down her face as she whispers to Colby.

"You're safe, monkey. I love you so much. You're safe. I've got you." She repeats some variation of the words over and over while I hold the two most important people in my world protectively in my arms.

Lifting my head, my eyes dart to my brothers standing in front of the motel then to Lucy with Cece wrapped in her arms. Cash is standing close with a hard look on his face while Jude stands behind Lucy, a comforting hand on her back.

"We need to get them out of here before Nolan comes back," Barrett says.

"I don't want to leave you," Maizie whispers, looking at me.

"I know, baby." My hand cups the side of her face. "But we have to finish this."

God, I want to stay with my family and try to comfort them after everything we've been through the last few hours, but there is no way in hell I'm going to leave Nolan to anyone else. It's my family he fucked with, and it's my justice to carry out.

I nod toward Barrett, who reads the request on my face loud and clear.

"I'll drive you back to the clubhouse," he says, and I walk with my arm around Maizie's shoulders as she carries Colby to the van, Lucy and Cece following behind us.

Colby doesn't let go when I help her in the back or when she sits down. Not that I can blame him. I hope to God he didn't see anything more than what is already sure to scar him. The anger I feel toward Nolan, that he put Colby in that situation to begin with, is one of the biggest reasons I'm staying to finish that fucker off.

"Barrett is going to come back for us and Linc is going to stay at the clubhouse with you until I get back." Maizie nods, her worried gaze piercing into my chest. "It'll be okay, baby. I'll be home soon. I love you."

"I love you, too," she replies.

"I love you, too," Colby says, tilting his head toward me.

I look at Maizie, who has a teary smile on her face.

"I love you, too, buddy. So much. You take care of your mom until I get back, okay? Don't let her go. She needs all the hugs in the world right now."

"Okay, Wyatt. I won't," he replies solemnly.

The lump in my throat is nearly cutting off my air supply as I shut the doors of the van. Barrett takes off down the road back to the highway, and I walk back over to my brothers.

"Surprised you didn't go with Cece," I say to Cash.

"I'm staying here to make damn sure that fucker doesn't have a heartbeat when you're through with him."

"That was never an option," I say as two black sprinter vans pull up in front of the motel. All of us raise our guns until we hear Jude call, "Put them away, boys. It's just my twat brother."

Liam Ashcroft opens the door of the first van and steps out with a broad smile on his face as though he wasn't about to be filled with lead only seconds ago.

"Little brother. Having all the fun without me?" Liam calls to Jude.

"You almost got your stupid arse shot up to bloody hell," Jude says as the part-time security expert, part-time mercenary makes his way toward us. "How did you know where we were?"

"Who used to own the van you drove here in?" Liam asks.

Jude shoots him a flat look. "And you still have the GPS on it?"

Liam scoffs. "Of course," he says as he walks past us and peeks his head in the room, eyeing the dead man on the bed. "Good thing, too. Looks like you're going to need some extra hands for cleanup," he says and walks to the other open door to find another dead Bone Breaker.

"Happy to have you here, Liam, but I need you to move the vans to the back. One of the guys left about ten minutes ago, and we don't know when he's going to be back."

"Yup," Liam says and waves at whoever is driving the second van toward the back of the building.

Without a word, the van pulls around the side of the building and disappears. It never fails to impress me how Liam and his team operate like a well-oiled machine.

"We'll set up out here to make sure this fellow you're waiting for won't get away." He looks up at the awning above the doors and notices a camera. "I'm assuming these are off?"

"Barrett talked to the owner. As far as he's concerned, we were never here and he had to leave for the night," Jude tells his brother.

"Alright. I'll have Sawyer double-check everything to make sure there's no digital proof that any of us were here." Liam walks back to his van and grabs a bag, handing it to me. "A few essentials for when the boy's father returns."

"I'm his father," I tell Liam as I take the duffel from his grip.

The man nods. "Duly noted."

He heads back to his van and pulls it behind the building.

"Fucking wanker," Jude mumbles under his breath as we head inside the room and shut the door behind us to wait for Nolan to get back.

CHAPTER TWENTY
WYATT

Fortunately, we don't have to wait long for that fucking asshole to come back to the motel. I'm not squeamish by any means, but the fucking dead Bone Breaker smells to high hell.

"Hope you're finished with the girl," Nolan says as he opens the door. "I brou—" his sentence cuts off when he sees me standing in front of the bed with a gun aimed at his chest and a dead body lying behind me.

"Hello, Nolan," I say.

He drops the bag of food and reaches for his belt, where I'm assuming he has a gun stashed. He doesn't have a chance to grasp it before Cash punches him in the side of the face, and he falls to the floor. Our treasurer is on him within seconds, landing blow after blow to his face and ribs. When Nolan stops struggling beneath my brother, Cash stands, taking Nolan's gun with him.

"Check him for more weapons," Ozzy says.

Cash pats Nolan down the front, then turns the unconscious man onto his stomach and repeats the process. "He's clear."

Ozzy grabs one of the chairs from the little table in the corner, then walks over to Nolan. He and Cash grab him under each shoulder and haul him into the chair. I grab the duct tape Liam gave me and wrap this fucker up nice and tight.

"Fuck, how hard did you hit him?" Jude asks, leaning against the wall while we wait for this piece of shit to come around.

"Not hard enough," Cash says, his eyes never leaving Nolan.

I grab the smelling salts that are in the bag Liam handed me. Fucking serial killers' wet dream in here.

I wave the salts under Nolan's nose, and his head jerks back. One eye is nearly swollen shut, but the other eye frantically looks around the room.

"No one is coming to save you," I say, stepping into his line of sight. "You really fucked yourself this time, asshole."

Nolan struggles against the duct tape, and I release a caustic laugh.

Nolan is seething when he realizes how tightly he's taped to the chair. "You aren't going to get away with this. My club will find out what happened. We already know you killed three of our brothers last year."

"You think you fucking scare us? If you're so sure we were responsible for your missing brothers, then why the hell haven't they come yet? Is it because they know they'll never win against us?" I ask.

The Bone Breakers don't have much of a reputation other than being tweaker desert rats who raise hell occasionally in the small town they live in. Not much of a threat to any other club worth a damn.

"Red isn't scared of you," Nolan says.

"Then why isn't your president here?" I ask, holding out my arms and looking around the room before my gaze zeros back in on the beaten man in front of me. "He sent you to do his dirty work and is probably back in Arizona snorting crank of some nasty club skank you fuckers keep around. Face it, Nolan. He doesn't give two shits about you."

"Fuck you," Nolan spits. "When I don't check in with him, he's going to come looking for us."

"And he won't find shit. Just like last time," Jude says. "Bet you didn't know it was me and my old lady that took your brothers out. They were just as incompetent as you fucks."

"You think you can keep dropping bodies and there won't be consequences?" Nolan asks, as stupid and cocky as the stories I've heard about him.

"You think you can take my old lady and our son and live to see another day, asshole?"

Nolan glares at me through his one good eye. "The kid is mine."

"Wrong. Colby has never been yours." I grab a knife from my belt and plunge it into his thigh to make my point clear, then lean down so that I'm eye level with the soon-to-be dead man. "Colby and Maizie are mine, and you made the fucking stupidest decision you possibly could have when you threatened *my* woman and took *my* kid."

I stand and look in the bag sitting on the bed, spotting all sorts of shit. Needles that you can put under fingernails, pliers, a box cutter with extra blades, and a bottle of epinephrine with several syringes.

"Goddamn, Jude. Your brother is one sick fuck. I like it," I say, pulling out the pliers.

"I have some questions," I tell Nolan. "And we can do this the hard way"—I wave the pliers in front of his face—"or...well, the harder way. That's the one where I keep you alive with what's in the bag. Or you can answer my questions and I kill you without having a little fun first."

"Fuck you," Nolan says.

A deadly smile spreads across my mouth. "The fun way it is, then."

I grab the side of his face and wrench his mouth open, sticking the pliers inside and yanking out a molar. He lets out a bloodcurdling scream, then quiets when I drop the tooth on his lap, breathing hard.

"Who's helping you? Is it the Italians?" We know they were friendly before Finn Monaghan took over their organizations. Have a few of the men dissented?

Nolan spits. "Fucking scumbags bent the knee to that Irish piece of shit."

So, not the Italians.

"Was it someone closer to us? You seemed to have information about my woman that no one in this room would have told you." Namely, where she lived and that she and I were together.

"I'm not telling you shit," he sneers.

I nod as though I'm completely nonplussed with his declaration and look inside the bag again. "Did you know the human foot has approximately two hundred thousand nerve endings?"

Nolan stares at me.

I look toward Jude. "Take his boot off."

Jude bends and rips the boot and sock off Nolan's right foot.

"You should have just told him, mate," Jude says with a mild chuckle. He stands and slaps Nolan on the face a few times with a laugh.

I grab two thick needles and slide them both under the toenail of his big toe. Nolan screams like a little bitch. Can't hardly blame him, I guess. This one has to hurt.

"You have nine more toes, Nolan," I yell over his screaming. "And I have plenty of needles left. Is someone helping you find information about the club?"

"Fuck you!" he yells as sweat begins to drip down his face.

I shrug. "Have it your way. Jude, grab his other boot."

Jude kneels again, but before he gets the boot off, Nolan screams for him to stop.

"I don't know who Red has been talking to. But he's been dealing with someone out here. Someone who wants Shine and all the surrounding towns. They deal in pills and meth and know you keep that shit on lockdown."

"Who is it?" I ask, standing in front of him with my arms over my chest and a couple of needles in my hands.

"I don't know, man. Like I said, he's been tight-lipped. Paranoid. He's never been the type to share information outside of the officers, but even they have no clue."

I grab the knife sticking out of his thigh and twist it.

"Fuck! I told you everything I know," Nolan screams. "He wanted revenge for our missing brothers. He knew you had something to do with it, and he reached out to a couple people. No one wanted to help him because of your in with the Monaghans. He finally found someone who didn't give a shit."

"See, there was more," I say. "I just needed to jog your memory."

"That's it. I swear," he says in a tone that begs me to believe him. And I do. Nolan doesn't exactly strike me as the type his president would confide in.

"Listen," Nolan pants out. "My parents are loaded. If you let me go, I can get you money. Anything you want. You want me to sign over custody of the kid to you? Done. I'll never tell a single soul what happened here. I swear to you."

"Nice to know you'd be willing to sell out your club, you piece of shit," Ozzy spits at him. "Fucking just as worthless now as you were back in the day."

"Oh, Nolan," I say, grabbing the gun from my holster. "You don't have to sign shit over to me. Wanna know why?" He doesn't answer, not that I expected him to, but I'm still determined to make my point before I send him to his maker. "Because you hurt two of the people I love more than my own life. You took what wasn't yours to take. You threatened my club and my family. And you'll pay with your life."

I raise the gun and fire a bullet between his eyes. Blood oozes from the wound as his head falls back.

"There's someone other than the Bone Breakers who wants to bring trouble to our club," Linc says.

"Sounds like," Ozzy agrees. "Let's deal with one problem at a time. We'll get this cleaned up, then it'll be time to plan our attack on their clubhouse. Now that these assholes are taken care of, we bought ourselves a little time before we head out to Arizona."

Jude opens the door and waves at whoever is outside to let them know that we're finished here.

"Let's get going then. This place is a fucking mess," I say.

"We've got this, brother. You and Jude go home and be with your families," Knox tells us.

"I would argue," Jude says. "But fuck it. I want to check on Little Bit and Lucifer."

"You sure?" I ask.

Both Ozzy and Knox nod. "Go. Be with your woman and son," Ozzy says. "You get the next cleanup."

Liam comes walking in and sees the state of Nolan's body, nodding in approval. "Ah, I see you found the needles. Well done."

This fucking guy.

"I'm taking one of the vans back to the clubhouse," Jude tells his brother. "Lucy and Cece need me. Barrett should be back soon to help."

Liam reaches into his pocket, pulling out the keys and tossing them to Jude. "I'll be over when we're finished here," he says.

"Thank you," I tell him and turn to my brothers. "All of you."

"This is what family does," Ozzy says. "Now go make sure yours are okay."

CHAPTER TWENTY-ONE
MAIZIE

I t feels as though time is standing still as I wait for Wyatt. I don't think I took a full breath since getting in the van. Hell, since I found my son and Cece missing.

Wyatt: *On my way home to you. I love you.*

Me: *I love you, too.*

Tears fill my eyes as relief washes through me.

We've just gotten back to the clubhouse when Wyatt's text came through. The forty-five-minute drive nearly did me in. Colby sat in my arms, clinging to me. Not that it would have mattered if he wanted me to put him down. I couldn't have even if he'd tried.

We're lying in Wyatt's bed at the clubhouse. Barrett put us in here so we could clean up and get some rest. I gave Colby a bath and put him in one of Wyatt's shirts. Being surrounded by his scent brings me comfort in his absence, but I know he'll be here soon.

There's no doubt in my mind that the men who took Colby and Cece are dead. And I'm glad for it. Wyatt swore to me he would protect not only my heart, but my life as well, and Colby's. When my son told Wyatt that he loved him, I would have cried if tears hadn't already been streaming down my face from the relief of having Colby safely in my arms. Just like Wyatt promised.

There's a quiet knock at the door and Mia peeks her head in. "Hey, sister. You need anything?"

"I'm good," I whisper. "How are you?"

"I'm...not sure," she replies.

"I know he was your brother. This can't be easy for you."

She shakes her head. "Nolan was..." Her voice catches on the word *was*. We both know there was never a chance of him making it out of this with his life. "He made his choices a long time ago. And I made mine. You're my family. That guy"—she nods toward my sleeping son—"is my family. Whatever happens to anyone who threatens them is something they brought on themselves. I have no qualms about knowing what happened to Nolan. And honestly, if I were there with a gun in my hand, I can't say I wouldn't have done the job myself."

"I can't say I wouldn't have done the same thing either. When I got that text, I wanted him dead."

"That makes perfect sense. And it also doesn't make you a bad person. He took Colby and threatened the people you love. It's pretty black and white in my book."

I nod. "Guess it is in mine, too."

There has never been any doubt in my mind who the Black Roses are. The things that they've done and still do. These aren't law-abiding men, and their world can be dangerous. But they fiercely protect the people they love, of that I have no doubt.

Mia smiles and dips her head before shutting the door behind her.

I never thought I would fall in love with a biker. Then Wyatt and his warm smile and gentle heart broke through every defense I tried to put between us. The way he loves me is so powerful and complete. I didn't think I would ever find someone like him. Like what my friends have with their men. And I have never been happier to be wrong. In my darkest hour, when my worst fear came true and my son was in danger, he stood between me and the evil men who took my son. He rescued Colby, protecting us from ever having them get their hands on my son again. Wyatt kept his word, and I couldn't imagine anyone else keeping my heart safe, either.

Someone else knocks on the door, and this time, the face I see is the one I've needed all night.

"Hey, baby," Wyatt says, opening the door and stepping inside his room before soundlessly shutting it behind him.

"Hi," I breathe out and tears fill my eyes. "Fuck, I'm glad to see you."

He takes three long strides and sits next to me, leaning down to place a kiss on my lips.

I turn onto my other side so I can wrap my arms around him, but he stops me. "I'm filthy. Let me get cleaned up first. I just couldn't not kiss you."

"Okay. Did you talk to Mia and Charlie about Pepper?"

When we got back, the girls were here after having left the vet's office to check on the dog on their way back to the clubhouse with Braxton. Pepper has a broken leg like I thought, and the vet needed to do surgery to fix the break. He told Mia that he was going to keep him for a couple days to make sure there are no complications or infections and to help manage his pain. That dog is my fucking hero, just like the man sitting next to me.

"I did. We'll pick him up in a couple days, and I'm giving him the biggest fucking steak he's ever had in his life."

"According to Colby, he's partial to pizza," I say with a smile.

"I'm not partial to the gas." Wyatt chuckles and stands from the bed. "I'm going to go shower."

He walks into the bathroom in his room and shuts the door. When I hear the shower running, I turn toward Colby and tuck the blankets around him just how he likes, making him into a little sleeping burrito, then gently lift myself from the bed and walk to the bathroom.

I open the door and step inside, turning the lock after I shut it behind me. Stripping out of my jeans and the T-shirt I've been wearing all night, I look through the glass and see Wyatt with his hands against the wall and his head lowered under the spray. He isn't moving, but I see the way his entire upper body rises then lowers with each deep breath.

Opening the door to the shower, I step in behind him and place my hand on his back. He startles for a moment, but when he turns, he wraps me in his arms and pulls me against his chest, burying his face in my hair.

"Fuck, I was so scared," he says on a broken whisper. "When you told me that Colby was missing, it felt like the walls were closing in around me."

"You were so strong tonight, honey." My hands run up and down his wet skin. "Everything I needed you to be."

"I had to. I promised I would never let anything touch you, and I had to get our boy back. But holy hell, baby, it's all hitting me right now."

I feel his entire body vibrating as he holds me with the water beating against his back.

"Shh. I've got you. We're safe," I tell him.

There are times when you love someone and they are your strength, the immovable rock you can crash against. Then there are times when you have to be that rock for them. This is one of those times.

I pull away just barely and grab his hand, placing it over my heart. "It's still beating. I'm here, and so is Colby. We're okay. You made sure of that."

Wyatt presses his forehead against mine and takes a deep breath. "I love you so much, baby. If anything ever happened to you or our boy..."

"But nothing did. You saved him. *You*, Wyatt. You kept your promise."

His hand slides from my chest to the side of my neck. Wyatt leans in and places a kiss to my lips, his other arm flexing around my waist.

I deepen the kiss, needing to taste him, to feel him.

"I need you," I whisper against his mouth.

Wyatt doesn't skip a beat. He crashes his lips to mine, and his tongue plunges inside my mouth, tangling with mine. His kiss is desperate and frantic as his hand dives into my hair, flexing as though he can't hold on tight enough.

He spins us so that my back is against the spray, and he lowers himself to his knees.

"You have to be quiet. Our boy is sleeping in the other room. Can you do that?"

I nod.

"Good girl." He looks into my eyes as he takes his first lick through my center. His eyes close on a groan. "Always so fucking sweet."

"You have to be quiet, too," I whimper, my voice barely audible over the sound of the running water.

He leans forward again, and his tongue starts licking at my clit as he buries his face in my pussy.

"Fuck," I breathe out.

One hand presses against the shower wall while the other clutches his shoulder for support. Wyatt stands and turns us so that my back is against the tile then quickly kneels before me again and throws one of my legs over his shoulder. This time, when his face meets my center, he slides two thick fingers into my wet core.

His tongue lashes at me and his fingers pump in and out, filling me over and over. Wyatt curls his fingers and instantly finds the spot inside of me that makes me detonate every time. The orgasm rushes through me, so powerful and intense that I have to bite my lip to keep from crying out. Wyatt licks me through every wave, never easing up. When I come down, he rises to his full height and tips his head forward, taking my mouth in an almost brutal kiss.

"Goddamn, baby. You taste so fucking good. I'll never get enough of you."

"I sure hope not," I say with a light laugh.

He pulls away and stares into my eyes. "Never, Maizie," he says in a serious tone. "I need you like I need the fucking air I breathe. There aren't enough words in the English language to tell you what you mean to me. What you being here with me does for my heart. So there's no getting enough of you. There never will be."

Fuck, this man is more than I could have ever hoped for. More than I ever thought I deserved.

"Then show me. Instead of telling me, I need you to show me," I tell him.

Wyatt kisses me again, then spins me to face the tile.

"Hold on to the wall," he whispers in my ear.

He lines himself up to my entrance, then he pushes inside of me in one thrust.

"Shit," I hiss, stretching around him.

He doesn't move. "Okay?" he breathes out.

"God, yes."

"Give me your mouth."

I turn my head and Wyatt kisses me hard as he begins to move in and out of me at a furious pace. The kiss is sloppy and wet, each of us quietly moaning into the other's mouth as he fucks me so deep I'm already about to come for the second time tonight. He keeps one hand on my hip, and the other he lays over my hand that's clutching the tile wall, tangling our fingers together. I feel the walls of my pussy flutter around his thick cock.

"That's it, baby. Squeeze me hard. I need to feel you come while I'm buried so fucking deep inside of you."

He thrusts harder, going deeper than I ever thought possible, and I explode around him. My teeth bite into his arm to stifle the moans that I'm barely holding back from bursting from me.

"Fuck, that's it. Goddamn, you're so fucking perfect," he says as his cock jerks inside of me and he empties himself on a ragged breath.

He slows his movements, eventually stilling completely, but stays inside of me as we both catch our breaths.

"Holy shit," I whisper, looking at the deep teeth marks I left on his arm.

"I'm getting those tattooed there," he says and I laugh.

"They'll fade by morning."

"Then I'll have to make you come that hard again," he says and releases a growl into my neck.

Wyatt pulls out of me and spins me around, placing a gentle kiss to my lips that is completely contradictory to our furious lovemaking from moments before.

"I love you, baby," he whispers against my lips.

"I love you, too."

"Let's get cleaned up. I want to hold you and our boy while we fall asleep."

I nod, not trusting my voice not to break.

Our boy.

Wyatt washes my hair, which is an experience all on its own. I've never had a man wash my hair or give me the kind of care he does. My heart is beyond full as I run my hands over his body with a cloth, washing this night away from him. He glides his hand across my cheek, over my bare shoulders, and down my arms as I clean him. Our touches aren't meant to excite. They're meant to worship.

When we're finished in the shower and dried off, Wyatt wraps a towel around his middle and opens the door. "I'll be right back."

Moments later he returns with a T-shirt like the one I put Colby in after his bath. I slide it down my towel-dried skin as he slips on a pair of gym shorts.

"Let's go to bed," he says, holding out a hand once we're both dressed.

I crawl into his king-size bed and lie against the wall and Colby. Wyatt lies down on his side, on the other side of our son, and rests his arm across both of us, holding all of us together.

This is how it was always meant to be. Wyatt, Colby, and me.

A family of our own making.

A family I'm so incredibly proud to call mine.

EPILOGUE
WYATT

I t's been six weeks since the incident at the motel, and we haven't heard shit from the Bone Breakers.

Liam and his team cleaned up the scene. Everything was set back to rights as though no one had ever stayed in those rooms. They erased all evidence of them ever having been in Shine.

But the effects of their visit? That's still plaguing us all.

Maizie hugs Colby a little tighter than she used to before when she leaves for work, and he's having nightmares a couple times a week. Each time, I carry him into our room and lay him between us so we can all sleep in the same bed, wrapping my arms around them each time we fall back asleep. Maizie assures me it won't be forever, but as far as I'm concerned, he can take all the time he needs with us.

I've been staying with Colby every night when Maizie works. Cece has been...well, not great. Jude told me she's angrier than ever before, lashing out at her sister for the smallest things. She isn't home much and doesn't talk to anyone about where she spends her time. I know it's made Cash nervous, especially with the threat of the Bone Breakers still out there and whoever else may be lying in wait. But no one can tell her what to do or force anything on her. She may have grown up subservient and obedient, but she's still Lucy's sister, and I'm pretty sure angry rebellion runs through their veins. It just took Cece a little longer to find it.

It's nearing the start of the school year, so everyone is gathered in Mia's grandmother's backyard for an end-of-summer party. That's never something I've celebrated, but since Mia and Colby will be starting back, it was as good of an excuse as any to have a BBQ at Elaine's estate.

Cash, Knox and Jude are running around with Colby in an epic water gun fight while Pepper sadly lies at my feet. I know he wants to be out there running with his best buddy, but he still isn't up for it. The vet said a little walking is okay, but running is going to have to wait for at least a couple more months to give his leg time to heal. The first week he was back home with us, he had steak every night for dinner. But Maizie was afraid I was going to make him fat since he isn't able to get the exercise he once did. I conceded to going back to regular dog food, but that doesn't mean Colby and I don't slide him strips of bacon from our breakfast plates every now and again. As far as I'm concerned, this dog is going to be treated like a fucking king for what he did trying to protect our kid.

Colby comes running over, followed by a soaking Jude, and collapses next to Pepper.

"Who won?" I ask as Colby gives Pepper all the attention he's been dying for.

"Your kid is quite the shot," Jude remarks, pulling his wet shirt from his chest. "Although it doesn't hurt that you gave him the biggest water gun that was ever made. I was beginning to think it was never going to run out."

"You could have given up," I say.

"You mean surrender?" Jude asks, affronted by my suggestion. "Never."

I laugh as Maizie makes her way over to us with two towels, tossing one to Jude and laying the other over Colby's shoulders.

She steps between my spread thighs and bends to kiss me, letting out a yelp when I pull her by the hips, setting her on my leg.

"Hi, baby. Having fun?"

"Mm-hmm. I can't believe he's going into first grade in a week," she says, tilting her head toward Colby. "What am I going to do with my days when he's back in school?"

"I can think of a few things," I whisper in her ear so other, littler ears don't hear me.

"I walked right into that one, didn't I?" she says with a giggle.

There's a commotion that grabs all of our attention at the double French doors leading from Elaine's formal living room into the expansive backyard.

"I said I'm fine," Cece hollers as Lucy is trying to grab her arm.

"You're drunk," Lucy hisses. "And you drove here. That is not even in the realm of okay."

"I had one glass of wine. I'm hardly drunk. You drink all the time. We can do that now. Whatever we want. No one is going to tell us no, right?"

"I never get behind the wheel. And I guaran-damn-tee it was a bottle, not a glass, unless you filled a fucking flower vase and consider that one glass," Lucy shoots back.

"Goddammit," Jude mutters before he takes off toward the two scowling women, one of whom is swaying where she stands—and it's not Lucy.

"Mommy, is Cece okay?" Colby asks, looking at his mom with concern in his gaze.

"Not right now, honey. But we'll take care of her. Get her better. Okay?"

He doesn't look like he believes her. Can't say I'm not questioning it, too.

Cash stalks over to Cece and grabs her by the arm, leaning down to whisper something in her ear. Cece tries to struggle out of his grasp, but he doesn't let up. Then her eyes dart to Colby, and I see tears well in hers. She nods at whatever Cash is telling her and allows him to lead her back into the house.

Ozzy walks over to where we're sitting with Freya under his arm.

"Cash is handling it?" he asks, staring at the door the two just walked through.

"Guess so," I reply.

A buzzing noise comes from Ozzy's pocket, and he pulls out his phone. He looks down at the screen, and his arm drops from Freya's shoulders as he stands stock-still, the only movement is the ticcing of his jaw as he stares at the phone in his hand.

"Ozzy?" Freya asks. "What's wrong?"

Knox walks over, and Ozzy hands the phone to our VP.

"What does it say?" I ask, getting more and more worried the longer the two of them are silent.

"It's from that piece-of-shit Red—the Bone Breakers president," Ozzy says through a clenched jaw. "He said he now has six dead brothers and wants to know how many I'm willing to sacrifice. Otherwise, he's bringing war to Shine."

The End

Thank you so much for reading Wyatt and Maizie's story. If you enjoyed the book I would be forever grateful if you left a review where you purchased this copy.

Reviews are a wonderful way to support indie authors and to help us get the word out about our stories.

Do you want to read about what it was like for a few of my guys to grow up in Shine? My free prequel novella **Rose Colored Glasses** can be downloaded when you sign up for my newsletter at katerandallauthor.com or by scanning the QR code below! Don't worry, I'll never spam you.

<u>Stalk me on my socials!</u>

TikTok
Instagram
Facebook
BookBub
Goodreads

Or you can scan the QR code below for links to all of my socials and to sign up for my newsletter!

Also by Kate

The Ones Series
The Good One
The Fragile One
The Other One

The Black Roses MC
Linc
Jude
Ozzy
Knox
Wyatt
Cash

The Boston Syndicate
Finn
Luca
Eoghan
Cillian

About Kate

Kate is a lover of all things books. It doesn't matter what sub-genre, as long as there's a HEA, she's in. She started reading romance in high school and would hide novels in textbooks to read during class. Becoming an author was always a dream she had and finally decided to put pen to paper (or finger to keyboard) and write what she loves. She grew up in the beautiful upper peninsula of Michigan then became a West Coast girl where she lives with her amazing husband and hilarious son. She would love to hear from readers so check out all her socials and sign up for her newsletter so she can keep you up to date on her books and whatever other ramblings come to mind.

ACKNOWLEDGEMENTS

First of all, I want to thank YOU for going on this ride with me. I absolutely love writing my anti-heroes, and Wyatt is no exception. Thank you for taking your precious time to read my stories. I will be forever grateful for you.

Thank you to Kiki, Megan and Anna at The Next Step PR. You ladies are wonderful at what you do, not only for your authors but for the book community as a whole. Seriously, I would be lost without you!

Thank the gods for Victoria, my editor extraordinaire. You make my books shine with your your suggestions and I love it when you fight with my choices in the comments. You can never, ever, EVER leave me!

I have the most amazing proofreader, Rose. Seriously, your eagle-eyes astound me, and I'm so happy I found you.

Thank you, Megan for being on my beta team of one. LOL. I'm so happy we get to swoon over fictional men together!

Of course, I have to give many, many thanks to my husband. You go through this with me every single day.

You're always there for me to bounce ideas off, and you keep this machine working when I'm stuck in a writing cave or daydreaming about fictional characters. I love you so much.